"Kel, I see . . . I think

"What!"

"The dragon. I think it's dead. It's dead, Kel! It got licked in the fight. All those scales! We're rich, Kel! Come on up, and . . . oh-oh."

"What is it, Jon?" His heart thumped. His throat dried instantly.

"Oh, Kel, it's alive, but I think it's almost dead. I think we can kill it and—"

"Jon, come away from there!" If the dragon was alive, but badly injured, they might be able to escape.

"A fortune, Kel! A fortune! Kel, I'm going to sling a rock at it."

Total folly! "No, Jon, no!" Kelvin croaked, his throat so tight with fear he could hardly speak.

But the intrepid little sister was already twirling her sling. With the skill of long practice and a natural knack she let fly and followed through with her usual "Got him!"

Kelvin couldn't speak; his horror had closed off his throat entirely. He held his breath as Jon stared down the opposite side of the pile. What was she seeing there, anyway?

"It sees me, Kel," her voice came back, rising with sudden alarm. "It's awake. It—Kel, it's coming for me!"

Look for all these Tor books by Piers Anthony

PIERS ANTHONY
AND ROBERT E. MARGROFF

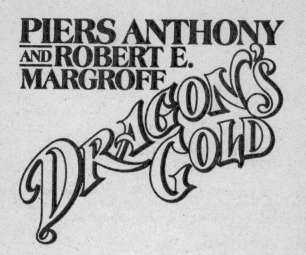

A TOM DOHERTY ASSOCIATES BOOK

DRAGON'S GOLD

Copyright © 1987 by Piers Anthony and Robert E. Margroff

All rights reserved, including the right to reproduce this book or portions thereof in any form.

First printing: July 1987

A TOR Book

Published by Tom Doherty Associates, Inc.
49 West 24 Street
New York, N.Y. 10010

Cover art by Steve Hickman

ISBN: 0-812-53125-6
CAN. ED.: 0-812-53126-4

Printed in the United States of America

0 9 8 7 6 5 4 3

Contents

PROLOGUE

THE FUGITIVE DID NOT know that his arrival at the small Rud farm was preordained. He would have scoffed at the notion, had he been told. All he knew was that his injured leg hurt abominably, that he was so filthy he was disgusted, and that he was too tired to fight or flee if discovered.

It was night again. He had hardly been aware of the passage of time since his escape, except for the awful sun by day and the cruel chill by night. Dehydration and shivering, with little between except fear and fatigue.

Yet this was a decent region, he knew, if viewed objectively. He heard froogs croaking loudly in the nearby froogpond, and corbean stalks rustling in the breeze. Appleberries and razzelfruits perfumed the air and set his stomach growling. The natives claimed that these bitter fruits could be charmed to become sweet, but he refused to credit such impossible claims. He was not yet so far gone as to believe in magic! But they certainly looked good! Hunger—there was another curse of the moment!

But thought of food had to be pushed aside, as did dreams of a hot bath and a change of clothing. He had come here, he reminded himself sternly, to steal a horse. He hated the necessity, for he regarded himself as an honorable man, but he seemed to have no choice.

He crept nearer to the cottage, orienting on its single faint light. How he hoped that there would be no one awake to challenge him! He did not know how close the Queen's guardsmen were, or how quickly they would appear the moment there was any commotion. How ironic it would be to die ignobly as an unsuccessful horse thief!

He paused, studying the light. Far off there sounded the trebling screech of a houcat. His pursuers had lost the trail last night, and he doubted that they would swim the river to pick it up again. There were hazards in that water as bad for guardsmen as for thieves, and only a truly desperate man would have been fool enough to risk it. Perhaps the guardsmen thought him dead already. This fool, for the time being, was almost safe.

He came close and peered cautiously in the window. A slender girl sat reading by the flickering light of a lamp. He gazed at the coppery sheen of her hair, and the planes of her somewhat pointed face, and the gentle swell and ebb of her bosom as she breathed. How lovely she seemed! It was not that she was beautiful, for by his standards she was not, but that she was comfortable and quiet and clean. A girl who read alone at night: what a contrast to the type of woman he had known! There was an aura of decency about her that excited his longing. He could love such a girl and such a life-style, if ever given a chance.

For a moment he was crazily tempted to knock on the window, to announce himself, to say, "Haloo there, young woman, are you in need of a man? Give me a bath and some food, and I shall be yours forever!" But he was not yet so tired that no reason remained. If he did that, she would start up and scream, and the guardsmen would come, and it would be over.

He ducked past the window and tiptoed to the barn. He held his breath as he tried the latch on the stable door. It opened easily, without even a squeak. This was a well-maintained farm. He felt a certain regret that this should facilitate the theft of an animal. It might have been more fitting to steal from a sloppy farm, but a squeaky door would have been an excellent guardian.

From inside came the scent of horse and hay. He

felt around in the dark just past the door and found the halter exactly where it should be. The arrangements in good Rud barns were standard.

There was the snap of a broken twig. He turned.

She stood there in the wan light from the window, garbed in a filmy nightdress and a shawl. The first thing he noticed was the way her firm slim legs showed in gauzy silhouette.

The second thing he noticed was the pitchfork she held at waist height, aimed at his chest.

He swallowed, trying to judge whether he could dodge aside quickly enough to avoid the thrust of those sharp tines, and whether he retained the strength to wrestle the implement away from her. And if he did, what, then? How could he hurt a girl he would rather embrace? Perhaps it was a trick of the inadequate light, but her eyes seemed to be the exact color of violets back on his native Earth.

"Speak!" she said. "What is your business here?" Her voice sent a thrill through him; it was dulcet despite its tone of challenge.

What use to lie? He hated this whole business! "I came to steal your horse. I would rather have stolen your heart." And what had possessed him to say that?

"You are a thief? A highwayman?"

She hadn't thrust her fork at him. That was a good sign. He decided to tell her the rest of it. "I'm not an ordinary thief, not even a good one, as you can see," he said with difficulty. "I just had to have a horse. I know you won't believe that I'm not a criminal."

"Why didn't you come openly to my door, then?"

"I—I looked in your window, and saw you reading. You were so—so *nice*! I thought you would scream if you saw me. I—I'm a fugitive from the Queen's dungeon. I know that doesn't make me a hero, but maybe it carries a bit of weight."

"You have round ears," she said, her voice assuming a soft, strange quality. "You cannot be of this planet. Certainly you are no ordinary thief. Introduce yourself, Roundear."

She seemed to have no fear of him, only a certain caution. It was almost as if she had been expecting him! "John Knight, of Earth," he said.

"A name may be an omen, Knight," she said. She smiled a mysterious witching smile and lowered the fork. "You may call me Charlain. We shall be married on the morrow."

He stared at her. Then, tentatively, he smiled. She returned the smile. Then, unaccountably, he laughed, and she laughed with him.

She took him inside the house and gave him a bath and some food, and when he was clean and fed she kissed him and took him to her bed. He was so tired that he fell almost instantly to sleep despite the presence of her warm body beside him. He didn't even care that this might be a ruse to lull him, so that she could safely turn him in to the Queen's guardsmen. He had to believe in her.

Thus did John Knight first encounter the woman he was to marry. She practiced fortune-telling, so had known he was coming: a round-eared man who was a fugitive from the Queen. She had told no one of this vision, so knew that his arrival was no trap by the Queen. She had known that the man would be completely unprepossessing, but would be the one she could truly love, and that though he had known a woman before her, he would never know one after her.

They married on the morrow, in a secret ceremony, and that evening he was enough recovered to remain awake in her bed for some time. Their life together had begun abruptly, but had an unspoken understanding that was at times mysterious and at other times thoroughly natural to him.

The following year their round-eared baby was born, and two years after that their point-eared baby.

The prophecy that John Knight had not known about was on its way to fulfillment. His life was relatively placid after he settled; not so, that of his children.

CHAPTER 1
Dragon Scale

THE ROAD WOUND LIKE a twisting dragon's tail.
Through rank underbrush and skeletal trees. Past
boulders the size of cottages. Along a sparkling mountain stream bordered with high piles of debris left by
the late spring floods. It did not look like the setting
for the beginning of the fulfillment of a long-term
prophecy.

Two slim figures walked the road, carrying travelsacks and leading a donkey. One was sixteen, tall
enough to be handsome were it not for his round ears.
The other was fourteen but looked twelve, with
pointed ears. Both wore the garb of Rud rustics: heavy
leather walking boots, brownberry shirts, greenbriar
pantaloons, and lightweight summer stockelcaps
whose long tips ended in tassels of blue and green
yarn. They could hardly have looked less like folk
destined to commence the fulfillment of a significant
prophecy.

Kelvin, the elder one, played on his mandajo as he
walked, picking out the accompaniment to "Fortune
Come a-Callin'," a Rud tune of great antiquity. The
three-stringed lute of Rud could be beautiful when
properly evoked, but Kelvin was not playing it well.
Some had magic that related to music, and some did
not; some thought they had magic when they did not.
Kelvin was of the latter persuasion, but he wouldn't
have cared if he had realized. His thoughts were far
away.

Jon, the younger one, brushed back long yellow
hair. A stranger, looking at Jon's alert greenish eyes
and large ears and face that showed no hint of a beard,
would have dismissed this as a lively boy. The strang-

5

er would have been mistaken, for Jon was Kelvin's sister. Because it could be dangerous for a girl to go alone into the countryside of Rud, the parents had tried to restrict her to the farm and village. But Jon was an adventurous sort, always eager to go out exploring. Realizing that she could not be restrained, they had finally yielded with two stern strictures: always go in company with Kelvin, and go as a boy. That suited Jon just fine, for though she would die rather than say it, she looked up to her brother, and wanted to share his activities. She also rather liked masquerading as a boy, for though her parents had been happy to have a girl, Jon herself envied the freedoms and prospects of the other sex. She had become almost letter-perfect at the masquerade, but now nature was playing on her a disgusting trick. Her hips were broadening and her breasts were swelling. It was getting harder to look the part, and it would be impossible without her solid shirt. What would she do when her rebellious front became too pronounced to conceal? She was disgusted, and the very thought put her in a bad mood.

Now Jon peered into the underbrush and up into the branches of the trees, looking for trouble. She carried a sturdy leather sling whose pocket held a carefully positioned rock of the required squirbet-braining size. Just let one of those creatures show its snoot now . . . !

"Fortune come a-callin', but I did hide, ah-oo-ay," Kelvin sang with imperfect pitch. "Fortune come a-callin', but I did hide, bloody saber at my side, ah-oo-ay, ah-oo-ay, ay."

"You call that old pig-gutter you're packing a saber?" Jon demanded. She spoke with deceptive good humor, her eyes wandering over to her brother. To the dark handle of the war souvenir protruding from its worn and cracked scabbard.

Kelvin lowered his instrument. His thoughts leaped ahead to the deepening gloom and the forbidding mountain pass. "We're not riding either," he said, referring to another verse.

"No, but we would be if you hadn't let that horse dealer swindle us," Jon said. She lifted the halter and made a grimace of distaste at their pack animal. "A horse to ride would be great, but you, you jackass, had to buy a jackass!"

"I thought," Kelvin said lightly, his attention focusing a bit, "that I could put two of them to work. You and Mockery."

"Mockery's the name for it!" Jon snapped. "Anyone but you would have been put off by the name, but you had to go and hand over our last two rudnas for it!"

"Jon, Jon, show faith in thy elder," Kelvin teased. "We hadn't the money for a horse, and Mockery was cheap. We'll need his strong back, and yours, to pack out all the gold we'll find."

Jon made an uncouth noise. "If he ever lets us load! It took us half the morning to get our pitifully few supplies strapped to his ornery back. He's got a kick like a mule! I suppose when we want our tent, he'll start all over."

"Not so, little brother Worrisome Wart!" Kelvin always referred to her in the masculine, maintaining the masquerade; what started as a game had soon enough become second nature. "It's only that he's jealous. *We* have the lighter loads. Smart animal, Mockery. Smart enough to know when we're in dragon country. Anything that smart, including me and possibly ye, knows the danger."

"Do we, Kel?" Her voice was almost pleading.

Kelvin narrowed the bluish eyes that seemed almost as strange as his rounded ears, in Rud. This was not like Jon. Usually she tried with pretty good success to appear more recklessly masculine than any ordinary boy could be. Until today she had seemed if anything too confident. What was bothering her?

"Jon, if you're afraid—"

"Ain't that!" Jon snapped. "Not any more than you

are, anyway. But curse it, Kel, if I'm going to get et up
by a dragon, I at least want a chance."

"Few people have a chance," Kelvin retorted.
"Dragons are big and strong and mean. If you run
into one, it will devour you fast. Once it bites off your
head, which I'm sure it will do early on, I can promise
you that you will hardly feel a thing."

"Great!" Jon said, not appreciating the humor. "So
we just stay away from it?"

"That's all anyone with any sense does. Or," he
added, giving a slight nod at Mockery, "any*thing* with
sense."

"But dragons have been killed, haven't they?"

"A few times by heroes with armor and war-horses
and lances. You know that, Jon. A few have fallen, but
not to the likes of us."

"But if we had a good sword, and a war-horse, and a
lance—"

"We'd get et, just the same," Kelvin said confident-
ly. "You ever see me ride a war-horse? Or use a sword
except for hacking brush? It takes training, Jon; it
doesn't just happen."

Jon subsided into silence as they plodded on. The
road was becoming narrower with every mile. The
debris piles were getting higher and higher. Now the
mountain walls seemed to lean inward. The sun hid
its face behind the peak of the mountain to the west.
The air became noticeably cooler as the bird and
animal sounds became more hushed and were heard
less often.

"I don't like this place," Jon said, looking about at
the tangled masses of trees the flood had left. "It's
ugly."

"Nobody comes here for a picnic, Jon. Riches
aren't found in the nicest places. If we're to get gold,
we have to put up with ugliness."

Jon flushed a little and looked away. Now and then
something Kelvin said did have a noticeable effect.
But he wondered whether he should caution her about
showing any color; that was a trait associated more

with girls, and could give her away. He decided to keep quiet; Jon didn't like to have her female mannerisms pointed out. There was a certain irony in this, because in truth she was becoming a rather pretty figure of a girl when she let herself be.

Kelvin estimated the time. It was getting to be late in the afternoon. Soon they would stop to build camp, and then early tomorrow they'd find gold. Or at least they'd search for it. If the spring floods had washed it down from the high mountains, they might find nuggets of it along the stream. That was their hope; that was what made this an adventure instead of just a chance to explore. A chance for Jon to be a boy —perhaps one of the last chances, for soon there would be no easy way to conceal her nature.

He wondered how he would feel if he knew that he was really a girl, and would have to resign himself to becoming a homemaker and never going out exploring again. He shuddered; he knew he would hate it. He wished he could at least express some sympathy for Jon, but he couldn't; it would come out all wrong, and she would be furious.

"Gods, Kel, look what I found!"

He blinked as he strained his sight to see what shone so brightly in Jon's hands. His eyes were not the best; if Jon's curse was being a girl, his own was being inadequate in various ways like this. Jon had reached down into a clump of ugly brown weeds, and now held something that filled her cupped palms.

Carefully, Kelvin took it from her, bringing it close enough for a decent focus. It was a scale that could have come from a dragon's neck. It had the heft of gold, and some luster through the grime. It could be very valuable.

"It's a dragon scale, isn't it? Isn't it?" she demanded, hopping about in her excitement.

"Easy, Jon, easy," he cautioned her. "Don't shout or do anything to attract a dragon's attention. This could be fresh, and—"

"Think I'm crazy?" Jon asked. Then, "It is, isn't it?

Gold that migrated to the scale from the nuggets swallowed by the dragon? It's just as the books said! Just like the shellfish that get metal in their shells from ingesting bits of metal and then become unfit to eat! We're lucky, oh so lucky!" She was dancing again.

Kelvin stopped her with an upraised hand. "Quiet, fool! The dragon could be in hearing distance!" For the scale of a dragon meant danger as well as wealth, and suddenly he was quite nervous about this aspect.

"Around here?" Jon whirled happily. "If that's so, why isn't smart-ass Mockery a-rearin' and a-rarin' and kicking up his heels? You know dragons shed scales! It probably happened weeks ago."

"Yes," Kelvin agreed. "But we can't be sure. We can't be sure it's not lurking and waiting for us."

Jon gave him a look of contempt. She had always been bolder than he. "Hah. Do you think that was just dropped?" She pointed to a pile of dried dragon dung.

Kelvin looked at the bits of white bone sticking out of the dung, and shivered. That, he thought, could be the remnant of a human being.

"We have to be careful, Jon," he said. "We have to check around here to make sure there's no fresh sign. If a dragon's been around in the last day or so, we want to move out. If we don't find fresh sign, we'll set up the tent, cook the squirbet you bagged, eat, and get a good night's sleep. Then, first thing tomorrow, we'll search." His hands felt clammy as he put the scale into a pocket of his pantaloons. The very notion of a nearby dragon gave him the cold sweats.

But Jon was already climbing a high mound of rocks and weeds and piled-up tree trunks. As usual she did not appear to have heard a word Kelvin said.

CHAPTER 2
Dragon Ire

CONTROLLING HIS FEELINGS AS much as he could, Kelvin petted Mockery and made plans for putting up the tent and cooking the squirbet Jon had knocked over earlier during the day. He took off Mockery's pack, put hobbles on the beast, went to the nearest sapling, and cut a sturdy tent pole with his incredibly dull sword.

"I found another! Two more!" Jon cried from halfway up the pile.

Kelvin's heart leaped. He controlled it. Careful, careful, he thought. Move too fast, make too much noise, and the two of them could become bones in dragon dung. Were those other bones human? Had the dragon eaten the last intrepid gold-hunters to brave this place?

"Kel, there's six of them! All in a bunch, and stained! The dragon must have been in a fight with another dragon."

So that was why so many downed trees, Kelvin thought. The flooding river hadn't done it all; dragons had added to the carnage of this region. He shivered in spite of himself as he imagined the size of the beasts. Two of them? That would account for the ground being grassless over there and for the dirt showing. Where would the loser go afterward, he wondered, and thought again that he really should be curbing Jon's noisy explorations.

"Let's make our camp now, Jon. Please." He hated sounding like a coward, but the possible presence of a dragon made him feel very much like one.

Jon ignored him, clambering nimbly on up the rockpile. *She* had no foolish concern about monsters!

11

He picked at a blister on his hand as he waited for her to finish with the pile and come down. Just how was their tent to be constructed? And what would they eat? The appleberry bushes had been savaged, too; even his most ardent charm was unlikely to make their fruit edible here.

"Kel, I've found . . ." Jon's voice trailed off, forcing Kelvin to look around for her. He spotted her atop a jumble of boulders piled amidst tree trunks, the rock coated with decomposed vegetation and sandy soil from the river bottom.

"Kel, I see . . . I think I see the dragon!"

"What!"

"The dragon. I think it's dead. It's dead, Kel! It got licked in the fight. All those scales! We're rich, Kel! Come on up, and . . . oh-oh."

"What is it, Jon?" His heart thumped. His throat dried instantly.

"Oh, Kel, it's alive, but I think it's almost dead. I think we can kill it and—"

"Jon, come away from there!" If the dragon was alive, but badly injured, they might be able to escape.

"A fortune, Kel! A fortune! Kel, I'm going to sling a rock at it."

Total folly! "No, Jon, no!" Kelvin croaked, his throat so tight with fear he could hardly speak.

But the intrepid little sister was already twirling her sling. With the skill of long practice and a natural knack she let fly and followed through with her usual "Got him!"

Kelvin couldn't speak; his horror had closed off his throat entirely. He held his breath as Jon stared down the opposite side of the pile. What was she seeing there, anyway?

"It sees me, Kel," her voice came back, rising with sudden alarm. "It's awake. It—Kel, it's coming for me!"

Kelvin's voice tore loose from his constricted throat. "Run, Jon, run! Back here!"

He heard the scramble as Jon moved. Her head

appeared at the crest. She seemed to be moving slowly, but Kelvin realized that this was really the effect of his terror: the world seemed to have slowed almost to a standstill. Now it came to him: this huge pile of debris had been kicked up by the fighting dragons!

Fighting? Then why wasn't the loser dead? A dragon never left prey or an enemy alive; he would chew it to bits just out of spite, even if he wasn't hungry. Dragons *liked* to kill, to make blood splatter! Everyone knew that! When they fought each other, the loser always died, because no dragon ever fled from anything. It couldn't have been a fight!

Then what had happened? Obviously this dragon had been only sleeping. But why had it scratched up such a mountain of refuse? For he was sure now: the natural hill here had been enhanced by more than flood refuse. Dragons were known to be as lazy as any other creature; they saved their energy for important things like pursuing prey and fighting and—

And mating. He remembered the stories now. The mating of dragons was almost indistinguishable from a fight to the death. It seemed that the females never did mate voluntarily, so the males had to run them down and subdue them and rape them. It was said that the effort of doing this tired out a male dragon more than any other activity, and that some dropped into deep sleep on the spot. That must have been the case with this one. Probably it would have slept for several more hours if Jon hadn't jolted him with a rock on the snoot.

But even a tired dragon was a worse threat than any other living creature. There was no telling how long this one had had to recover; it might have slept for several days, and now be largely restored, and plenty hungry. And they, like the fools they were, had blundered in, thinking the scales that had been torn off in the ecstasy of rut meant that the dragon was gone.

Jon was coming down the ragged slope, slip-sliding

across slime-slick stones. The dragons probably hadn't even noticed the havoc they wrought on the landscape! The male had finally tamed the female, probably holding her down with his huge teeth and claws while it rammed into her torso. There would be blood galore, his as well as hers. Once the male's urge was spent, his grip would have relaxed, and the female would have torn free and departed. This was the one encounter in which dragon did not kill dragon; she had to go gestate, and he had to let her go. So, worn but satiated, he slept where he lay ... until this moment.

With a cry of despair and fright elevated to unadulterated terror, Jon turned and dropped, screaming as she slid through loosely piled debris and river-borne brush. She had fallen into a hole in the pile!

But her cries were drowned out in a moment by the loudest and most drawn-out hiss Kelvin had ever heard or imagined. It was the sound of the biggest, most dreaded reptile ever to slither through a nightmare. Then a scrabbling noise, as huge claws dug at smooth rock to find a foothold. No worn-out dragon, that!

Kelvin looked wildly around for safety, spotted none, and turned to his faithful steed. The donkey, amazingly enough, was chomping grass. Obviously the animal was stone-deaf; this was the first time Kelvin had realized it.

"Kel, Kel! He's going to get me, Kel! He's going to get me! He's climbing up, Kel! He's climbing!" Jon's former boldness had been completely dissipated; now at last she understood what he had feared when he saw the first golden scale.

What does one do when one's sister is in dire danger from a menace that cannot be opposed? One does what little one can.

Raising the old sword in his already sore hand, Kelvin rushed madly for the pile. A tree trunk lay next to some smaller rocks and made a regular staircase that Jon had followed. Kelvin's running feet found it of their own accord. Panting, he reached the spot where Jon had fallen, looked down between stacked rocks and tree trunks, and saw her frightened face.

"I can't get out in time, Kel!" she screamed tearfully. "I'm trapped! Save yourself, Kel! Save yourself!"

Kelvin, in a rear portion of his mind, recognized this as one of his sister's better ideas, but somehow he wasn't satisfied with it. Whether he would have taken her up on it he could never afterward be certain, for at that moment the golden-scaled, elongated snout of the dragon appeared over the pile's top boulder. The thing was simultaneously awful and beautiful: deadly living gold. He had known that dragons were monstrous, but from this range that was an appalling understatement. He judged that this one could swallow both of them in a single gulp. He could not see the main torso, but guessed that its size must be equivalent to that of six or seven large war-horses. No wonder so few men had ever dared face such a creature! The wonder was that any who had done so had survived.

The monster levered itself up on gigantic scaled claws. Its entire head was now visible, and the front of its body. Kelvin could see the crest on the head and the short, leathery wings. He knew he should be afraid, but his emotion seemed to have shorted out that stage, leaving him strangely clearheaded.

Kelvin raised his sword. His arm shook so that he seemed to be fencing. He wished he had scoured off the rust and put a razor edge on the blade. He couldn't imagine what he could do with a sharp clean sword, let alone this dull dirty one, but now was not a good time for imagination anyway.

Ping!

His arm went numb. Something serpentine and leathery and wet curled three times around his sword blade and twice around his wrist. He lurched backward in horror—and was promptly pulled forward by the long, forked tongue.

Some sword! he thought, insanely hacking with the

edge of his free hand at the tongue's forked tip.
The edge of his hand came down precisely right, and
he yelped with pain and disgust as he numbed his own
wrist. The dragon seemed unaffected by the hand
chop that had all but fractured Kelvin's good right
arm. He got his feet wedged in a crack of a boulder
and pushed back.

The tongue uncurled from his arm, and the sword
went with it, up and into the cavernous mouth. Those
teeth—they were the size of short swords! The breath
—a poisonous hot wind from a fetid swamp.

Kelvin was falling backward. Then he saw the
sword spinning in midair, and he heard a splatting
sound. The dragon had simply spit out Kelvin's best
and only weapon. And now . . .

The ground closed in about him. He was falling
through the same hole that had swallowed Jon! His
arms spread out reflexively to catch hold of the edges,
but his fingers only tore out hunks of brush and sand.
His descent slowed, but did not stop.

There was an "Ooof!" of protest. He had landed on
something soft. His sister's body had filled out more
than he realized.

They scrambled to separate. It was dark in this hole
and smelly.

"You hurt?" he whispered.

"Just bruised," she gasped. "You?"

He didn't answer, for he heard a scrabbling sound
on the rock overhead. Could the beast move the
boulders? Could it dig them out? How tired was it?

"Kel—"

"Quiet!" he hissed. Surely the dragon *could* dig
them out, since it had formed this miniature mountain. But *would* it? In its fatigued state it might decide
it wasn't worth the energy it would take to roust out
these two little morsels.

"There's a hole here," Jon whispered. Already she
was reverting to normal, ignoring his strictures.

Kelvin felt Jon's hand in the dark, and she moved it
to the place. There was indeed a hole—an aperture

formed by two large tree limbs near ground level. A way out, possibly, but not necessarily to safety. If the dragon discovered it, he could reach in with that long tongue and lick them out as if they were only ants!

This hole was more danger than help! Kelvin tried to think of a way to seal off the opening and keep the dragon's sinuous tongue outside. His hands went out in quick desperation and snagged on a broken branch. He felt along the branch and encountered a smooth, rounded surface. Further investigation informed his senses that here was a boulder that wasn't supporting anything. If he and Jon could somehow move it and use it as a plug for the hole . . .

"Look!" Jon whispered, nudging him urgently.

In the dim light he saw the dragon's clawed foot, just as it lit on something with a sound like a bursting bladder. A moment later there was a loud hiss; then the frantic snort and squeal of a suddenly alert donkey.

"There goes Mockery," Kelvin said. He had an ugly picture of the donkey in the jaws of the dragon, and he hoped the monster would hurt his teeth on the hobbles. Mockery was unable to run; if only he hadn't put those restraints on!

But he realized that this just might have saved his life and Jon's. The dragon had found easier prey.

Jon whimpered. Kelvin hardly noticed, but suddenly he realized that his sister was worming on past him, blocking his light.

"What—Jon . . . ?"

"I won't let it! I won't let it!" Jon screamed. "It can't have Mockery. Mockery's ours!" Evidently she had had a change of heart about the worth of the animal.

Kelvin grabbed hold of a slim leg above and below a boot top and pulled her back. "You want the dragon to discover this hole?"

Jon subsided. Kelvin breathed a silent sigh. Now, if the incipient scream of the donkey didn't set her off—

He felt a foot on his back. "There's a root here," Jon said. "Or something. I think it can get back up."

A loud hiss that sounded like escaping steam drew his attention back to the hole at ground level. The dragon had moved. Now he could see the little donkey hobbled near the riverbank. It no longer mattered whether Mockery could hear; certainly he could see and smell! The donkey's eyes were rolled back, the nostrils flared.

Then suddenly there was a loud hiss as the dragon's awful, golden-scaled head moved directly over the animal. Slowly the long, serpentine neck lowered, hunching, and the mouth gaped to display the deadly teeth. The forked tongue shot from the mouth and just touched the donkey's flank.

Throp!

It was a magnificent donkey kick that landed with stunning accuracy on the huge snout. A man would have been killed by that strike, or a war-horse disabled. The dragon didn't even seem to notice. Seemingly bent on tasting before devouring, it closed its front teeth in a dreadful snap on Mockery's tail. The tail came off in a little shower of blood.

Kelvin closed his eyes, dreading what the dragon would do next. There was nothing he could do except let it happen.

"Bite my ass, will you! Take that!"

Kelvin's eyes popped open as the childish scream of defiance ended and a walnut-sized projectile struck the dragon's bloodred eye. The rock seemed to go into the eye like a froog into mud, then eject and lodge just under the eye's huge lower lid.

The dragon let out a hiss that hurt Kelvin's ears. The neck twisted the head around to stare at the pile of debris and at the small human figure. A great claw lifted to the lizard face and delicately flicked out the rock from beneath the eye's lid. The slow thought processes were almost evident. This tiny creature was trying to attack!

The dragon hissed again as the neck went back in

striking position. *This is the end of Jon,* Kelvin thought, for the moment too stunned to act.

Then Jon jumped down into the hole, landing on him. Kelvin felt the wind go out of his chest, and a heel bruised his left ear, and a foot hit his hand. He was glad his sister didn't weigh more than she did!

"I got him, Kel! Got him in the eye! Right in the big, bloody eyeball!"

"You've gotten us killed," Kelvin gasped as soon as he could talk. "That thing might have been content with the donkey, but now—"

Nearby snorting interrupted him. A huge, open nostril was sucking up dust at the ground-level hole. Certainly the dragon smelled them now! In another instant the tongue would intrude, would search them out, and then . . . dragon fare!

"Jon, help me roll this boulder!" Kelvin strained at the rock, trying to get it between them and the flaring nostril. He strained, and then he remembered a broken branch he had felt before that might serve as a pry and a smaller rock that might serve as a fulcrum. Quickly he got the smaller rock and the branch positioned, and got Jon's small hands on the branch next to his.

"Heave, Jon, heave!"

He strained until he saw stars. Beside him, Jon groaned. The rock quivered ever so slightly. It was free—broken free of the dirt. Now if it would just *move.*

"Kel, it's got me!" Jon said. At that moment Kelvin realized that a rough and living rope had shot to the side of the boulder and fastened on Jon.

"Where does he have you?" he asked quickly.

"M-my leg."

"Hang on to me. I think—" He threw his back into the effort and then all his weight, buttressed by hers. The dragon was pulling her, and that was actually helping them to put pressure on the lever. It had to be now, he thought, or else there would never be another chance.

The boulder moved. Kelvin scraped up a bit more strength from somewhere and put all he had into it.

The boulder rolled grudgingly over the soggy ground. Now if only—

It had! The boulder had partially blocked the hole, and—

"I'm free, Kel! It let go! But—"

A terrible hissing outside—and something moved next to Kelvin's shoulder. He jerked away with revulsion, even though he knew what it was and what they had done.

The dragon's long tongue was *under* the heavy boulder—a rock the weight of perhaps two very large men, or one very small donkey. The tongue was pinned!

The tongue vibrated at its unpinned tip. Saliva rained into their enclosure, and a breath that was dizzying in its putridity came with a most stomach-turning gagging sound.

"We got him, Jon! For now! Let's get out of here before he forgets how he's hurting and starts using his legs to roll that rock off his tongue!" For though the dragon could readily have moved the rock with its legs or even its head, it was too stupid to make that connection. It was trying to free its tongue by reflex, snatching it back into its mouth. That way would never work!

Jon led the way. They helped each other out of the trap and to the top of the pile where Jon had first sighted the dragon. The beast lay almost level with their faces, its eyes glaring hatred. Kelvin stared back, almost hypnotized by its stare.

Jon picked up the fallen sword and handed it to him. "You've got to, Kel. If you don't, it may get loose. Or it could just die here."

Kelvin's urge was to flee immediately, but he realized she was right. If the dragon was truly pinned, and never figured out how to escape, it would die a lingering death that shouldn't be wished even on a monster. If it did escape, the two of them and the

donkey would be in immediate danger, for the dragon
would sniff them out and pounce on them long before
they got home.

He took the old sword, held it tight, and considered
the best place to attack. An eye, probably, but would
the sword penetrate all the way to the beast's brain?

Gnash!

A large clawed foot came up as he hesitated, striking within an arm's length of Jon. Jon leaped back and
almost slid down the hole again.

The sword was inadequate, Kelvin concluded. He
needed a lance.

"Jon, that long tent pole I cut—can you bring it to
me?" Kelvin didn't dare move, in case the dragon
decided to ignore the pain of its tongue and rip free;
then he would have to try with the sword, however
hopeless it seemed.

"What do you want it for?"

Damn her impertinence! "Just get it! Hurry!"

From the corner of his eye he watched her scamper.
He stood just outside the range of the monster's leg. It
was unnerving to be this close, but if he retreated
farther he would not be in position to strike at the eye
if that became necessary.

Jon paused to examine Mockery's tail stump. "Jon,
Jon, Jon!" Kelvin said to himself in frustration. But
finally she brought the pole.

He used the sword to sharpen the end of the pole to
a near needle point. The dragon's eye watched him
with unnerving intensity. Did the monster know what
was coming? If so, why didn't it simply wrench out its
tongue and free itself? That would be less painful than
a stake through its eyeball! But of course it was an
animal, unable to plan ahead. No creature as powerful
as a dragon needed much in the way of intellect,
ordinarily.

It would be better if he could fasten the sword to the
pole. But then there was a haft on the sword that
would surely stop it from penetrating. The pole, if he
put his weight behind it, would stab through the jelly

of the eyeball and on through, into the pulsing,
seething brain.

Suddenly Kelvin felt faint. The vision of that brain
—could he do it, even to save his own life? Could he
kill so messily in such cold blood?

Jon watched as he put down the sword. Her face
bore a peculiar and undefinable expression. "Kel, let
me do it."

"No. It's dangerous, and I doubt you're strong
enough. I'm not even sure that I'm strong enough."

"That's what I'm afraid of. You look as if you're
about to conk out."

"No!" Stupid sister! Kelvin took the pole firmly in
his hands, balanced it until it felt right, took a deep
breath, and ran the few steps to the dragon. Staring
into the bloodred eye and trying to visualize the
location of the brain in that reptilian head, he drove
the pointed stake with all his strength.

The point hit true. The eye was so large that it
would have been difficult to miss.

It went through the pupil, sending blood and gray
stuff squirting back at him.

There was a frightful scream. The dragon's head
jerked violently. The pole snapped up into the air,
hauling Kelvin with it, for he was so frozen with fear
that he could not let go. Then his hands lost their grip
and he flew. He had a glimpse of Mockery and the
river and trees.

There was the sensation of air moving across his
face. He knew he had done all he could. Had it been
enough?

He felt only a timeless waiting, as for unknown
hands . . .

CHAPTER 3
Memories

"MAMA, WHY ARE MY ears so small and so round? Why aren't they like yours? Why are they like Daddy's?"

He sat in the bath and put questions to his beautiful mother. Even as a small child, he knew what a lovely creature she was. Her hair was the hue of copper, and her eyes of violets. Her skin was translucently white, and her ears were large and pointed. What more could a child ask for?

"Because, my dear, you are very special," she said.

"Special, Mama?" He knew she didn't mean it to hurt, but it always did. He didn't want to be special, he wanted to be normal.

"Your father is special. That is why you are, too."

"But . . . why?"

"He's from another world, dear. A world just a little bit different from ours. There are many such worlds, many such existences, universes. They lie side by side, touching as the skins touch on an onlic. Each skin subtly different, yet subtly same. We can't see the worlds that interpenetrate ours, but they are there, and they are real to the people or beings living there."

"There?" He didn't understand her explanation at all. He only knew that he hated the pungent taste of onlics.

"Here. All about us. Your father talks of atoms and the great spaces between the stars, but the wise ones in our world have different explanations."

He looked around their cottage, at the furniture and at the water he had splashed from the tub onto the polished yellow wood floor. "Here? Another boy? Another boy in another world in another tub?"

"Perhaps many boys in many vessels on many

23

worlds touching and almost a part of ours. It has to be. That may be how myths start, and superstitions, and stories and tales from the imagination. It's the closeness, the nearness, the very near identity." Her fingers, so strong and shapely, soaped his chest. "You'll understand when you're older, dear. When you are old enough to begin to fulfill the prophecy."

"Prophecy? What's that, Mama?"

She dried her hands on a towel, crossed the room to his father's desk, opened it, and took out the vellum-covered book with the bloodstain on its cover. She brought it to him, opened it, and turned the pages so he could see the strange, straggly letters.

"This," she said, "is the Book of Prophecy. It was written long, long ago by Mouvar the Magnificent, who saw ahead, and who wrote ahead, and who became godlike in the process. Mouvar, who fought the great battle with the dark sorcerer, Zatanas, and who will live, some say, forever, if Zatanas does not finally kill him and eject his essence from our continuum. I'm going to read to you some of Mouvar's words written long, long before your father and I were born."

"Is it about me, Mama?" Excitement tingled his hands and feet as though he had grasped an electric bug and been shocked.

"Yes, darling. It's about you. It's in rhyme, like all the prophecies. It doesn't give your name, but it's about you." Squeezing one of his small hands in her larger, stronger hand, she read:

> A Roundear there Shall Surely be
> Born to be Strong, Raised to be Free
> Fighting Dragons in his Youth
> Leading Armies, Nothing Loth
> Ridding his Country of a Sore
> Joining Two, then uniting Four
> Until from Seven there be one
> Only then will his Task be Done

Honored by Many, cursed by Few
All will know what Roundear can Do.

"That's pretty, Mama. What does it mean?"

"That you will fight dragons. That you will rid Rud of its tyrant Queen, Zoanna, daughter of Zatanas. That you will first join two of the Seven Kingdoms, then unite with four. That you will finally join and unite into one land *all* the Seven Kingdoms."

"How will I do that, Mama?"

"When the time comes, you'll find a way. It's prophecy. Prophecy may be misunderstood, but always comes true. Always. If not in our world, in another almost like it."

"True about dragons, too?"

"Yes, darling. About dragons, too."

"Dragons . . . with claws and teeth and a long tongue and scales?"

"Yes, darling. And the scales will be gold, just as in the story I read to you."

"And will I marry the princess and will we live happily together ever after in a great big palace? Will we have servants and courtiers and jesters and acrobats and ponies?"

"You may," she said with an affectionate smile. "But the prophecy leaves us to guess about such details. I don't have the complete prophecy; no one does. Bits of it are scattered around the globe. Some talk of gloves, and some of round-eared girls, but those may not be valid aspects of it. But I know enough to know that you are the one."

He pondered that. "Did you know all the details when you married Daddy?"

She laughed. "I hardly knew any, dear. I simply knew that I had to marry a roundear if I was to have a roundear child, and even then the chances were only even. I hoped he would be a good man."

"You *wanted* a roundear son?" he asked incredulously.

She drew him into her and kissed the top of his left

ear. "I did indeed, Kelvin! But had I known he would
be you, I would have wanted him even without the
prophecy."

He found himself crying, and she held him close,
comforting him. But these were not tears of grief, but
of relief. Now, finally, he could accept being special.
He had secretly feared that his point-eared little sister
had arrived because his mother was unsatisfied with
him.

His father finished twirling the rope and tossed it
over the peg. A jerk of the line and the peg shot from
the ground and followed the rope to his hands.

"All right, Kelvin. Now you try."

But Kelvin had his hands over his eyes. "It's magic,
Daddy! It's magic!"

"It's *not* magic!" Stern blond eyebrows, stern face.
"Magic is simply natural law that hasn't been explained. There's no such thing as magic in this world
or any other. Do you understand?"

"Y-yes, Father." He watched the adult roundear,
frightened, as the lasso was placed in his hands.

"Now you practice, and you practice, and you
practice. This is the only skill I had before I went into
the army, and it's the one skill I can leave you with."

"What good is it, F-father?"

"You saw me lasso the cow the other day."

"Yes, but she would have come anyway."

"Someday there may be something that won't. Now
you hold the loop in this hand, and—"

They worked at it for a very long time, but finally he
could rope the peg nearly as well as could his father.

The door flew open with a bang, scaring Kelvin as
he played with fortune cards on the cottage floor. His
father rushed in, trailing a cold wind and a swirl of
snow. He limped across the room, favoring the leg the
wild bull had kicked long ago while he was trying to
separate it from their cow.

Mama looked up from the coat she was mending,

her expression the one she wore when she was expecting something to happen that happened.

"Charlain, I saw them again," his father said, taking his mother's hand. "They've tracked the rumors to the village. Now I *have* to go. I won't endanger you and the boy any longer!"

His mother lodged the needle in the coat sleeve, stood up, and put her arms around his father. They held each other for a while. By and by she said, "Your travelsack is ready. Will you take the horse?"

"I can't take your horse," his father said. "I couldn't take it the first time I came here, and I can't do it now. You'll need it for plowing. Those cursed tax collectors . . ."

"I'll fix you a lunch."

Kelvin looked at his father and together they watched his mother go into the kitchen. Suddenly his father was kneeling by him, holding him up against his chest. A noise came from that chest, or perhaps his father's throat, and it was not a sound a big, strong man was supposed to make.

"Don't cry, Father."

But his father merely said, "Son, I want you to listen. Listen to me now, even if you never have before. Your mother's head is filled with nonsense. Don't believe her, son. In my world they understand —about atoms and the spaces between atoms. That prophecy is nonsense. Foolish! You're just a boy, son. You won't have to fight a dragon and fight with a sword and lead armies the way she says. If I can, I'll come for you someday. All three of you. If we can, we'll go home to my world. It's not as nice as this world in some ways, but then in other ways . . ."

"Father—" He felt confused, lonely, and scared. What was happening? Why did his father have to leave?

"It will be, son. It must be. Promise me you won't try to live out her prophecies. She's a fine woman, but—"

"Here's your lunch," Mommy said. She held out a

small packet that gave forth the smell of freshly baked bread, and a jar of the bright red razzlefruit wine that Kelvin was not yet allowed to try.

"Charlain, oh, Charlain!" his father said, and then the two were hugging as though there was never to be any more of it.

"I don't want to go. I really don't. But——" There was such anguish in his father's voice.

"It might as well have been written," she said. She seemed so calm, so certain of her facts. "It's as true that you have to as . . . as the prophecy itself."

"Yes." He smiled, wiping at his eyes. His tone seemed to add, "But we both know I don't believe in that nonsense."

"Kelvin," Mommy said, placing her hand on his head, "you stay inside and keep an eye on your sister. Play with your cards. Read your fortune, and your father's, and mine. I'll come back to you before it is suppertime."

Kelvin watched them out of the house and into the barn where the horse was kept. When they did not immediately emerge, he did what his mother had told him and sat down with the cards. His sister, only two years old, was sleeping, so she was no trouble.

He looked at the painted pictures and swirling symbols on the cards. Could these tell anything about what the future would bring?

"Sometimes," Mommy had said, "if you look at them and think about them."

"Nonsense," Daddy had said gruffly. "Nonsense. All of it nonsense. Don't you believe her."

But Mommy had countered Daddy with a conspiratorial wink. She knew what she knew, however tolerant she was of the ignorance of others.

The woodsman's face was grim when he brought the news. Watching him and his mother, Kelvin felt that she really didn't look surprised. She looked, in fact, much as she had the day his father left.

"Nothing much to bury, ma'am. They cut the big

bits into little bits, the filthy highwayman or whoever did it. The wild things had been feasting, but it was no wild thing that was to blame."

She nodded, understanding perhaps more than her son did or could imagine. After a painful pause, she said, "I dreamed it would be you, Hal Hackleberry. You to bring me the dread news, and more."

"Ma'am?"

"Charlain. I want it to be Charlain again." She picked up a stockelcap that his father had sometimes worn under protest, patting it as though it were alive. She looked at what she was doing, then back at the woodsman.

"He didn't believe," she said. "Never. Never once, even after Kelvin happened. He just wouldn't believe."

The woodsman shifted his feet. "I understand, ma'am. Some men are like that. It's nothing against them, you understand."

"I know. Not against them. Some things just have to be. Would you care for some wine?"

"Why . . . yes, ma'am, I would. But—"

"But I have already grieved," she said. "I knew when he left that I would never see him again in this life. I grieved, and now . . . now I am ready."

"Ma'am?"

"For a new life. A life that maybe was only interrupted for a time."

Kelvin was surprised to find tears dripping from his face. The woodsman might be a good man, he thought, but Daddy—Daddy was special.

"Roundear, Roundear, Roundear," taunted the circle of reddish faces. They moved closer, reaching out to poke Kelvin in the stomach and ribs with stiffened fingers.

"You stop that!" cried eight-year-old Jon. Her fists were clenched, and she was all fury as she turned round and round to face the tormentors. But the harder she shouted, and the more angry she got, the

bolder the teasing became. "You stop that or my
brother will fight!" Jon told the biggest and roughest
boy of the bunch. "You're just jealous 'cause he can
charm the berries better'n any of you!"

"Jon!" Kelvin said with alarm. But he knew there
was no stopping her youthful indignation. It was true
that he had developed a way with plants, being able to
encourage them to flower and to sweeten their fruit,
but that wasn't anything he cared to advertise. His
natural father would have called it magic, therefore
invalid.

"He's a hero! A big hero! Mama said!"

"Fight? Fight? You want to fight, Roundear?" the
thirteen-year-old with the tooth out in front demanded.

Kelvin shook his head, remembering what father
John Knight had said about the stupidity of human
beings fighting. *Only if there's no other way, son. Only
if there's no other way.*

"You're afraid," said the bully. "Aren't you?"

"Yes." Kelvin said it before he thought. He always
spoke the truth except to his mother when they were
pretending.

"Ha! Some hero! Come on, boys, let's go to the
pond and skip rocks."

Kelvin breathed a shuddering sigh of relief.

"He'll fight *you*," Jon said. "And he'll lick you,
too."

"Jon, shut up," Kelvin muttered. But he knew that
the unsayable had been said. Now, as his father had
said, there was really no other way.

"Your mother's a witch, Roundear!" the big boy
said, pushing his face close to Kelvin's. "Your sister's
a nasty little frog, and you're a scared and stupid
squirbet."

"Sticks and stones," Kelvin said, reciting the charm
his real father had taught him. "Sticks and stones may
break my bones, but words will never—"

The fist landed on his cheek, hurting terribly. The

boy was all strength and no bluff, and happy to demonstrate it.

Kelvin hit back, almost by reflex. By good luck he hit the bigger boy on the mouth. The boy stood back, putting a hand to his bruised lips where a trickle of blood showed.

"Now you'll get it!" the boy exclaimed. He leaped at Kelvin, swinging with one hand while he grabbed with the other. Kelvin tried to twist aside, and that was partially effective as the fist grazed his ear, but the boy's other hand caught him and hauled him roughly in. Kelvin tried to jerk away, and only succeeded in winding himself into a tighter hold. He pushed forward, the only way he was free to go, and this overbalanced the bigger boy. Their feet got tangled together, and they fell on the ground.

They rolled over and over, while the other boys cheered their hero and Jon shouted advice, mostly inappropriate. Perhaps it looked like a good fight from outside, because of all the motion, but it was really just Kelvin trying desperately to get away while the big boy sought to pin him in a position for some more effective punishment.

Kelvin was getting the worst of it. Now the bigger boy was on top of him, hitting him more often and with greater force. Kelvin was losing his ability to avoid or fend off the blows, and each one hurt awfully.

The bigger boy paused. "You eat horse dung, don't you, Roundear!"

This was Kelvin's chance to capitulate, cutting down on his punishment. But he couldn't lie, even now. "No."

Fists rained down on his face, bruising, hurting, scaring him silly with the thought that he might lose teeth or even an eye.

"I'll help you, Kelvin!" Jon cried. She piled onto the bully's back, fists raining as hard as an eight-year-old girl could manage.

The bully was distracted. It gave Kelvin a chance.

He struck upward, his fist catching the bully's turned head.

He had scored directly on the nose. Blood exploded from a rupture. *"Aahhhh!"* the big boy screamed.

Now his face, so close and ugly, was turning as red as the blood from his nose. Kelvin had won the fight, amazingly, for the bully was unable to do anything except react to the pain and horror of it. It seemed that it had never occurred to the bully that *he* might get hurt. The other boys would not interfere, for there was a code: it had to be one on one. Jon had violated it, but she didn't count, being a girl.

But in that moment before it broke up, a bright shaft of sunlight lit the bully's features, turning them to gold, and that was the image that was to remain most firmly in Kelvin's memory. Because that color was—

Dragon's gold.

Jon and Kelvin had been working beside Hal, their replacement father, grubbing out some tree stumps so that they could plant more grain. The sound of horses' hooves on the hard road and a plume of summer's dust warned of the approach of guardsmen.

Hal nodded toward the woods. "Better you get out of sight, Kel, just in case." He was not their natural father, but he was a good man, and had always treated them well and looked out for their welfare. Charlain had chosen well, both times she married.

"I'll go with him," Jon said.

Hal glanced at her. "Maybe that's best. You're growing up, girl, and there's no telling what guardsmen might do."

Jon flushed, hating to be reminded of her nature. But it was true: the Queen's guardsmen had been known to do things to young girls that couldn't be done to boys. That might be part of what she hated about being a girl.

They went behind some duckberry bushes and crouched, waiting. Kelvin breathed on the leaves and stems, and the bushes moved to provide better concealment. Shortly the guardsmen were there on their war-horses, talking down to Hal.

"You're behind on your taxes, farmer!"

"It's been a bad year."

"You'll pay a fine. A big fine."

"I'll get the money. But if I sell our horse, there'll be no money to buy more seed grain." He patted the large gray animal hitched to the stump. Hal was kind to animals, too, and worked well with them.

"That's your worry, farmer." The guardsman's voice rang with contempt. "Scum like you have to pay. If you don't pay, we set fire to your house and seize your boy to sell in the boy market."

"I'll pay." It was evident that though Hal was technically subservient, he had no real respect for the agents of the Queen. "I just have to chop some wood, and—"

But the big guardsman's face was turning redder and then golden in the rays of the sun. Squinting through the bushes, Kelvin began to see him with a snout like that of a dragon. What was the big difference between a guardsman and a dragon? Both brought destruction on common folk!

The matter of dragons was looming larger in Kelvin's mind. He feared them terribly, but their scales were gold, and represented wealth that could free the farm of debt. He would really have to do what he had talked about to Jon. They would have to leave here and go after gold.

Dragon's gold.

CHAPTER 4
Highwayman

"JON! JON!"

The girl looked up at him with eyes that shone from her face nearly as brightly as what she held in her bloody hands. What she held was palm-size yellow gold, and had belonged to the late dragon.

"Gee, Kel, I thought you were dead!"

"So you were getting the gold anyway." What kind of creature was this sister of his? Sometimes it seemed to him that if anyone was a changeling, it was Jon.

"Well, I couldn't reach you very well, and I thought I might as well start getting the scales. They come off hard, Kel. It's going to be a lot of work."

Kelvin wormed his way off the tree branch, held himself poised, then swung clear and dropped. He lit with a shock to his feet and legs that surprised him. Dragon scales, he remembered, were far from soft, even if gold was supposed to be a soft metal.

"I looked about some," she continued. "There's a funny little patch of berries—"

"You didn't eat strange berries!" Kelvin exclaimed, alarmed. "You know that many of the wild plants out here are poisonous!"

"Of course I know," she said in an aggrieved tone. "I can't charm them into edibility the way you can, with your round ears. I didn't eat any. But for all I know, they might be good, so I saved a few to show Mommy."

Kelvin relaxed. At least she had had some sense! "But what's strange," she continued, "is that they look, well, tended. Almost as if the dragon was taking care of them. His prints are all around the patch, and there's a path leading to it, which is how I found it.

A dragon path. I was going off to—you know."
She never liked to refer directly to natural functions, partly because she couldn't perform them in
quite the manner she deemed proper for a boy. "So I
followed this path, because it was easy, and there
was this patch, almost like a garden, and the dragon could've tromped all over it, but didn't. Isn't
that funny?"

It was indeed! Why would a dragon protect a simple
patch of berries? "You did right to save some," Kelvin said. "Dragons know about some things we
don't."

Feeling trembly and far from good, he let his legs
collapse beneath him. He sat down on the flat area
between two short wings. The dragon's tongue was
still protruding from its mouth and entering the
debris hole, but now a long pole was embedded in its
left eye socket. Evidently he had scored on the brain,
but he shivered to think how close a call it had been. If
he had not thrusted hard enough, or if the dragon's
death throes had hurled him into the trunk of a tree
instead of onto a branch . . .

Could he really have a charmed life, the way his
mother insisted? She had been right about his magic
with plants, after all, and if he really *was* destined to
be the hero of the prophecy, then this was not the
coincidence it seemed. Yet his father had been such a
practical man, making so much sense, that it was hard
to believe he could have been wrong about magic.

Jon came close, bringing Kelvin's sword. "You get
them off, Kel. It's far too much work."

"For you, you mean," he said, disgusted.

"Uh-huh. You're the biggest, so—" Then her composure disintegrated. She flung herself into his arms,
almost stabbing him with the sword. "Oh, Kel, I
thought you were *dead,* maybe, and I couldn't even
reach you!"

He felt her tears soaking into his shoulder. So it had
all been an act, her nonchalance. Unable to help him,
she had gotten to work, hoping he would recover, and

when he had, she tried to remain tough, but wasn't able to carry it quite all the way through. How glad he was of that; she had almost fooled him!

In a moment she recovered her composure. "Oh, I'm getting all icky," she said. "I'm sorry."

"I'm not," he said. "Do you think I like the notion that you don't care at all what happens to me?"

"But it's not manly to cry."

"Jon, someday you're going to have to accept the fact that you're not—"

She cut him off with a bad word.

He dropped that aspect. "Anyway, I'd sure cry if *you* got killed. But you're right; we've got to get to work here. There's a skinning knife in the pack. I'll use that and you use the sword and with luck we'll get the job done."

"When?" Jon asked somewhat sourly.

"Before nightfall if you work hard. You're not going to be girlishly squeamish about dirty work, are you?"

"No!" She hefted the sword, suddenly ready to use it.

"I thought not. Here, let me see how it works." He took the sword from her, stuck it under the nearest scale, and pried. Grudgingly, it came up. Then he cut at the leathery flesh holding it.

This would take longer than nightfall, he realized. Even a dead dragon was tough!

He hacked the scale free and held it up. "There we are—easy as pie." He returned the sword to her and went to fetch the knife.

He was correct. Three grueling days later they had finished as much of the unpleasant task as was possible without turning over the dragon, and were on their way out of the pass. It was just as well, for the huge carcass was decomposing, and the vultures were circling ever lower; soon the attention of other predators or even men would be attracted, and that would be no good for the two treasure-hunters. They had to get away with their prize, and back to the farm unobserved.

Bobtailed Mockery was in tow with two very heavy travelsacks. They had scraped the scales as clean of attached flesh as possible and washed them in the river, but still some odor accompanied them. Jon had to walk behind Mockery and swat the biting flies that landed on the beast, because the donkey threatened to dislodge the load when tormented by flies he could no longer flick off with his tail.

"Do you think we should have dumped all our stuff?" Jon asked. "Those pans and those blankets were still good, even if Mockery did roll on them in the river."

"We can buy more. One scale should buy all the pans and blankets we'll need in our entire lives."

"If we don't live too long," Jon said, liking the notion.

"Of course, Brother Wart."

They plodded on. They were out of the pass now and the sun was shining and it looked to be a glorious day for two rich youngsters. Kelvin was thinking that they hadn't much of a worry in the world. A few scales would pay off the errant taxes on the farm, and a few more would cover all the luxuries Charlain might want, and Hal, too, though Hal was a man of simple tastes. They would turn the scales over to him for safekeeping; he was honest, and would not cheat anyone.

Suddenly a huge black war-horse appeared as if by magic in the road ahead. It bore a man clad all in black. Some bushes swayed at the side; the man must have been lurking there. He leveled a sword that flashed golden in the sun and looked extremely sharp.

"Your property or your lives!" the man said in the time-honored manner of the highwayman.

Disaster! Kelvin swallowed. "We're without coin," he pleaded in the traditional way of the waylaid traveler. He knew that the brigand would check the travelsacks in a moment.

"No coin, just scale," the man said with the certainty with which Charlain announced anything after a look at the fortune cards. "What'd you two do, find a dead dragon?"

"No—" Kelvin started.

With a sudden swish the man's sword tip slashed through the lashings on Mockery's pack and sent the sacks falling. Golden platelets came loose from their stacks and rained down. Mockery went into a bucking protest.

Kelvin choked. He grabbed his sword, yanked it from its scabbard, and—

Watched as it spun through the air in response to the highwayman's quick and expert backhand motion. "Don't try that again, sonny, or it's your life! You!" he snapped at Jon. "Drop that sling, or you'll eat your ears!"

Mention of ears reminded Kelvin to check his own. Fortunately he had remembered to pull down the stockelcap, covering them. Years of getting beaten up had made this an automatic reflex, just as was Jon's concealment of her female attributes.

"Gods curse you, highway horse excrement!" Jon exclaimed.

The bandit swung round to her. "You do what I say, cubwhelp, or—"

Jon's sling started its defiant circle, but before she could let fly, the horseman had leaped his horse to within arm's reach and was leaning down, grabbing the girl by her shoulders. Once, twice, the bandit shook her, and Jon's head tossed helplessly and her long yellow hair flopped out of the cap. Then the highwayman thrust her aside.

Jon lit in the road and immediately scrambled back to her feet. She had dropped the sling as the bandit reached her, and now her face was very pale.

"You look like a damn girl!" the highwayman muttered. "Maybe I'll just lop off some of that hair."

Jon said a word that would have gotten her a hiding even at their liberal home. The bandit laughed. "But appearances can be deceiving, eh? Spoken like the man you'll someday be!"

He had not caught on! Kelvin gave a heave of relief. Bad as their situation was, it could have gotten worse.

"Both of you, load that scale back on that beast! Tie that strap together again so it holds," the highwayman snapped. "And hand your own packs up here!"

They worked, Kelvin knowing that his own face must resemble Jon's. If only the outlaw would make some mistake!

Finished, scales all in place on Mockery's and the war-horse's broad backs, the bandit rode over to Jon. Leaning down, he grabbed the girl and swung her up in front of him on the saddle.

"I'm taking this one to market," he said to Kelvin. "An overseer's whip will teach him manners. Snarly whelp!" He cuffed Jon, who had managed by a clever twist to bite his hand.

Jon said something that Kelvin did not hear but brought another cuff. Reacting at last to this new threat, Kelvin leaped for the war-horse's bridle. He grabbed the rein and raised an arm to try to deflect a blow from the highwayman's sword. He saw a twisted dark face, lips pulled back from yellowed teeth, an old red scar that reached from the right corner of the villain's mouth to the edge of his gaunt cheek below his right squinty eye.

A moment later he found himself lying in the partly filled ditch as a bird sang somewhere and the drumming of the war-horse's hooves pounded off in the distance. Once again, Kelvin had been absolutely ineffective.

CHAPTER 5
Captive

JON HAD CEASED STRUGGLING hours ago. She had realized very early that the more she resisted, the tighter the highwayman gripped her, and it would not be long before his hand or arm encountered aspects of her that were not normal for a boy. She now rode docilely ahead of the bandit on the huge black war-horse. Waiting, she told herself repeatedly, her chance to escape cleanly.

"Not so chipper now, little foulmouth?" the highwayman asked. It was a taunt, she knew, not a question. "You know where I'm taking you? You know what's going to happen to you?"

"You said the Boy Mart," Jon said. She knew of it. Runaway boys, delinquent boys, boys seized for their fathers' nonpayment of taxes, possibly even kidnapped boys were sold like livestock to be slaves. To work someone's plantation, or mine, or. to row a galley. It was all legal in Rud, and boys remained slaves until they reached the legal age of manhood: twenty-five. Quite a number, it was said, failed to live to that age.

There was, however, one thing worse than the Boy Mart. That was the Girl Mart. The girls, it was said, generally lived out their terms, but hardly wanted to. The lucky ones became housemaids or servant girls, but many were sold to brothels or to sadistic old men. Suicide was the leading cause of death among them. Already Jon knew that if she didn't manage to escape, she had better protect her secret, because the Boy Mart was the better bet.

"Yes, the Boy Mart," the bandit repeated, taking her silence for natural dread. "Best thing in the

world for you. The *only* thing in the world for you."
He laughed. Jon looked around at the towering cliffs
and the stunted trees and the new twisting path that
led through brambles and brush and on into more
bleak land. It was semidesert ahead. That was what
was called the Sadlands—a region fit only for scorpiocrabs, giant spiders, and snakes. Outlaws such as this
one reportedly lived there, though why they should
choose to do so was a mystery.

Well, perhaps not so big a mystery. Since honest
folk stayed well clear of the Sadlands, that made it
relatively safe for outlaws. If they had good horses, as
this one did, they could range pretty far out, raiding
better regions and returning. There was a story that an
outlaw had aggravated the Queen once, and she had
sent a party of guardsmen into the Sadlands after
him, and they had never returned. Maybe it wasn't a
true story, but it had an authentic ring. Actually, the
Queen's guardsmen were little different from crimi-
nals at times, so maybe they had simply gone into
business for themselves. Maybe this one was one of
them.

"Whoa," the highwayman called, pulling on his
reins.

Jon made her decision to fight, to the extent she was
able without risking betraying her nature. Whatever
the outlaw wanted, he was not going to get much
cooperation.

The bandit slipped a dark bandanna over her face.
"Can't have you seeing where we're going for the
night, whelp."

So that was it! The outlaw was not very smart for
telling her, Jon thought. One way or the other she was
going to see through the bandanna, or over it or
around it. Since she was destined for the Boy Mart, she
probably would not be hurt if she behaved; then
when she escaped, she could tell Kelvin where the
highwayman's hideout was, so they could steal back
their gold.

But the bandanna was tight. Twice folded over her

eyes, it let in not a bit of light. The outlaw, unfortunately, knew his business.

The horse resumed its steady walk. Jon thought they were going uphill, not down, then down, not up. But she wasn't sure; it could be the other way around. She tried to edge a hand up to the bandanna, but got it slapped down promptly.

"None of that, I tell you," the bandit said. He didn't even sound annoyed. Maybe he took such efforts as a matter of course.

But she had to see, Jon thought. She *had* to.

An insect buzzed loudly near her left ear. She shook her head, and as she did, an idea struck.

Her ears. She could wiggle her ears. Girls weren't supposed to do that; therefore it was one of her proudest accomplishments.

If she could wriggle her ears just enough, the bandanna just might be coaxed down a bit. The right side of the blindfold wasn't folded evenly at the top. If she could work the single thickness down, she could see through it. If the bandit didn't stop her.

Slowly, Jon turned her head until her right ear was directed frontward. The outlaw might not see it now. With luck.

"Flies bothering you? Here!" The highwayman's slap almost took her head off. Her breath hissed in with pain—but while she shook her head in reaction, she made her right ear twitch.

"Huh, missed the fly, hit your face. Hah."

Had he seen, Jon wondered? Could *she* see, now that the bandanna had slipped a little?

Through her right eye she picked up a little light. She could make out the bright sunlight and its sheen on two towering rocks—one on either side of the horse. They were going a different way than into the Sadlands. This was back the way they had come! So the bandit *was* trying to deceive her!

Now she detected the scent of the bilrose tree, and remembered the grove they had passed through earlier. Then she heard water, and knew they were back at the river.

The horse was taking another road, into the mountains. It was the only turnoff place near the river; Jon was certain because she had walked every step into dragon country. It went up above the village of Franklin and then into the mountains and then somewhere she had not been.

The horse plodded now. The outlaw was taking his time. That meant he felt secure from discovery.

They were up in the mountains, and Jon knew the road they had taken. The highwayman had said he didn't want her to see where they would spend the night, and now he seemed satisfied that she didn't know where they had gone. So the camp or cave or whatever must be close. How criminally clever, to have a hideout close to a traveled road, while pretending to stay far away!

Now she heard the *clip-clip-clip* of the war-horse's hooves on rock. Then they were definitely going down a steep path. The outlaw's hand clamped on her shoulder just as she seemed about to pitch off headfirst.

"Well, we're here," the highwayman said. With that, he pulled the blindfold off.

Jon blinked. A rude log cabin was there, set in a box canyon. Cactus trees were nearby. It could indeed be the edge of the mountains in the Sadlands. The outlaw expected her to think they had ridden on and that this place was far away from where they had left Kelvin.

Kelvin? What had happened to him? Was he struggling out into the Sadlands trying to track the highwayman down? He would get himself lost and die of exposure! Kel was a decent brother, but sometimes he was short on common sense.

But now was not the time to worry about Kelvin, whom she could not help. Now was the time to think about herself. Once she got free, she could see what she could do for Kelvin.

"Marta! Marta!" the highwayman called, startling Jon. "Come look at what I brought."

A big, slovenly woman with a wart to the side of her large nose appeared in the doorway. She could almost be this outlaw's sister, judging by her looks. But the way the two embraced indicated otherwise. It seemed odd that a violent criminal should have affection for a stupid fat wife, but it was evidently so.

"Another boy?" the woman said, her voice as abrasive as her appearance. "Can't you do better than that? There's a glut of them on the market; they don't fetch the prices they used to."

Jon knew what *did* fetch good prices: girls. She had to protect her secret!

"I did do better, woman!" the outlaw said cheerfully. "Take a look at these." He held out scales that still had some messy flesh attached, despite Kelvin's and her own best efforts.

"Uck! What?"

"Scale, love, scale! This one and his brother found a dead dragon and pulled its scales off. They've loaded them for me. In those bags on the donkey and in here." He tapped his saddlebags.

"A *dead* dragon?"

"Must have been. The pup and his weakling brother were still alive."

"Some people have all the luck!"

"Yah. *Us!*" Laughing at his own supposed wit, the highwayman shoved Jon stumbling to the back of the cabin. A rough cage stood there with open door.

Jon knew better than to argue. She climbed inside the cage and watched him lock the door.

"She'll bring you a few corbeans and a jug of water," the highwayman said. "You sleep on that old blanket in the corner. And don't try to escape!"

"Suppose I do?" Jon asked, morbidly curious.

"Then I'll slice off your legs and leave you for the wild houcats and the bearvers. That's if I'm in a good mood. If I'm in a bad mood, I'll do something mean. Har, har, har!" He really thought he was being funny.

Jon sat in the cage and stared at the back of the cabin, knowing that it wouldn't be smart to try anything now. She might be able to pry out part of the cage and squeeze through, but that would surely make noise, and they would be alert. The highwayman might indeed be expecting some such attempt, and have a punishment in mind. He wouldn't cut off her legs, for that would ruin her value on the Boy Mart, but he might rip off her clothes and beat her. Except that once he ripped off her clothes, he wouldn't beat her, he'd think of something worse.

The light faded. The woman brought her a plate of stew that smelled somewhat like urine, and a jug that smelled of the liquor it usually held, but now it had only water. The woman did not bother to speak, only motioning her to stay in back of the cage while she set the food inside.

After the long and rough day Jon had had, the stew did not taste nearly as bad as it might have. She ate and drank.

Then she became aware of the need to relieve herself. Would they let her out at least to urinate? But if they did, they would surely watch her, and that would be extremely awkward. If she tried to stand and do it like a man, she'd only get her pantaloons soaked, and they'd know. But if she didn't get out pretty soon, she would have to soil herself right here in the cage.

She pondered, and decided on a course that had a better than even chance of success. "Hey, I gotta go poop!" she called out in the crude masculine manner.

"Just stand up and do it through the slats," the highwayman said, laughing.

"Not in my house!" the woman exclaimed angrily. "It stinks bad enough already!"

"Then *you* take him out," the man said.

"I don't want no woman watching me!" Jon protested loudly. "What do you think I am?"

"Aw, she's seen it before," he retorted. "We sure aren't going to let you loose outside!"

The woman got up. She fetched a length of rope

from a peg on the wall. "He won't be loose." She came and opened the cage door. "Put your head in this," she said, showing a noose at the end of the rope.

Jon obediently put her head forward, and the noose slipped over. The woman tightened it just enough to be snug on the neck. "You try to run, you know how fast this'll tighten," she said.

"I know," Jon agreed. She would be choked in an instant. She climbed carefully out of the cage and walked across the room to the door. The woman had the other end of the rope coiled twice about her hand; she would not let it slip accidentally, and could twitch the noose tight at any moment.

It was getting dark outside. The woman showed the way to a rotten log some distance from the house. There was a trench beyond it, and the smell made clear its purpose.

Without a word Jon pulled down her pantaloons just enough and stuck her bottom out over the trench. She put one hand down in front as if to direct the aim of a member there. The dusk and the hand effectively concealed that region of her body. Fortunately she did have solid as well as liquid wastes to deposit, so the woman had no reason to be suspicious. Men did squat when they had to do both.

The woman proffered something white. It was paper—a fragment of some old wrapper. Jon took it and used it, then quickly pulled up her pantaloons, as if embarrassed that any male anatomy might show before a woman. It would have been far more awkward if the highwayman had come with her, for then she could not have justified her concealment.

They returned to the house. She had made it! They had thought she might try to escape, but she had just wanted to get her business done without destroying her masquerade. Escape had to wait on a better opportunity. Meanwhile, she would have to go easy on what she drank, so that she wouldn't need to urinate again until she could do both together. Until darkness, again, if she didn't manage to escape first.

Back in the cage, she lay down on the smelly blanket and peered out through the cracks in back at the canyon wall outside. By twisting her head to the side she could just manage to see some stars.

When the highwayman and his wife slept, she could get up and pry her way out and escape. If she could do it silently.

But when she slept, she was so tired that she never woke till morning. Her chance to escape had passed. She would be stuck with her luck in the Boy Mart.

CHAPTER 6
Hero

KELVIN RECOVERED HIS SWORD from the ditch, sheathed it, and began what he knew was going to be a long walk. The war-horse's hooves had made plenty of tracks, but the road got harder ahead and the tracks vanished. It was hot and it was uncomfortable and his head hurt.

He would have to have help. There was no way he could rescue Jon by himself. No way that he could even hope to find the highwayman. He had to get to Franklin. That was where the Boy Mart was. The highwayman had said he would sell her, and he wouldn't ride to some more distant market when Franklin was convenient. Kelvin hoped. But when he did get there, what could he do but get himself arrested and sold along with his brother?

There had to be help somewhere. Guardsmen were not to be trusted since the start of the reign of Queen Zoanna, but once they had been good and dependable defenders of the land. Things had been different back before his father's time. His father—his natural father, John Knight—had run afoul of the Queen in some way, and that had led perhaps to his death. Kelvin had a morbid curiosity about that, but it wasn't something his mother liked to talk about.

He would have to go to the guardsmen's barracks outside Franklin and tell about the highwayman and ask and hope. He would have to be very polite and servile, because otherwise he would be seen as a runaway and a vagrant and taken to the Boy Mart as merchandise.

The bandit probably had a shack out in the

Sadlands, Kelvin thought, sniffing the spicy scent of bilrose blossoms from the grove ahead. He would take Jon there, and then tomorrow take her to the boy market. There Jon would be sold, to work at something hard and degrading and unworthy of her sharp brain. If she managed to conceal her sex. That was a special problem, and Kelvin didn't know what complications it would lead to, but it made it all the more urgent that she be rescued promptly.

He thought of Jon, hiding her nature, and being forced to work at hard labor until she was twenty-five years old. Not all boys survived that long, and Jon would have twice as much trouble. The rich merchants and plantation owners and shipping company masters supported the Queen in order to keep the custom alive, so they could have cheap labor. Other lands had long since rid themselves of every type of slavery, except (some wits claimed) that of matrimony. Rud was a fit land for a hero of prophecy to start!

He didn't feel like a hero. Not now that he was out of dragon country, and not even before. It was all nonsense, this prophecy. His father had said as much, and he had believed. Many, many times, he had believed in the invalidity of the prophecy, despite his mother's certainty.

But he had slain the dragon, a perverse thought came.

Luck! Just dumb luck. If there hadn't been that haven in the debris pile, that rock and that stout branch, a deaf donkey . . .

But how, then, do you think prophecy works? It's the stacking of fortune cards, the loading of prediction dice. One has a little extra bonus in the game folks call life.

He shook his head. He didn't like the way his thoughts were going. It must have been that blow the bandit had given him. That and the heat. It was pointless to argue with himself!

Ahead were the two sentinel rocks flanking the

road, like waiting highwaymen. Such imagery came readily now! Straight ahead were the Sadlands, while dragon country was back the way he had come, and the road to Franklin was to the right and across the bridge.

He had no choice but to go right. It was almost as if it had been prophesied. But that laugh was ringing somewhat hollowly in his mind now.

The appleberry bushes by the bridge parted just as he got there and a large, woolly, red-coated bearver waddled out. The animal looked at him, sniffed, caught the scent of dragon's blood, and turned and ran.

Kelvin heaved a sigh. If he had been forced to face the bearver in a bad mood with only this old sword, he knew he would have ended up as the bearver's meat.

That's no way for a hero to think!

Who's a hero?

I'm a hero.

Shut up!

He had to keep walking even though he was tired and depressed and everything seemed crazy and hopeless. His tongue felt swollen and his head whirled so that everything shimmered in the heat haze. He had to go under the bridge and wash his face and get a drink.

His legs felt like cooked lengths of pasta stalk, wobbly and weak. Slowly he made his way down to the water. A mooear raised its handsome big-horned head, sniffed, caught the scent of dragon on him, and abruptly turned tail and went.

Dragon is good for one thing, anyway.

That's more than I am right now.

He knelt on the muddy bank and looked at his reflection. He had dirt all over his clothes and all over his face. He should wash both body and clothes before going into Franklin, he realized. Otherwise he would be arrested as a vagrant for certain. Then he would go to the Boy Mart, but not as a rescuer. Jon would cuss him out roundly, before they were separated forever by the auction.

He scooped up some of the water and drank. It was muddy-tasting, but very cold, like snow from the high mountaintops. His hands tingled and hurt from their contact with the cold.

If only he had some money, he thought. If only . . .

He stripped off his clothes, sloshed them in the river, tossed them aside, and then went to work on himself. Without soap, it was difficult, but he scrubbed himself with his wadded-up clothing and managed to get some of the dirt off each. The dragon's blood had accumulated on his boots and was caked and noisome; that was his hardest struggle. When he was done he was shivering blue, with welts and bruises showing up much better now that their covering of grime was gone, but at least he didn't look as if he had just wallowed in a mud hole and rolled around in dragon filth.

As he was redonning his garments, something scratched his right hand. He looked in the hip pocket of his pantaloons and found a single golden scale. It was the first dragon scale Jon had found. He had slipped it into the pocket and forgotten it.

So at least I can't be arrested for vagrancy. Not as long as I hold that.

Luck!

Stacked cards. Weighted dice.

He had to get on to Franklin.

As he started back up the bank he spied a battered plant. The mooear had trampled it when fleeing. But this was no ordinary growth; it was a shade-blooming spicerose! Those were extremely rare and valuable, because the scent of their blooms was supposed to send the one who sniffed one into a few minutes of utter ecstasy.

There was a rose, on a broken stem. Kelvin lifted the flower and sniffed. It had a very pleasant aroma, but it didn't transport him. Either the story of the power of a spicerose was exaggerated, or he was immune to it. As a roundear he had a number of attributes that differed from those of pointears, including his facility with plants; this could be another example.

Too bad he couldn't heal the trampled plant! But his magic, if such it was, was limited to facilitating health in a living plant; he could not restore a dead one. He felt guilty, because if he hadn't come down under the bridge, into the shade that the spicerose required for its blooming, the mooear would not have spooked and the fine plant would not have been damaged. Well, he might help the rose a little; he could save the flower, and breathe a second blooming into it for some other person, later.

He tucked the rose into a pocket, where the direct sunlight would not touch it and destroy it, and resumed his climb.

As he reached the road again, he felt better than at any time since the highwayman rode off and left him in the ditch. Maybe the spicerose *had* buoyed him!

As he started walking he wished that he had his mandajo. He didn't feel like playing or singing, and yet it would be company. Alas, the highwayman had it, along with the donkey and the gold and his sister.

A squirbet chattered at him from an oaple tree.

He looked up at the fuzzy, short-tailed rodent and thought how good the last one had tasted. Jon had been responsible for that: Jon and her sling.

Well, at least he could eat one of the fruits of the tree. Oaples weren't the most luscious fruits, but he could make do. He reached up and put his hand on a low-hanging one. "You are the oaple of my eye," he said to it. "I long to eat your delicious substance. May I pluck you?" He tugged, and in a moment the tough stem let go. Like most fruiting trees, this one was subject to flattery. Kelvin knew his father would have said it was superstition, that he just knew how to pick the ripe ones, but the fact was that any fruit Kelvin touched tended to ripen and sweeten when he praised it, and to turn sour when he condemned it. His mother had the same ability, and she had no hesitation about calling it magic. "Of course it is, dear! My family has always been good with plants." Which meant, he reflected, that his round ears were not after all responsible. Did it matter?

He plodded on, step by step, eating the oaple, trying harder and harder to think that the prophecy his mother so firmly believed in would enable him to win out. To believe that his mother was correct. After all, if she was right about one thing, why not another?

His lovely mother, Charlain. His homely, sturdy, decent stepfather, Hal. What were they doing now? Kelvin and Jon had planned for an exploration of a week's duration; it had taken them two days to reach the dragon, three more to get the scales off, and this was the sixth day. They would not even be missed until tomorrow or the day after. Unless Charlain read the cards, and realized. But what could she do, assuming that the cards worked? No, this was Kelvin's own mess to muddle through, somehow.

After an eternity on the road, he brushed sweat from his eyes and saw the grimy barracks building ahead. He dreaded what was likely to happen there, but he knew he had to do it. He was, after all, supposed to be some kind of hero.

"Ho, ho, ho! Took your little brother, did he? Said he'd take him to market, did he? Heh, heh, ho!" The burly guardsman clasped his sides and wiped at the tears running down his florid cheeks.

Kelvin swallowed as he looked at this blue-and-gold-uniformed representative of law and order. He was at the guardhouse outside the village of Franklin. Beyond the guardsman were others, similarly uniformed, similarly slovenly. Open collars and dirty undershirts seemed to be the order of the day. Even if the guardsmen were competent, they were an unlikely lot to ask for help. But he had to do it. Hanging on to his slipping courage, he persisted: "You do arrest highwaymen?"

"Certainly, my boy, certainly. Every now and then when one of them doesn't divide the loot."

"Shut your fat mouth, Carpenter!" a guardsman wearing sergeant's stripes ordered. He glared at the man until he sobered, then swung round to Kelvin.

"Tell me, boy, was there anything of value taken?" His tone was freighted with contempt. "Besides that valuable brother of yours?"

Kelvin thought quickly how not to lie. He hadn't actually said Jon was a boy, just that the outlaw was taking Jon to the Boy Mart, and the guardsmen had jumped to the obvious conclusion. He knew that if he told them about the gold, they would lose what little interest they had in justice and go for the wealth. "Our donkey, sir. We paid out two rudnas in good coin for him. He's bobtailed, and he's deaf. Stone-deaf, sir, though we didn't know that when we bought him."

"Deaf? A deaf donkey," said the first man Kelvin had spoken to. "A skinny boy to act as a scullery hand or stable boy! A skinny boy and a deaf-as-stone donkey. Ho, ho, ho!"

"Carpenter!" roared the sergeant. "The next time you bray like that you'll do a donkey's work! You hear?"

"I hear ye, Sarge."

"Sergeant! Sergeant, you impudent jackass!"

"Sergeant," the man agreed after a pause.

Kelvin looked from private to sergeant and then about the small guardhouse. Only one face, that of a young guardsman only a couple of years older than Kelvin, showed any sign of sympathy. He thought he would prefer to talk to this man, but the sergeant was staring straight into his face.

"You know the consequences of lying to a queen's guardsman, don't you, boy?"

"I, ah, yes, sir."

"I can hang you or cut off your ears or cut off

anything else I fancy. A guardsman must not be lied to—especially by scum. You understand?"

"Y-yes, sir."

The sergeant paused, glaring at him, and Kelvin thought to himself that he recognized him as one of the tax collectors who had come to his farm.

"What did this highwayman look like, boy?"

Kelvin thought fast. "He wore black, and he had a black horse."

"That describes half the highwaymen in Rud. What else?"

"A—a scar. From here"—his finger traced a line on his face—"to here."

"This scar—was it deep red?"

"Yes, sir."

"Cheeky Jack!" Carpenter said suddenly. "That rascal owes me a drink or six! I thought he moved out to the plains, and here he is, plying his trade just like he's been since the day he left the barracks!"

"Carpenter," the sergeant said evenly, drawing his sword, "stick out your tongue."

"What?" Carpenter's face paled. He had evidently pushed the sergeant too far this time.

"Stick out your fool tongue. It's flapping too much. I believe I should shorten it."

"No, Sergeant. Please!" The man was really frightened.

"Are you refusing a direct order?"

"N-no."

"Stick out your tongue!"

Carpenter's tongue protruded from his bulbous lips. He looked sick. He wasn't laughing now. Sweat stood out in globules on his greasy forehead. Kelvin was suddenly conscious of the odor the man exuded of cheese and beer and a long-unchanged undershirt. Here he had been concerned about his own appearance, and the guardsmen were just as bad!

The sergeant's sword rose and flicked, its point just lightly pricking the man's tongue. A single drop of blood fell to the unswept floor of the barracks. Carpenter's eyes rolled, their whites showing in terror. It was obvious that the sergeant could have done much worse damage if he had chosen to.

"Let that be a reminder," the sergeant said, sheathing his blade. "Now you," he said, turning quickly to Kelvin. "Get out."

"Sir?"

"Out!"

"But this Cheeky Jack—will you catch him?"

"Out! I don't want to see your baby face again. Ever. And, boy, if I find you've lied to me, whatever happens to your brother will be nothing compared to what I'll see happens to you. You understand me, boy?"

"Y-yes." There went hope, he thought.

"Then get!"

Kelvin ran outside, looking wildly around at the dusty road and the collection of houses and shops on the adjoining street. There was no help anywhere. For him or for Jon.

A burst of laughter from the guardhouse set him walking. At the end of the street was a shade tree and a bench, empty for the moment. He made for it, reached it, and sank down on it with a sigh that made him feel much older. Sixty, perhaps. He sat and gazed at the grass, wishing the sergeant were under it. If only he had such magic, to rid Rud of such monsters! If only there *were* such magic! He'd give anything to have such power instead of this worthless prophecy that was only getting him in trouble.

"Ah, there you are! I was hoping I'd catch you."

Kelvin rose, ready to run, but it was the young guardsman he had seen watching him. The man was empty-handed and looked human. Of course after Carpenter and that sergeant, *anyone* would look human.

"Stay there. I'll pretend I'm chewing you out for sitting where only guardsmen are allowed to sit. It's not a law, but the officers have made it one. Some such as Carpenter would beat you for sitting here."

Kelvin stared at the fellow, but there was no mockery in the man's manner. The guardsman was leaning over, staring him directly in the face.

"We're not all like that. The trouble is, with such as Sergeant Kluff, we have to pretend to be. If I didn't, well, then I'd be beaten, or worse. I'd like to help you, but I'm not sure I can. You go into Windmill Square and find my father. He's got the biggest, widest shoulders of any man you ever saw. He looks like me, but heavier and older, with graying hair. You talk to him. His name's Morvin Crumb. I'm Lester Crumb. Friends call us Mor and Les Crumb. Crumbs, it's said, from the same loaf."

"I'm Kelvin Knight Hackleberry. Friends call me Kel."

"Knight? What an interesting name! I wonder if it means anything, prophecy-wise. Well, go to Windmill Square. Just follow that side street." He nodded with his chin. "Wait by the speaker's platform and eventually my father will show. He's a rough man, and stern, but you'll like him. Most people like Mor Crumb."

"I—I thank you," Kelvin said. He felt overwhelmed by this unexpected kindness.

"You just do it, Kelvin Knight Hackleberry." Les Crumb gave him the friendliest smile yet, a smile made brighter by a ray of sunshine that momentarily turned his face to the color of a dragon's sheen.

"Maybe, just maybe," Les added as Kelvin started to get up, "Father can help you to recover your brother."

CHAPTER 7
Gauntlet

KELVIN SAT ON A bench in the park called Windmill Square and listened to his growling stomach. It was getting louder than the sounds of the gathering across the square! It was difficult to decide whether his worst complaint of the moment was hunger or fatigue, but the longer he rested, the more the balance shifted toward hunger. He had eaten only the single oaple this afternoon, and there were no fruit-bearing plants in sight. What was there to eat? He had to wait here until Mor Crumb showed up; if he left even for a few minutes, he might miss the man. And if he cared to risk it, where would he go for food? To some shop where they would charge him so much that he would have to use the dragon scale for money, and then they would cheat him of most of its value? No, he really needed some honest help, and the young guardsman's father seemed like his best bet. But when would the man ever show?

He gazed up into the beenut tree nearby. Maybe there would be some beenuts. They were not his first choice of food, because of the extreme difficulty in cracking them open, but they would certainly do for now, and the tree was close enough to the bench so that he could watch it from there. This was the remnant of a once-magnificent tree, with thickly spreading foliage to the sides, but a sadly marred trunk. Lightning had wounded it, leaving an oozing cleft. As a gust of wind moved the leaves about, he saw into that cleft. There was something wedged in it that reflected a glint as the sunlight briefly penetrated to it.

Curious, as well as hungry, Kelvin got up and walked to the tree. None of the people in the vicinity paid him any attention. The ground beneath it was a tangle of weeds and briers; no one had come here recently. But there, at about twice the height of a man, was the wedged object. It seemed to be some kind of heavy glove, with metallic reinforcements.

Well, where there was one glove there might be a pair, and gloves could always be useful. Kelvin suppressed his fatigue and set about climbing the tree to reach it.

The bark was rough, so that he found fingerholds and toeholds. He hauled himself up, and in due course reached the glove. He took hold of it and hauled it out of its cleft. It was more than a glove; it was a massive gauntlet, fashioned of good quality dragon leather, with reinforced studs of silver metal across the knuckles. That was what had reflected the gleam. This must have been one expensive piece of equipment when new!

He felt around for the companion glove, but couldn't find it. He climbed higher and inspected this entire part of the tree, but there was nothing. Just this single gauntlet for the left hand. How strange that it should have been left here alone!

Still, half a pair was better than none. Might as well use it. He shook it out to free it of whatever bugs might have taken up residence inside, and slipped it on his hand. The thing fit marvelously well; it was as though it had been made to his measure. It seemed about time that something went his way!

He climbed down. His right hand felt the abrading roughness of the bark, but his left hand was quite comfortable. The gloved fingers gripped with surprising accuracy and force, greatly facilitating his descent. His hand felt as if it had infinite power.

He reached the base. Now he observed the beenuts scattered on the ground, dropped by the tree. Those should be edible; maybe he could after all crack some open and get a meal of sorts.

He picked one up and brought it to his mouth. His teeth clamped on the hard shell and bore down, but it would not give. This nut was too tough for him; he would have to bash it open with a rock.

Naturally there were no rocks around. No big sticks, either. Well, he could bash it with the haft of his sword. Of course that would probably either make it explode into far-flung fragments that would be lost in the briers, or crush shell and nutmeat into one inedible mass. What he really needed was a nut-cracker.

He held the nut between the thumb and forefinger of the gauntlet and squeezed, wishing it could be that easy.

The nut cracked.

Kelvin did a double take. Oh—he had probably happened on a flaw, catching it just right. He picked out the meat and put it in his mouth. It was slightly bitter, but tasty enough. Had he picked it fresh from the tree, he could have charmed it into a better taste, but the fallen nuts were beyond his power to improve. However, he was not about to climb way up to the tips of the bearing branches to reach growing nuts; he would probably fall and break his neck if he tried.

He picked up another and tried it similarly, between the gauntlet's thumb and forefinger. This one cracked open as readily as the first. Good enough!

He tried the third with his right hand. He got nowhere. He tried it between his teeth, but it was impervious. He tried it with the gauntlet, and it opened as if its shell were made of paper.

Now, this was interesting! He experimented, and verified that the glove had power that the rest of him lacked. When he linked his right hand to the gauntleted left and squeezed, carefully, his right soon was hurting, while his left never felt the pressure. Apparently the glove amplified the power of any motion his fingers made—enormously.

He reached out to grip the tough bark of the tree. He squeezed—and the bark crumbled. He put several nuts in the glove and squeezed hard—and they compressed so quickly and thoroughly that juice spurted.

What remained when he opened his hand was just dry mash.

Kelvin gathered as many beenuts as he could hold and returned to the bench. There he methodically cracked them open and ate them, feeling steadily better as his stomach got back into business. What a discovery this gauntlet was! How strange that it had remained lodged in that cleft, and nobody else had noticed it or, if they had, bothered to fetch it down. All the people here, constantly passing through, yet none of them really looking at the tree! Who would have thought that the accidental acquisition of a single glove could have brought him a decent meal!

"Young man—"

Kelvin jumped, turning. The man facing him had the reddest countenance he had ever seen. His shoulders were as wide as the rest of him, and the rest of him was as broad as the back of a war-horse. His ears shone pinkly at the lobes and had little tufts of dark hair at their tips.

"Morvin Crumb?" Kelvin asked after a moment, recovering from his surprise. He had gotten so involved in cracking nuts that he had tuned out the world!

"That's right, youngster. And you're—"

"Kelvin Knight Hackleberry. Your son said—"

"Yes, I know." Morvin brushed a pile of beenut shells from the bench and sat down beside him. Then, speaking in a conspiratorially low tone, he said, "We've had a small group of vigilantes here in Franklin. Crumb's Raiders, we call ourselves. Now and then we can help someone, but it all depends on who they are and how bad they deserve help. What's your loss?"

"My sister," Kelvin said, thinking of nothing else. "A highwayman named Cheeky Jack has her, and—"

"A girl? How old is she?"

"Fourteen. But she—"

The man shook his head sadly. "Then it is already too late to help her. Don't you know what outlaws

—and guardsmen, too, for that matter—do to girls that age?"

"Yes, but she's masquerading as a boy. So with luck Cheeky Jack doesn't know."

Mor considered. "So you two aren't entirely naive about traveling, then?"

"Not entirely," Kelvin agreed. "But we still got ourselves into real trouble. If that outlaw finds out—"

"Better hope he doesn't. Then at least she has a chance."

"He said he was taking her to—"

"Yes, yes." The man rubbed his bristly chin. "The highwaymen stock the Boy Mart all the time. We've had little luck in preventing it."

"Then—"

"Maybe. If Les can help. He's a good lad. Too good for the likes of the Queen's guards."

"Then why—"

"Listen, Hackleberry, we may not have much time. The speaker up there on the platform has been trying to stir up trouble." He jerked a thumb, indicating the region. "He's a windbag, and none of us noticed what he was saying until we started noticing the crowd. He's got about twelve listeners besides several Raiders, and that's too many if—"

"I don't see any guardsmen." Kelvin looked about. All he saw were farmers.

"They come disguised. And there are informers."

"Do you really think—"

"Any moment. That's why we have to leave. Now."

A clatter at the end of the park caused them to turn. Three guardsmen, one of them Private Carpenter, another Sergeant Kluff, were bearing down on the platform and the speaker.

"You, Speaker, you're under arrest!" the sergeant shouted. "And you, Crumb and the boy, you're under arrest, too."

Crumb's eyes stood out in his red face as he bellowed back: "Good people, none heard me speak today! I was but listening to the talk and enjoying the shade! There's no cause for my arrest!"

"None for mine, either," Kelvin squeaked. He hardly sounded like any hero now!

"Boy," Crumb said, "they mean to slay us. I'll fight them, but they're mean. That sergeant's fast! I want you to hold back and watch your chance. Maybe I can get one or two of them, and if I do, you get away. Hear!"

"I need your help!" Kelvin gasped.

"*I* need someone's help," Crumb said, disgusted. "They must have followed you."

"If I had a good sword—"

"Lad, this is nothing for a boy, this is something for a man. Get away if you can. Save yourself, and then maybe some other time you can save your sister. Or somebody's sister."

Kelvin picked up his old sword. He raised it in his right hand and the gauntlet on his left and tried to look as defiant and fierce as Crumb. "Now I'm armed," he said, but his attempt at a bold statement came out as another squeak.

"Look at the fool!" cried Private Carpenter of the pricked tongue. "Thinks because his name is Knight he's a warrior. You protected by magic, boy?"

"Gods," Crumb exclaimed, staring at Kelvin. "Hackleberry, that gauntlet—where did you get it?"

"Found it in the beenut tree," Kelvin replied, wondering at the man's intensity. "It was in the wood where the lightning struck."

"Lightning? Lightning! Gods! Hackleberry, off with your cap!"

"What?"

"Your stockelcap, man! Off with it!"

Hesitantly, then defiantly, Kelvin reached for his cap. He pulled it off, feeling it yank at his ears.

Crumb gave a great sigh. "A roundear! Could it be the Roundear of Prophecy, come at last?"

"That's just a wild story!" Kelvin protested. "I'm no hero!"

"We'd better assume it's valid, because otherwise

we're finished," Crumb muttered. Then his voice rose, booming across the square. "The Roundear of Prophecy came to lead our fight!"

"But—" Kelvin protested weakly.

"Treason!" shouted Sergeant Kluff, taking a step forward.

Now Crumb's stance and voice took on the appearance and sound of the seasoned orator. "Good people," he cried in a voice that really carried, "are you willing to live and let your children and grandchildren live under the rule of a tyrant? We've got a champion here—or the start of one. Think! Act! Now!"

Suddenly hands were raised and the three guardsmen were surrounded.

"Back! Back!" the sergeant ordered. "Back, or I'll split the lot of you!"

But the man was given a hearty shove in the back and he stumbled forward. Crumb backed away, calling over his shoulder. "Hackleberry, lad, I want you to take my sword."

"But—"

"Just take it, son. Don't think about it. Just think about your left arm and using it to protect yourself."

Kelvin feared his legs would go out from under him, they felt so rubbery, but he took Crumb's sword and let Crumb take his. Crumb looked at him and made a motion. Carpenter and the other guardsman were suddenly grasped by willing hands. Only the sergeant remained free.

Then, to Kelvin's astonishment and alarm, Crumb did an amazing thing. Sheathing the old sword, he said, "You take him, Hackleberry."

"W-what?"

"The sergeant here. Or would you prefer to battle all three?"

"At once?" Kelvin squeaked, terror constricting his throat again.

"Look how scared he is," said the sergeant. "He can't take me, gauntlet or no gauntlet."

"Think left hand, Hackleberry," Crumb whispered.

Kelvin hardly had time to think. As the sergeant's blade swished out, he raised the gauntlet in what he knew was a futile effort to stop him.

With blinding speed the gauntlet got between the sergeant's blade and Kelvin's otherwise unprotected face. He felt nothing but a slight tap on his wrist. Then the sergeant's blade rebounded.

Kelvin looked at his intact left hand. That hand should have been lying on the ground! He took a deep, shuddering breath, raising that hand again as the sergeant drew back his blade for another strike. The man's teeth were gritted; he intended to make sure that he lopped off Kelvin's entire upper section this time!

The blade struck forward. The gauntlet moved like a snake striking a bird. It caught the blade, then wrenched the sword expertly from the sergeant's hand.

Kelvin, numbed by this occurrence, still managed to raise Crumb's sword, posing its blade in front of the man's throat.

"Still don't believe it's his gauntlet, Sergeant?" Crumb asked the disarmed man.

The sergeant looked at the sword point, at Kelvin's trembling arm, then turned pale as the belly of a frog. He dropped to his knees. "Don't slay me. Don't!" he pleaded.

"Slay him, Hackleberry!" Crumb ordered.

Kelvin's hand shook. "I c-can't!"

"He needs slaying. He would have slain you, and me. And any other who got in his way. He enjoys slaying. He has no mercy, and deserves none. You know that!"

Kelvin did know that. Still he couldn't do it. "I—"

"Hackleberry, is it possible that you don't know the meaning of that gauntlet?"

Kelvin shook his head. He had never felt more certain that he was unsure of anything.

"Gods!" complained Crumb. "What do they teach

younguns these days? It's a gauntlet once owned by Mouvar the Magnificent, he who wrote the Book of Prophecy. You *have* heard of the book?"

"Of course." Some of Kelvin's uncertainty was replaced by ineffective indignation.

"And you do remember the story of his battle with Zatanas, Prince of Evil, sorcerer and father of our unwanted Queen?"

"They flew," Kelvin said. "According to legend."

"And Mouvar dropped his gauntlets. When they are found, Zatanas will be properly vanquished."

Now Kelvin remembered. There had been such a story in another section of the fable Charlain had read to him. He had not made the connection before. Could this really be one of those fabled gauntlets? "According to legend," he said weakly.

"Right. What else?"

"'And the gauntlet great shall the tyrant take,'" he quoted. It seemed impossible that this could be one of those! His father, John Knight, had always pooh-poohed such legend, despite his mother's belief, even though the legend was the reason his Charlain had married him. Could she be right, after all?

"That's the scripture, lad!"

"The gauntlets are supposed to contain the souls of brave and powerful knights."

"Right! With them, you cannot be defeated."

"But—" Belief was starting to seep in. "But I have only one."

"A detail," Crumb said. "Maybe both gauntlets were seeking you, and this is the one that found you. Now is the time for you to take command. To lead your people. To excise the sore on this our gentle land."

"I, uh—"

"To start with, what are you going to do about this?" Crumb lightly touched the sergeant with his foot.

Kelvin looked at the man groveling before him. So

this was what it was like to be a hero and a puppet of prophecy!

"I—I give him his life." It was what any hero would have done in any old storybook.

"You *what?*"

"I g-give him his life, if he—"

"Hackleberry, hero or no hero, you've got rocks in your fool head!" Crumb took back his sword with a sudden grab. Then, as the sergeant made a triumphant half-leap with an extended knife, Crumb swiftly and expertly deprived him of his head. He gave a quick signal and the men holding the other two guardsmen used daggers on their charges in silent unison.

"You," Crumb said to Kelvin, "have an awful lot to learn about being a hero."

Looking at the two dead men oozing blood, and at the headless, spurting body of Sergeant Kluff, Kelvin felt a sudden great illness.

The beenuts he had so avidly consumed chose this moment to erupt from his mouth.

A moment later, Kelvin stood clutching his aching stomach. The park and the men and the body were whirling round and round and round.

Learn to be a hero. Learn to be a hero.

If he could. If only he could!

CHAPTER 8
Boy Mart

Jon looked around at the circle of boys. Some were older than she was, and some were her own age. But she looked younger, because she was not a boy. How long could she maintain her masquerade? Here there seemed to be no private place for natural functions, and if they required the boys to strip . . .

The boys clustered around her the moment the guards closed the door and departed. She had only a moment to look around, noting the small barred windows. There were three pails in the corners; one seemed to contain water for drinking, and the other two—

Oh, no! They were what served for elimination! Right out in public. That was certain disaster for her.

So this was the Franklin Boy Mart, she thought as she wondered what she was going to say to the crowding boys. At least, this was one of the holding pens. The odor was bad; the boys were all dressed in rags, and seemed not to have bathed for weeks. Still, she hadn't had a bath either, since Mockery rolled in the river. Her dirt was now excellent protective costuming; she did look like one of these boys.

"You," the biggest, meanest-looking boy said, poking her in the stomach with a thumb. "You know who's boss?"

"Not me," Jon said. It would do her no good to fight here. If she fought anyone, it would be whoever purchased her. If she couldn't manage to escape first.

Her answer seemed to puzzle the boy. "You new? This your first time?"

"Yeah," Jon said, trying to get some masculine husk

68

into her voice. "I've never been here before."

"Newly pressed?" another boy asked. This one was a bit shorter than the first, but looked just about as mean.

"Newly brought by a highwayman," Jon said. "I've always been free. Never bound."

"Lucky!" the big boy said.

Jon examined the faces. Most, underneath their dirt, seemed unnaturally hard. Village boys didn't usually look as though they never laughed.

"I'm Bustskin," the big boy said. "I'm boss until somebody knocks me down."

"Boss of what?" Jon asked.

"Here."

"Here? This room?"

"Yeah."

"That's not much."

"You want to challenge it?"

"No. You're the boss."

"You sure, Newskin?"

"Newskin? What's that?"

"You. When you're new, just ready to be bound. Newskin."

"Oh. Yeah, I don't want to fight anyone. I had enough fights before I got here."

"Yeah? Who with?"

"The highwayman. And a dragon."

"Dragon?" Bustskin was incredulous. "You?"

"And my brother. We both fought it."

"Liar."

Jon considered. She didn't like being called a liar. She might have to fight this fellow, lest the boys take her retreat as a sign of unboyishness, but she didn't want to. She was older than he took her for, and she did know a trick or two that she had taken pains to learn after being so ineffective when trying to help her brother in the past; she just might be able to surprise him and knock him down. But her risk was much greater than just victory or defeat. If she won the fight, but her clothing got torn and revealed her nature, she would be a worse loser than he. What was the course of least danger?

"You going to let me call you a liar, Newskin?"

Jon shrugged. "You could lick anyone here," she said, hoping he wouldn't notice the change of subject.

"Yeah. And don't you forget it, Newskin." The big boy half turned, as though to leave, then suddenly slammed a rock-hard fist into her stomach.

Jon doubled over, gasping.

"That's just for being a liar. For being a Newskin."

"Fight! Fight! Fight!" several of the boys chanted.

Jon found tears in her eyes. That fellow could really hit! At the same time, she was thankful he hadn't struck her in the chest. How awful it would be to be bound with him on the same plantation! Judging by Bustskin's darkened skin and ruddy complexion, he had never been in a mine, and he didn't look as if he had ever rowed a galley. Chances were he would get a foreman's job bossing field workers, and just possibly he would survive to reach twenty-five. If someone didn't slay him first.

"You going to fight, Newskin?" the bully asked.

"Don't do it, Jon! Don't!"

Jon blinked. It was a red-haired lad she remembered from the village. He was a decent sort, but had been given up for a tax penalty a year before. His parents and brother and sisters had all cried.

But he represented perhaps a worse threat to her than the bully did. Because he had called her by name. He knew her—and therefore knew she was a girl. If he gave her away—

"Tom? Tom Yokes?" She had hardly recognized the boy, so changed was his appearance. He had scars on his arms and legs; both his eyes were blacked. "He did this to me," Tom said, indicating the scars and his eyes. "If I couldn't lick him, then you sure can't. I'm bigger than you, and stronger."

Because he was a boy. He had avoided reference to age, knowing they were the same age, so as not to betray her. He was keeping her secret.

Jon wished fleetingly that her brother were here. Kelvin didn't like to fight, but he could when he had to, and he was almost as big as Bustskin. Bustskin deserved a lesson.

But she was not the one to give him that lesson. Not now, not this way. Slowly Jon straightened, letting go of herself. Her stomach still hurt. She hadn't balled her fists, and she knew that with Bustskin standing there so eagerly that it wouldn't be wise.

"Tom . . . can I talk to you?" she asked. "Over there in the corner?"

Tom nodded.

"You win, Bustskin," Jon said. "I ran away from home. I was caught by someone on a black horse. I never saw a dragon and I never learned to fight."

Several of the boys broke into a halfhearted cheer. It irked her to lie. Kelvin, she knew, would have stuck to the truth or kept his mouth shut. She really respected Kelvin for that, but she just couldn't do it herself.

Bustskin drew back his fist and waved it in front of Jon's mouth. "I should hit you once or twice for lying to me."

"You did," Jon said.

"No, Bustskin, don't!" Tom cried.

Bustskin whirled on him. "You want some more, Redhead?"

"N-no. We're going to be sold soon, Bustskin. Now's not the time to fight. Besides, you've licked everyone here."

"Yeah, I have, haven't I?" Bustskin turned and clapped another boy on the back. "Let me tell you about the girl I had on the Finch plantation. She was the overseer's daughter and she brought us slops. One day when she came too near and the overseer was away, I reached out and—"

As he spoke, he turned again and reached out by way of illustration, grabbing the closest material available: Jon's dirty brownberry shirt. This could not have been accidental; probably he intended it as one final humiliation. He hauled in and up, pulling it out of the waistband. The material was too tough to tear, but the jerk did cause her to stumble forward, and as her head came low, he pulled the shirt up over her head, blinding her.

There was an abrupt silence. Quickly Jon brought down her shirt, but she knew it was too late. They had seen.

"I'll be damned!" Bustskin exclaimed. "It's a girl!"

Jon tried to bluff it out. "So I didn't want them to know," she snapped. "It's not so bad, being sold as a boy. You don't have to tell."

"Tell? Hell!" Bustskin's eyes were round. "I've got better things to do with a girl than tell!" He stepped toward her. "Give me some of that skin, honey. I don't have to talk about what I did to that plantation girl; I'll *show* 'em!"

"Not with me, you don't!" Jon retorted.

"Oh, yeah?" He grabbed for her again.

Now Jon really had to fight. She kicked him in the shin, knowing the pain would be enough to double him over. But he was tough; he only winced, and hung on, hauling her into him again. "Let's just get those pants down," he said, pawing at her pantaloons.

Jon brought up a knee, aiming for the groin. But the bully was street-wise, and twisted his torso to the side, so that the blow missed. He caught her raised leg and held it, drawing on the pantaloons, pulling them down around her bottom.

"Yeah, that's nice, very nice!" he grunted, his hands squeezing at her buttocks as he continued to work on the pantaloons. The other boys watched, fascinated by the proceedings. Most of them were young enough so that this would be their first such experience.

"You can't do that!" Tom Yokes protested, trying to interfere.

Bustskin paused just long enough to slam Tom in the gut with a backhand fist. "You knew her—and didn't tell!" he said savagely. "I'll pulverize you —after I finish with her!"

Tom clutched his front, his breath knocked out. It was clear that he was unable to fight the bully, no matter how proper his instincts were. But this distraction gave Jon time to regroup.

When Bustskin turned his attention back to her, she let him have a prime smash in the nose, just the way Kelvin had done it to another bully years before.

But again the bully's experience saved him. Even as her arm moved, he jerked back his head, and the blow only caught him on the mouth. It smashed his lip against his teeth, and the lip started to bleed, but the injury wasn't serious enough to make him pause. Meanwhile, Jon's knuckles stung; teeth were hard!

Now the line of battle was at her thighs, as Bustskin struggled to get her pantaloons the rest of the way down and she clung to them to keep them up. Her head thrashed back and forth, her hair flying out, and she kicked her feet, but could not break free of the bully's grasp. She saw Tom retreating to the door, and with a fraction of her mind wished he had been just a little bit bigger, stronger, and bolder. He was a decent kid; that was his problem. He couldn't have helped her much anyway; if he had hauled Bustskin off, another boy would have hauled Tom off, and held him until Bustskin was through with her.

Slowly and erratically, the pantaloons came down, until finally they were all the way off, and she was bare-legged. Another snatch, and her ragged underpants were torn off. The watching boys could have been zombies for all the expression on their faces; it seemed that most of them had never before seen the thighs of a fourteen-year-old girl.

She kicked at the bully, then hunched over and butted him with her head, but he simply shifted his grip, threw her down, and pinned her to the floor with his body. Now he started working on his own clothing, to get the essential section open for business. It was evident that he had not been making up the story of the overseer's daughter; he knew how to get a girl down.

She snapped at him with her teeth, but this, too, was ineffective. Now he was ready below; he used a knee to wedge her legs apart. She was worn out from fighting; she could no longer resist him. But she refused to give up; she continued to squirm as much as she was able, hoping for a chance to hit him where it would do the most good.

Then the hulking shape of a guard loomed over them. A ham-hand caught Bustskin by the collar and hauled him literally up in the air. "A girl!" the guard exclaimed. "You idiot! Don't you realize that a virgin girl is worth ten times as much as you on the open market? You know what the penalty is for ruining value like that?"

Bustskin swallowed. His hands went to his front. He was getting a glimmer of the penalty.

The guard dropped him, staring at Jon appraisingly as she scrambled for her pantaloons. Obviously he had seen everything he needed to. "Definitely prime," he said. "We'll get a bonus for this discovery! Come with me, girl."

Jon really had no choice at this stage. She drew up her pantaloons and followed the guard to the door.

There Tom Yokes stood, cringing. "Sir, remember—"

The guard paused. "Yeah, you did call us," he said.

"They'll kill me now, if—"

"Okay, you get a separate cell," the guard decided. "Come on out."

"It was the only way—" Tom said to Jon as they left the cell.

She touched his hand briefly. "I know."

Then she was hustled off to the section that was the holding pen for the Girl Mart, while Tom was taken to his solitary cell. She didn't know whether she would ever see him again.

CHAPTER 9
Girl Mart

THE BOY MART had smelled of unwashed bodies and manure-coated boots. The Girl Mart was cleaner, but Jon feared it more. Boys were sold for work, but girls could be bought for play, and that could be much worse.

The boys had been rowdy and rough. The girls were quiet—too quiet, for it was the silence of despair.

Jon found herself in a dusky chamber where eight or ten girls sat, each isolated by her own thoughts. She had endured the impersonal preparations: the stripping by a matron, inspection of her private parts to verify that she was healthy and was indeed a virgin, a stiff shower and scrubbing, and garbing in a rough smock and slippers. Now she stood before the desolate girls of all ages, feeling naked under the smock, for she had no underclothing anymore. Obviously girls were supposed to be rendered naked at short notice so that buyers could appreciate their assets.

She had salvaged one small vestige of her pride, however. She had saved the handful of dragonberries in her pocket by putting them in her mouth. She hadn't needed or wanted those berries; she had done it simply as a matter of principle, to prove that they could not fathom *all* her secrets or deprive her of all her possessions. Actually, the berries tasted awful, though she neither chewed nor sucked on them; her cheek had become numbed by their presence. But she had carried them past the gauntlet of inspection and changes, and so they represented her small victory. After all, they could have been gold coins if she had had any to save.

She took a step forward—and reeled, abruptly

dizzy. She almost fell, then caught herself, then reconsidered and collapsed to the floor.

An older girl got up and came to her. "I know it's rough, honey, the first time. Did they beat you?"

Jon opened her mouth, but couldn't speak. Instead the sodden berries dribbled out.

"God! Don't tell me—!" the girl exclaimed. "Are those what they look like?" She squatted to pick one up. Her smock hiked up over her knees, and Jon saw that she, too, was naked under it. "They *are*!"

"I just didn't want—" Jon said, but then her voice failed her again, and more berries slid out.

"Did you swallow any of those?"

"No, I just—"

"Grackle! Tanager!" the girl cried to the other girls. "Come here, haul her up, take her to the bucket and wash her mouth out good! Quickly! Maybe it's not too late!"

Two husky girls came and hauled Jon up by the arms. "But I didn't even swear," Jon protested weakly.

The leader girl laughed. "Swear! Who cares about that! Don't you know what those berries are?"

"No, I just found them near a dragon lair."

Grackle and Tanager got her head down by the bucket. "Take a mouthful, spit it out," one said.

Jon obeyed, and did it again, and again, until all trace of the berries was gone, though her mouth remained sore.

"I guess you'll live," the girl said. "What's your name? Mine's Thornflower."

"Jon, just Jon," Jon said, feeling somehow inadequate. Their names were so fancy!

"We make up our own," Thornflower explained, catching on to Jon's confusion. "To conceal our shame. So news doesn't get around about what happened to us, you know."

"Oh. But about those dragonberries—"

"They're poison! One of them makes a person sick, two puts her in a coma, three will kill her. You had a dozen in your mouth! Whatever possessed you to do that?"

"I'm just ornery. I wanted to hide something from them, just to prove I could do it, and the berries were all I had."

Thornflower shook her head. "I understand, I suppose. But dragonberries! Of all the things to put in your mouth! Why, just the juice from their hulls will make you sick."

"I know," Jon said wanly. "Now."

"You better pick a room and lie down. You need to recover your strength for the auction tomorrow, because if you're sick they'll think you're faking, and they'll beat you. No malingerers here! Which do you want?"

"I get a choice?" Jon asked, amazed.

"Any room that has a free bunk, if the other girl doesn't object. We're not boys, you know; we're halfway civilized."

Jon stood unsteadily and looked at the rooms. They opened off the main chamber, and each had two beds. Girls were lying on some, or sitting on them with their heads in their hands. The accommodations were much better than those of the Boy Mart, probably because the proprietors didn't want bruises or dirt to interfere with the marketability of the girls.

In one chamber a girl sat hunched in a corner, her hands over her ears. "What's the matter with her?" Jon asked.

"That's Flambeau. She's really bad off. She's a roundear. That's why she covers—"

"A roundear?" Jon asked, coming abruptly alert.

"You know, one of the offspring of some intruder from that other planet. They're pretty much like us, except for those horrible ears."

"I'll room with her," Jon said.

"She won't talk to you," Thornflower warned. "She just wants to die."

Jon stooped to pick up the berries that had washed out of her mouth. "Well, if these really do—"

"Say, that's one tough notion!" Thornflower said admiringly. "But don't let the guards know you gave them to her, because—"

"They'll beat me," Jon finished. "No one will tell?"

"No one will tell," Thornflower promised.

"Thanks. I like it better here than at the Boy Mart."

"You were *there?*"

"I was pretending to be a boy. Bustskin found out, and tried to—"

Thornflower sighed. "The first time's the worst. I remember mine, when I was ten."

"You were raped when you were ten?" Jon asked, appalled.

"The first time, yes. By a middle-aged man. He wasn't too rough, actually, but he was so dirty and clumsy, I felt like dying."

Jon glanced again at the huddled girl. "Is that why—?"

"Sure, I thought you realized. She's a roundear, so isn't worth much on the market, so the guards knew there wasn't anything to lose."

"The guards?"

"Didn't you know? No, I guess you didn't, because they don't do it to virgins, of course. Just to us who can't lose that kind of value."

"You mean—you, too?"

"All of us. Or at least any they want. If we cooperate, they give us little things, like extra rations or clean water. If we don't—well, then it gets ugly."

"And Flambeau—"

"Didn't cooperate," Thornflower finished. "She's new here, like you. She didn't understand."

"I guess I'm pretty well off, after all," Jon said, shuddering.

"Depends how you see it," Thornflower said, shrugging.

Jon thanked her, and went to the room. She sat down near the huddled girl. "Flambeau," she said.

There was no response.

"Flambeau, listen to me," Jon said. "My brother is a roundear."

Slowly the girl lifted her head. She had black hair and brown eyes, and would have been quite pretty if the hair weren't matted and the eyes swollen from crying.

Then she dropped her face again. "Don't tease me!" she said, and her body was racked with renewed sobs.

"No, he really is. I'm half roundear, too, only my ears came out like my mother's. When they said you were one—"

Jon stopped, because the girl's hands were clamped tightly over her ears, effectively blocking the sound.

Well, if she really thought she wanted to die, Jon would just call that bluff! She opened her hand and put it down under the girl's nose, showing half a dozen dragonberries.

Flambeau saw them. She snatched at them, surprising Jon. In a moment, she had swept up three and popped them into her mouth.

"Wait!" Jon cried. "Those are—"

The girl lifted her head again. She swallowed. "I know. Thanks."

Jon had not meant to have the girl really commit suicide! Now what was she to do?

Well, she could alert the other girls and have them haul Flambeau to the bucket and poke a finger down her throat to make her vomit up the berries. That would save her life. But to what purpose? If she really did want to die, maybe it was better to let her do it in peace. Jon knew how rough it could be on a roundear, because of Kelvin, and how it could be for a girl. So maybe Flambeau had reason.

Her alternative was to let nature take its course. She was in doubt, so she did nothing—which meant the second choice. She did not feel at all easy about it, but that was it. If she was cooperating in a death, maybe that was just the way it had to be, here in this awful place.

Lunch came. Thornflower supervised the doling out of portions of the rough bread and thin soup. It wasn't much, but no one complained; they were all aware of how readily and capriciously it could be cut off.

Flambeau remained on her bunk, where Jon had laboriously hauled her. The girl had a well-fleshed body, and would have been a real prize on the market if it hadn't been for her round ears. At least what little she would have brought would now be denied to the owners of the Marts. That was a very small consolation; Jon now wished she hadn't ever shown her the deadly berries. But what was done was done; she reacted as she had when she wasn't sure whether Kelvin had survived the dragon's toss: she went on with her business. What else was she to do?

But after about three hours, Flambeau stirred. She was alive! Jon went to her. "I'm sorry I gave you those dragonberries!" she cried. "I didn't think you'd really—"

The girl opened her eyes. "I found him," she said.

"What?"

"I found your brother. With the round ears. He's a hero."

Jon laughed. "You were dreaming! My brother's a great guy, but he's not really a hero. Just the notion of fighting puts him in a cold sweat, though he does it when he has to."

"Kelvin," she said. "He has a gauntlet."

"Kelvin doesn't have any such thing!" Then Jon did a double take. "How did you know his name? I never told you!"

"I was there. I ranged out from my body and found him. He was easy to find, because he's the only other roundear in the vicinity. All I could think of was what you said, so I just concentrated on those round ears, and suddenly I was there. He's handsome!"

"You what?" Jon understood the words, but they weren't making much sense.

"I went out and found him. I could see him and

hear him, but I couldn't talk to him, because I was only a ghost." Then Flambeau did a double take. "What am I saying?"

That was better! The girl was as confused as Jon was. "You swallowed three dragonberries and almost died. I guess you could have been a ghost! But you weren't, because you recovered, and here you are. How do you feel?"

"Very weak," the girl said. Then: "My name is Heln."

"They told me—"

"My given name. After my roundear mother, Helen. Heln Flambeau."

"Oh." Jon was disconcerted. "I'm Jon. Jon Hackleberry."

"I know. Kelvin spoke of you. He means to rescue you."

"You dreamed all that?"

"I don't think it was a dream," Heln said.

"You mean to say that the dragonberries didn't poison you, they just sort of sent your soul out wandering for a while?"

"I suppose so. I didn't exactly wander, I could go anywhere I wanted. I just sort of flew, only I could get somewhere without even flying, just by *being* there. So I decided to be where there was that roundear you spoke of, just because—" She shrugged. "Now I don't think I want to die anymore. I—I got—something terrible happened, and I really wanted to die, but now I have something back that sort of makes up for it. It's as if I've entered a whole new realm, and what happened in the old one doesn't matter so much anymore. I've left that old, spoiled life behind. Now I want to live, and travel astrally again."

"Better not," Jon said. "Those berries kill most folk, and if you took too many, too fast—"

"Yes. I'll wait. But now I have something to live for. I want to meet your brother, in the flesh. Kelvin's nice. He's my age."

"He's nice," Jon agreed. Could she really believe this? She decided to be forthright. "Look, Heln, this is hard to believe all at once. I really don't know if you were dreaming or if you really did it. Could you tell me more about my brother?"

Heln smiled. "His eyes are sort of blue, and his hair brown. He's thin. He wants to rescue you, and get back some dragon scales, but he got all caught up in being a hero, because of the gauntlet."

"What gauntlet? He doesn't have any gloves!"

"He found it somewhere. I came along after that, so I don't know where, but everyone says it means he's the hero of the prophecy. I don't know what the prophecy is, though."

Jon realized that there was no way Heln could have known all that unless she had been there. Obviously she hadn't been there physically. So she must have been spiritually. "But the berries are poison! Why didn't they kill you?"

"I don't know. Unless—did your brother eat any?"

"No. Why?"

"Maybe they don't work the same on roundears. Maybe they kill the folk of Rud, but just separate the souls of roundears, because our metabolism is different. Where did you get them?"

Jon explained about the garden near the dragon.

"Why would a dragon tend a garden? Do they like to eat berries?"

"Those few little berries wouldn't feed a dragon more than a second!" Jon exclaimed. "They eat hot flesh."

"But they must have some reason to tend those gardens, if other dragons have gardens. At least that one did. Suppose it had the same effect on a dragon? Made it able to explore without going anywhere? Wouldn't that help it forage for prey?"

"It sure would!" Jon agreed. "I always wondered why it's supposed to be so hard to catch a dragon! When hunters get together in big parties and try to run a dragon down, the dragon's never there. We thought it was because the dragons heard them coming, but maybe—"

"I think we've just discovered the dragon's secret," Heln said. "No one knew about it, because the dragons are able to guard their gardens pretty well, and anyone who ate the berries died. Just as I meant to die, because—" Here she faltered. It seemed that despite her words, she had not yet let go of the bad experience.

"Thornflower told me what happened to you," Jon said. "I'm sorry. I almost got, well, the same thing. So I guess I understand. But you know, the other girls seem to have survived it all right."

Heln considered. "Kelvin—would he—?"

"He wouldn't rape anyone!" Jon exclaimed, horrified.

"I mean, would he—would he be able to like a girl who—"

Oh. "I'm sure he doesn't judge by that sort of thing. I mean, he knows how bullies are. It wasn't your fault. And I came to you because you have round ears, like him. I think he'd really like you, if he met you."

"I'm glad. Because I think I really like him. He was so confused, but trying to do the right thing, instead of being so brutal the way the others are. Unsure of himself."

"That's my brother!"

"Yes. While the others—they don't seem to care anything about—they just use—"

"Yeah," Jon said, understanding. "He's not like them."

"But of course we're both going to be sold in the auction tomorrow. If only I could have told him! But I couldn't say anything to him; I was completely invisible and silent. He knows you're here, because someone told him, but—"

"Kelvin will rescue me somehow, I know it!" Jon said stoutly. "And then he'll get back our gold. And when he rescues me, I'll tell him to rescue you, too. I know he'll want to meet you, and you can help him so

much if you can do that thing with the berries again."
She paused. "But suppose they only work once? And
the second time they really do poison you?"

"Next time I'll only take one berry. That's not
supposed to kill a person anyway. I'll see if it works.
But I think not today; they did leave me rather washed
out."

"Well, you could be hungry, you know. You missed
the noon meal."

Heln laughed weakly. "I suppose I could be. I'll
make sure to eat all I can tonight."

CHAPTER 10
Auction

MOST OF THE POTENTIAL bidders were buyers for the larger plantations. Here and there on the tiers of seats forming a half circle around the ring was to be seen a seaman in search of new galley hands. The seamen's blue shirts and trim sea trousers contrasted with all the brownberry shirts and greenbriar pantaloons. The seamen's flat, tight-fitting caps shone like white rocks in the tossing sea of bobbing green and yellow stockelcaps.

Back where Queeto sat, the noise was the steady murmur of men talking crops and the buying and selling of crophands. Feeling a sliver from the plank seat digging into his squat behind, tasting the bitter bile that always rose in his throat amid such surroundings, Queeto retreated into his favorite fantasy. In his mind the clouds of hatred roiled thick and black as he imagined himself with the money to buy boys for his own purpose. In this favored daydream he did not have an enlarged and humped back, but instead was straight and tall, with a high, black-crowned forehead. In fact, in this vision he resembled the one he was proud to acknowledge Master: Zatanas, Confounder of Righteousness, Defender of the Ugly and Misshaped.

At last the auctioneer made his appearance. Standing tall, dressed in black, he was almost the picture of an ancient prophet with his gray, flowing beard. He cleared his throat at the lectern, banged his gavel twice with reports like exploding skulls, and waited for silence. Then, having achieved it, he began.

"Some of you have come from distant kingdoms and may not know all of our Rud customs governing the Boy and Girl Marts. Some of our stock have been seized for nonpayment of taxes; others are convicted felons. Most were young vagrants who have been properly and legally impressed."

Queeto squirmed, reminded that he, too, had been a vagrant, though not one a bounty hunter would have taken for sale at a Boy Mart. As a lad, his had been a hard lot: tormented constantly by smooth-cheeked boys and ugly soldiers; in constant flight from those who knew he had stolen something; eating whatever and wherever he could. In those days he had to eat, unlike the days following Master.

"And now," the auctioneer was saying, "our first lot of six boys from MacGregor Plantation. Used for one season and now to be replaced with fresh hands. These still have a lot of work left in them, gentlemen, and seasoned as only MacGregor seasons them—"

In the center ring, prodded by the overseer's whip, six lanky boys with whip marks and protruding ribs walked the circle. Obviously they had been recalcitrant and repeatedly disciplined. Useless, because of one year of hardness, for Master's (and Queeto's own) exacting purposes.

The boys were sold to one of the smaller plantations. The purchaser was a man of such evil countenance as to be identified as such even by the approving dwarf.

Small lot followed small lot, and soon it was down to single, broad-shouldered farm boys seized for their father's nonpayment of taxes. Watching their misery, remembering the torments of his long-ago youth, Queeto felt a little, though only a little, avenged.

But none of these were quite suitable for Master. Queeto knew better than to buy any boys that weren't precisely right. He sighed; he would just have to report no purchases, this time.

"And now," the auctioneer announced, "the Girl Mart."

Immediately the lagging attention of the buyers

revived. Even those who had no intention of bidding liked to look at the girls!

The girls were herded out, in their slippers and smocks. Most were motley, not attractive despite their youth and the management's evident effort to get them prettied up. It took more than the combing of the hair and washing of the face to make a hardened young slut into an attractive package! But a few were interesting. One had an excellent chassis and good face, marred only by a stockelcap someone had inexplicably pulled down around her ears. Another looked to be thirteen or fourteen, with good lines, long fair tresses, and a bearing that indicated her spirit had not yet been broken. She was exactly the kind Master wanted!

The auctioneer hauled a girl out of the bunch. "And what am I bid for this fine specimen of womanhood?" he asked rhetorically. "Let's start it at ten rudnas."

"Five," a seaman said.

The girl made a gesture at him with a finger. She was no innocent youngster! That of course lowered her value; the average buyer preferred to degrade a girl in his own fashion, rather than wrestle with one who had already been broken in. Queeto watched in silence.

Finally the auctioneer brought out the lively young one. Her yellow hair glistened in the sun, and her smooth skin was marked only with a purpling bruise across her face. Her cheeks were healthy and ruddy. She was full of the good red juice of life. Yes. Exactly what his appetite craved and the Master specified. Either sex would do, as long as it had the right attributes.

"And here's a fresh virgin, age fourteen, just turned in by a public-spirited citizen. She was caught trying to steal a donkey."

"I was not!" the girl retorted. Oh, she was a prize!

"Fourteen rudnas," the auctioneer said, acknowledging a bid from a wide-shouldered, red-faced man accompanied by two younger men on Queeto's right. "Who will make it twenty?"

There was a pause. This one was obviously worth more, but the buyers were still appraising her, deciding how high they should go. Meanwhile the girl, looking at the first bidder, did a double take. Did she know him? That could be good for her, or bad, depending on the nature of the prior contact.

"Twenty," a plantation buyer said. She would get plenty of use in a hurry if he took her home to the farmhands!

"Gentlemen, let's get serious," the auctioneer said. He whipped off the girl's smock, rendering her abruptly naked.

The body thus revealed was full-hipped but still light in the breasts. She was just coming into her prime, with some growing yet to do. Her half-defiant, half-chagrined attitude spoke more clearly than any words the auctioneer could say of her naivete. Oh, she was certainly a prize, probably abducted directly from some farmer's house!

There was bound to be heavy bidding here. Queeto decided to preempt it. "One hundred rudnas," he called. This was a princely sum, but money was of no consequence to him or to the Master. This borderline child would never again be at this stage of innocence!

"One hundred and two rudnas," said the big man.

Queeto was shocked. He hadn't expected to be bid against at this level. He had made a preemptive bid! But he hesitated only a heartbeat, then called, "One hundred and twenty-five."

There were gasps from all around, and murmurs, and even a few snickers. They knew he had gone over the limit for even the most delectable of young flesh. It wasn't a matter of money now, but of propriety. Why fatten the Mart's percentage beyond what was reasonable? Queeto clenched his teeth, and hoped the other man wouldn't force him into further embarrassment by bidding again.

The girl, still naked, was signaling frantically to the

big man. She pointed to the girl with the cap. What
was she trying to do, get him to bid on someone else?
Well, the other man could have the capped girl, who
was obviously concealing some serious flaw under
that cap. Otherwise the auctioneer would never have
put it on her.

"One hundred twenty-five going once," the auctioneer said happily. "One hundred and twenty-five going
twice, one hundred and twenty-five going thrice. *Sold*,
to the gentleman with the sack of gold between his
shoulders!"

That was a punnish reference to Queeto's obvious
hump. The auctioneer would not be so frivolous,
Queeto thought, if he had known him to be an
immortal.

The next girl up was that capped one. Suddenly,
defiantly, she reached up and tore off the cap. The
audience gasped. Her ears were round! That destroyed her value. No wonder it had been concealed.
The auctioneer was furious; any play he might have
made had just been destroyed.

There was only one bid for that one, of two rudnas,
and the big man took her. Well, at least she was cheap!
Queeto wondered what use the man would find for a
nonvirginal roundear girl; no matter how sweet her
shape, she simply wasn't worthwhile.

After the silently glaring young purchase had been
placed, securely shackled at ankles and chained at
wrists, into his specially appointed carriage, Queeto
found the bile subsiding in his stomach. After all, he
had prevailed, and the chattel was his. Perhaps it was
just as well that the stupid man had bid against him,
because it had given him a chance to prove that such
opposition was hopeless. Such reminders were in
order, periodically.

The wind out here on the open road blew fresh,
carrying tree smells and grass odors. The stars shone
down, twinkling. Owlarks hooted and whistled.
Froogs chirped. Queeto smiled as best he could,

thinking of Master, of good red juice, and of what lay in store for his purchase. A healthy, spirited virgin —that was the very best kind to degrade, because there was much more reaction for the effort. Master would be very pleased.

"Hold there!"

What was this? Three men. Highwaymen? Yes, all had bandannas round their faces. How did they dare? He thought all highwaymen knew that the Master's tribute could become the Master's vengeance if they molested one of his own. A stern warning should suffice.

Then, by the light of the stars, he recognized the big, broad-shouldered bidder at the Mart, and the two who had been with him. Obviously some amateur going into business for himself. The fool!

"I represent someone of great importance," Queeto said loudly. "If it's gold you want, I have little left after the Mart." Thanks, he thought, to the man's idiot bidding.

"It's not gold we're after," said the big man. "It's the girl."

"My master—"

"Damn your master!"

Queeto's shock was renewed. Such disrespect for persons of power was almost unheard-of! Had the man no concern for his health or his sanity, let alone his life? But he was in no position to fight; he would simply have to tolerate this affront, and make a full report to Master.

Queeto watched as the two stockelcapped young men sheathed swords, dismounted, and threw open the door to the carriage compartment.

"Kel!" cried the girl who had cost a fortune.

"Brother Wart," said the young man. That was odd indeed; why call a girl "brother"? Then, to the other, "She's shackled."

"Key, dwarf!" the big man ordered.

Queeto knew better than to argue. These were rough men showing little caution; anyone who would waylay a carriage of the Master would hardly hesitate to slay the Master's underling. He tossed the big man the key ring, who caught it and quickly transferred it to the slighter built of the thieves.

With a jingle, they released the girl. Then the big man cut the harness on the carriage's horse.

A moment later they were gone, one horse carrying double. Queeto was alone on a lonely road with an empty carriage. They hadn't even had the decency to steal his animal, he thought bitterly, but instead had left it for him to catch—or to try to catch.

"Damn!" Queeto said, wishing himself adept in magic. "Master isn't going to like this. Master isn't going to like this at all!" That was of course an understatement so gross as to be humorous, but he wasn't laughing. There was no telling against whom Master's rage would first strike.

CHAPTER 11
Leader

WELL AWAY FROM THE carriage, they slowed to a walk, so that the double-loaded horse would not be unduly fatigued. Kelvin, riding with Jon behind him, introduced her to his new friends: the father-and-son team of Morvin and Les Crumb. "They are members of the Raiders," he explained. "They oppose the Queen and her evil policies. But they have to operate in secret, or the Queen's guards will wipe them all out."

"What about Heln?" Jon demanded. "You bought her, didn't you?"

Morvin Crumb laughed. "How could we fail, after you signaled so strongly! Then when she took off her cap, and we saw she was a roundear, we understood. That had the incidental effect of ruining her value; the auctioneer was furious!"

"We had to hurry down with the money," Les agreed. "Otherwise we knew she'd be severely beaten."

"Then where is she now?" Jon asked.

"She was very tired," Kelvin said. "I think she'd been sick. She said something about eating dragonberries, and how glad she was to see me, and then she just, well, slept. So Mor carried her to his horse, and took her out to a hideout cabin he has in the wilderness, and got a girl to tend her, and that's where we're going now. How did you find her? Where did she come from? Why did she seem to know me?"

Jon explained about her discovery and removal to the Girl Mart, and how she had picked Heln Flambeau for company because of her round ears. "I knew right then she was the perfect match for you, Kel!" she said, and Kelvin felt himself blushing. Then she told of what she had learned about the dragonberries she had saved, and how Heln had tried to commit suicide with them.

"Suicide!" Kelvin exclaimed. "Why?"

"She had been raped, Kel. She's a delicate girl, always treated well before; when that happened, she just wanted to die. I told her it wouldn't make any difference to you."

"Of course it makes a difference!" Kelvin said. "Who did it? We'll have to kill—"

"I mean in the way you feel about her."

"But I don't even know her!" Kelvin protested, blushing again.

"You must have seen her ears—and her body," his sister said. "What more do you need to know?"

Kelvin shut up, knowing that she was baiting him. Indeed, he had seen her ears and her body, and been somewhat smitten on the spot, but hadn't wanted to admit it. "I—of course it wouldn't make any—if I—" He faltered to a stop.

"Just make sure you tell her that," Jon said firmly. "She likes you, Kel."

"But she never saw me before!"

"She saw you. The berries didn't kill her; they only sent her into a trance, and her spirit left her body and traveled around, and she saw you. She liked your ears, of course; there couldn't have been any other reason, could there?"

She was still teasing him. She was certainly back to normal! Kel did not protest any further.

But Mor Crumb was interested. "She traveled astrally? I thought that ability was lost centuries ago!"

"We think maybe it was her ears," Jon said. "That maybe the berries kill the folk of Rud, but only stun those with Earthblood, so their spirits can travel for a while. Maybe if Kel ate some berries—"

"No!" Mor cried with surprising vehemence. "He's the hero of the prophecy. We can't risk him on poison berries!"

"I told Heln she could be very useful, because she can travel anywhere, see and hear anything. That's why I signaled you to buy her."

"You did well, girl," Mor Crumb said. "The Raiders can really use a talent like that! We can spy on the guardsmen, on the Queen herself!"

"But if the berries are poison—" Kelvin said weakly.

"We'll have to find out what the minimum number is she can take that will let her spirit travel, without harming her," Mor said. "Obviously the effort takes a lot out of her, so we won't overdo it. But what a tool!"

Kelvin could see the point, but remained troubled. He didn't like thinking of a beautiful girl like Heln Flambeau as a tool.

They reached the cabin in due course. Mor knocked in a code pattern on the door, and the girl opened it, then slipped out and disappeared into the darkness. They went in.

Heln Flambeau was up, having recovered from her fatigue. By the wan, flickering light of a lone candle Kelvin saw her face, round ears and all. She had brushed out her black hair, and now it shone beside the candle, and her half-shadowed face was lovely. She had been bedraggled and then unconscious before, not presenting her best aspect; now, animate, she was beautiful.

Jon nudged him. Kelvin opened his mouth. "I'm, uh, beautiful," he said.

"You jackass!" Jon hissed.

Morvin Crumb burst out laughing. In a moment everyone was laughing.

Heln approached gracefully. "I'd like to be your friend, Kelvin," she said. "Did your sister tell you—"

"No difference!" he exclaimed.

". . . about the experience I had with the dragon-berries?" she finished.

Kelvin choked. "I did," Jon said.

"I saw you with the gauntlet. I realize you are a hero, but if there's any way I can help—"

"I'm no—" Kelvin began.

"You sure can!" Morvin said. "We need information on the whereabouts and activities of the Queen's guardsmen. If you can spy on them without their knowing—"

"I think I could," Heln said. "But I would need more berries, and I don't think I could do it too often, because it really took the strength from me, that one time."

Kelvin tried to get a grip on himself. "You actually saw me and heard me?"

"Oh, yes," she agreed. "Of course it was all rather confused, because you weren't explaining anything, you were just going somewhere, but everyone was saying you were a hero, and something about a prophecy, and I couldn't stay long. I never did this before, I mean going about in astral form, and I suppose I'm not very good at it."

"I'm not very good at being a hero!" Kelvin blurted.

She smiled. "I think we have a lot in common."

"Round ears," Kelvin said.

"That, too."

For some unaccountable reason he felt himself blushing again. He hoped the dim light masked it.

"We'd better bunk down here," Morvin said. "We're going to be busy, the next few days. You two girls better take the bed, and the rest of us'll lie on the floor."

They settled. Kelvin was tired, but also buoyed by the rescue of his sister, and by the discovery of Heln Flambeau. He had never dreamed of meeting a roundear girl, let alone a beautiful one his own age! And she liked him! It was almost too good to be true. He hated to think it, but it seemed that the highwayman's abduction of Jon had been a net blessing.

Morvin Crumb's face got very dark, his heavy eyebrows knitting together like dark caterpillars. He stared at the bedraggled farmer and the pinch-faced woman Kelvin guessed to be the man's wife.

"Say that again, Jeffreys," Crumb said, making no move as yet to dismount from his horse.

"They burned my barn. Ransacked my house. Carried away everything they wanted and smashed and destroyed the rest. We watched them from the woods."

"Damn, and I suppose that's just the start!"

"Must be," Jeffreys said. "I heard one of 'em say they would hit Al Reston next. You know what it's about, Morvin?"

"Revenge," the big man said.

"I—I smell smoke!" Jon said from the front part of Kelvin's mount. The big bay shifted on his feet and whinnied, as though he had caught the scent.

"That would be Gaston Hays," Morvin said. "Looks as if they're trying to get us all. All of us with the Raiders."

"Sir," Kelvin said, speaking determinedly. "If it's all because of me—because of what happened in the park—if it is, sir, perhaps I should, uh . . ." He swallowed. What had he been about to say?

Morvin glared at him, seemingly seeing into his very soul. "It had to come, youngster. Prophecy or none, slain bullies or no. We planted right, and now we reap the expected crop."

"They won't have killed many," the younger Crumb said, kneeing his dappled gray to within touching distance. "The Raiders were expecting it. Most have been setting watches every night for weeks, and every time there's trouble in the park everyone sets a watch."

"It's an excuse to play cards and read books late a'night," said Jeffreys. "Few will have been taken by surprise."

"Fewer yet, if I have my way," Crumb muttered, and Kelvin knew he was thinking of Heln, who remained back at the cabin. Obviously astral spying could do a lot to help them oppose raids like this. If they could learn exactly where and when each raid was planned . . .

"We will round up those who have suffered," Morvin said. "Then we disband Crumb's Raiders. What we have now we'll call Knights. That's appropriate, isn't it? Kelvin Knight Hackleberry Knights. Knights of the Roundear."

Kelvin felt himself blushing again. So absurd of Crumb—and yet there *was* the gauntlet.

"What does he mean, Kel?" Jon whispered. She was back in boy guise, feeling most comfortable that way, especially after what had almost happened in the Boy Mart.

Kelvin poked his sister lightly and explained all with a brotherly word: "Quiet!"

"We'll have to hide out for now," Morvin said. Kelvin realized irrelevantly that the man's chronically red face probably spared him the embarrassment of blushing; who would know the difference? "But when we can, we'll gather men and arms, and then, come good or come evil, we'll fight. This time to win!"

"What will you use for money?" spoke up Jeffreys' wife.

"What we have. What we can scrape up. If only we had some gold. Say half a dragon's worth!"

"I know where we can get gold!" Jon said, and immediately Kelvin wished his sister's captor had left her with a gag.

"That so?" Morvin asked. He sounded interested rather than disbelieving.

"My sister's just a child," Kelvin started, and promptly got Jon's elbow poked into his stomach.

"Let 'er speak, Hackleberry," Crumb said.

Jon sneezed, lightly, brushing some hair back under her stockelcap, and said, "Our dragon—the one Kelvin slew—"

"He slew a dragon?"

"Yeah. With a tent pole, right through the eye socket and into the old brain pan. That's where I found the dragonberries."

"Gods!" Morvin exclaimed. "And here he pretended to be afeard of a couple of mere guardsmen!"

That was exactly the reaction Kelvin had feared. He knew he was no hero, and that the dragon business had been mostly luck and desperation, as had the gauntlet business. What would he be in for now?

"Well," Jon continued blithely, "we packed out the gold, but Cheeky Jack's got it. He's the bandit who kidnaped me for the auction. I heard his name when—"

"Impressed you for the auction," Crumb said. "They don't call it kidnaping, because there's supposed to be a law against that. You wouldn't, eh, know where old Cheeky is hiding, would you, youngster?"

"You bet I would!" Jon said enthusiastically, while Kelvin cringed. He knew that more heroic business was coming up.

They saw Mockery grazing behind the lean-to shack, from the rim of the canyon nearly a quarter of a mile away. Morvin suggested an arrow to stop the equine's mouth, but Jon quickly protested, and Kelvin hastily explained that the donkey was deaf as a stone and unlikely to sound an alarm.

"In that case we'll slip down that steep bank behind those trees and come in from the southeast," Morvin said, pointing with his sword tip.

"Jack will be home. That's his horse," Jon said, indicating the black stallion hobbled near the door.

"Um, now, that one could make a bit of noise if we don't come in just right," Morvin said. "Any ideas?"

"My idea is that he won't," said his son. "Donkeys are the ones who make the commotions. Horses can be passed."

"Then let's pass," Morvin said. He turned to Kelvin. "Son, you got that gauntlet on right?"

"I think so, sir." Why was Crumb calling *him* son, he wondered? What must the man's actual son think?

"Good. Because I'll let you do the killing. You need the experience."

Kelvin swallowed in private agony. He had known that this was part of what leadership entailed. If there was one thing he did not want to experience, it was killing. Not even villains who would steal gold and sell his sister for a plantation hand.

"All right. Go," Crumb said, dispensing orders as naturally as everyone around seemed to take them.

After a downhill run, a careful descent, and a cautious walk, there was a silent crawl. They were almost to the black horse when Jack emerged from the shack and saw them.

"Well!" he said, his hand going for his sword.

"Take him, Hackleberry," Morvin said.

Kelvin found himself on his feet, good sword in right hand, gauntlet on left.

"Baby boy's brother," said Jack, "come to get his head split." He never had learned of Jon's deception.

"Get him, Kel!" Jon cried, sounding bloodthirsty.

Kelvin trembled, though he knew (he kept telling himself) how this should end. Magic was after all magic, and the fight in the park had convinced him that the gauntlet was that. If only it was for the proper hand!

"You fight with bare sword hand, sonny?" Jack seemed amused. "What's the mitten for? You going to use it to wipe something? Your nose, maybe? Perhaps your blood?"

"I'm ready, mister," Kelvin said. It was as brave a statement as he could muster. Yet the highwayman's taunts were making it easier.

"Are, huh? Well, in that case—" The sword swished and darted like a striking serpent.

To be caught and flung away with one lightning move on the part of the gauntlet.

Jack blinked and opened and closed his mouth like a fish drowning in air. "What—what—?"

Kelvin raised the tip of his sword to the highwayman's throat. "If you have anything to say, say it fast." *Because if this takes any time, I'll lose my nerve!* he thought.

"I didn't mean—I only wanted—" The eyes of the bandit were wild as they darted from sword tip to the face of the elder Crumb, to Jon's face, to his own sword still quivering in the trunk of a tree.

"Don't kill him! Don't!" It was a large slovenly woman standing in the doorway of the cabin.

"Watch her, men," Mor Crumb snapped.

Kelvin realized that this was the man's wife. Could he kill a man with a wife and maybe a child? Even such a man as this? After all, Cheeky Jack hadn't really hurt Kelvin or Jon, he had just taken their gold and sold Jon to the Boy Mart. All that evil was now being undone.

"You're sorry, aren't you? And you won't do it again?" Kelvin hardly realized what he was saying. He only knew that the Crumbs were watching him and that Morvin was trying to get him blooded: to shed his first human lifeblood.

Jack shook. "I never saw anything like that move! You just grabbed my blade right out of my hand! You must be—"

"You better believe it," the elder Crumb said.

The highwayman raised his hands, eyes now on the gauntlet. "It hardly seems fair. Magic—"

"You prate of 'fair'?" Crumb demanded. "You who attack nearly unarmed and unskilled boys? You who prey on them with no other object than enriching yourself? You who prey on the weak without a sign of conscience?"

"Kill me, then," Jack said, regaining a bit of defiance. "Kill me and get it over with!"

"Kill him, youngster!" Morvin said.

"Kill him, Kel!" Jon's shrill voice echoed the elder man's.

"Yes," the younger Crumb said. "Strike!"

Kelvin closed his eyes, bunched his muscles, and tried to will the deed. But Jack, trembling there with his bare arms raised, was now just as helpless as anyone he had ever slain. Villain he might be, but now he was helpless before a sword, and to strike now would make Kelvin feel like a murderer.

"Murderer!" the woman screamed, echoing his thought.

"Shuddup!" Mor said to her. "Another word, woman, and—"

She was silent. Kelvin could imagine the gesture Mor must have made.

"Go on!" Crumb said. "I swear I won't do't this time! Ye's got to do for ye'self!"

Do for myself and kill, Kelvin thought. Kill an unarmed man before a woman who loves him. This is how a leader acts?

Abruptly he lowered the sword point. "I give him his life," Kelvin said.

"What!" Crumb shouted, outraged. "Hackleberry, may I ask why?"

Because this hero wasn't cut out for murder, he thought. But he knew Morvin would snort at that.

"Because," he said, and fought to find some acceptable reason. "Because he's only a—a man. Only a highwayman. Only one bandit."

"What? Are ye daft?"

"Only one highwayman," Kelvin said, his mind racing with all the velocity of a slug. What was he trying to think of? "But there are others," he continued with sudden inspiration. "Many others—as your son has told me."

"What are you blathering about?"

"He can spread the word. He and his wife. About us. What we did today. We won't allow boys to be pressed any longer. Or girls. We won't allow anyone to rob and to steal and to kill as he has done."

"We'll do it! We'll do it!" the woman said.

Morvin silenced her with a wave. He raised a hand and rubbed his chin. "Hackleberry, I do believe you make a little sense. Let him spread the word to his friends, and if he's up to his villainy again, we disarm him and we gut him!"

"Right, sir!" Kelvin cried, weak-kneed with relief.

"Gods, but I believe you'll make a leader yet! Me, I'd never have thought of that."

Not that it mattered, Kelvin thought, but he wasn't sure that even he himself had thought of it. He had wanted to avoid killing, and somehow an excuse had come. An acceptable excuse, he had realized, even while making it, but nothing *but* an excuse.

Maybe, just maybe, there was something to the prophecies.

But somehow he still wanted terribly to doubt.

CHAPTER 12
Dragonberries

"BUT I CAN'T EVEN try it without more dragonberries," Heln Flambeau protested. "We lost the rest of them at the Girl Mart. I'm willing to try, if we can get the berries."

Kelvin had hoped she wouldn't be willing, but he couldn't say that. What would he do if she ate the berries again, and this time they poisoned her? Maybe it had been a fluke before.

"Then we'll just have to fetch more berries," Morvin Crumb said. "Actually, we'll need the rest of the scales from that dead dragon, just to be sure we have enough gold. Jon tells me you only got them from the topside of the beast, the easiest place to reach."

Damn his big-mouthed little sister! Now they would have to go back to the dragon, and Kelvin didn't like the notion of bracing even a dead dragon.

"We'll take a full crew, so we have the manpower to turn the critter over," Mor continued. "We'll get them all this time, to be sure! And Jon will get a whole basketful of the berries at the same time."

"Yeah!" Jon said enthusiastically.

"I should come along," Heln said.

"No!" Kelvin cried.

"But why not, Kelvin? The berries are for me."

"I don't want you in dragon country! There could be another dragon!"

"Well, yes, but—"

"Gods, Heln, the thought of anything happening to you—"

"Then you do care for me," she said as if it were a discovery.

"Of course I—" But then he got all tongue-tied.

103

"He's right, Flambeau," Mor said. "Dragon country is no place for women."

"Now, just a minute!" Jon protested. *"I'm—"*

"Or children," Mor added.

That didn't sit any better with her. "Now, I won't
let you exclude me! I found those berries, I know
where they are!"

"Right. I said you're coming. Let's get on with it."
He turned away.

Jon jumped for joy. Then she paused. "But what
does that make me? If not a woman or a child—"

"A Knight," the man said as he moved out toward
the horses.

"Oh. Yes." Abruptly pleased again, she hurried
after him.

Heln turned to Kelvin. "Please, be careful, hero,"
she said. "I don't know what I'd do without you."

Kelvin felt himself blushing yet again. Why was he
so helpless in her presence? She gave him chances
without end to say something meaningful, but he
always muffed it. "Uh, yeah," he mumbled, true to
form, and stumbled off to join the party.

There were thirty of them now: all the farmers and
townsmen who had called themselves Crumb's Raiders and now called themselves Knights of the Roundear. Dressed in their brownberry shirts, greenbriar
pantaloons, and lightweight summer stockelcaps, they
looked like anything but an army. Smelling of natural
fertilizing agents, they didn't even have the aroma of
an army, Kelvin thought as he rode along with the
Crumbs, Mor and Les, and with Jon sharing his big
bay mare. What an outfit, and what a mission! They
were going back to dragon country to find the rotting
carcass and get *all* the scales and all the berries.

"You play this?" Les asked, his horse sidling nearer.

"Huh? Oh." Lester held out the mandajo they had
found in Jack's shack.

"A little. It's mine."

"Play it. Now."

Kelvin hesitated but a second to test the tension on the strings. He knew he was not the best minstrel, indeed, not better than mediocre, but he enjoyed playing and singing and felt comfortable doing it, and there was much to be said for pleasure and comfort after the disruption and tension of recent events. He strummed a little, then burst into his favorite theme:

"Fortune come a-callin', but I did hide, ah-oo-ay. Fortune come a-callin', but I did hide, bloody saber at my side, ah-oo-ay, ah-oo-ay, ay."

Jon got out her new sling and a rock. As on their first trip into dragon country—such a short time ago, and yet seemingly so long ago—she seemed alert for squirbets. Or, Kelvin thought uncomfortably, something larger.

"You say it's along this bank?" Mor asked, leaning down from the extra-big plow horse he rode.

Kelvin nodded. They should be seeing buzvuls soon, he thought, looking at the overcast sky for the dark scavenger birds. Normally buzvuls were said to be an ill omen.

"There!" Les exclaimed, pointing. At the same time, the stench of the rotting carcass reached them on the breeze. Kelvin felt his nose wrinkle and his stomach lurch. Somehow the odor made him feel even less like a hero or leader; he had no nose and no stomach for it.

"Yup, that's dragon stink," Mor said with a smile as broad as his back. He might have been talking about a gentle perfume, or—Kelvin's gut tried to lurch again —a toothsome delicacy.

"I wonder—the buzvuls aren't landing. They're just hovering in the sky," Les Crumb remarked, glancing up.

"Who cares?" Mor replied. "The body's there, there's still scale to gather. That's what counts."

"There was another dragon," Jon said. "We saw its tracks. It looked as though they fought."

"Or mated?" Les asked.

"Much the same thing, with dragons," Mor said.

Kelvin put away the mandajo in his horse's saddle-sack. It was, after all, his. As usual no one had seemed to pay much attention to his playing. Mor and Les had come to the same conclusion he had: that the two dragons had probably been mating. Did that mean that the other would return to this vicinity? Farm animals, he knew, could require several matings before it took, and it could be the same with dragons. What would happen if the female came back and found men crawling over the corpse of her mate? The thought made him shudder, but no one else seemed concerned. Were they fools, or was he a coward? Somehow he didn't really like either alternative.

As they rounded the river bend, the word went back and forth from man to man, and soon all were craning their necks, reddened or dark-tanned as the case might be, as they strained to see the sight. Soon everyone who had been behind moved up front, leaving the Hackleberries and the Crumbs and Keith Sanders, the rabble-rouser from the park, and burly, graying Gaston Hayes.

Kelvin felt himself frowning. Something wasn't exactly right, but he couldn't quite pin it down.

"What is it, bold brother mine?" Jon asked brightly. As often was the case, Jon seemed to sense her brother's sensing.

Then he realized what it was. "The scales—they were scattered about like petals from flowers. I just had a glimpse, but—we didn't leave them like that. We loaded all we could onto Mockery, and stacked the rest neatly near the body. Wasn't that so, Jon?"

Her mouth grew tight. "Yeah."

"The other dragon!" Kelvin cried, his forebodings now assuming full force. "It's been here—feeding."

"You sure?" Morvin barked.

"The scales have been moved!"

"Maybe Jack?"

"He didn't know where the dragon was," Jon said.

"He could've smelled it," Mor pointed out.

"Then why would he scatter the scales instead of taking them?" Les asked. "Dad, I think——"

Abruptly he broke off, for a very live dragon's snout had appeared over the side of the dead one. Blood-stained jaws gaped, gobbets of spoiling flesh hung on the terrible teeth. The thing rose up on its front legs and issued a long and penetrating hiss. Its bloodred eyes seemed to fasten on them instantly.

"Gods!" Crumb muttered. If he hadn't taken the notion of a companion-dragon seriously before, he certainly did now.

"Run for your lives!" someone cried. It was, Kelvin realized a moment later, Keith Sanders. It seemed that the man was just as proficient at urging rabble to flee as urging it to fight.

"No! Stand and fight!" Lester called. His sword came out of its scabbard with the whisper of polished steel being bared for action. No coward, he!

The dragon gave a frightful snort that raised dust from the road's surface. It came charging, hard.

Men and horses scattered. Men shouted. Horses squealed. Men and horses screamed together as the huge jaws snapped, again and again. If there was one thing a dragon preferred to a rotting carcass, it was live meat. It also liked fighting better than sleeping. This dragon was having a ball.

The tail lashed, like a big, thick rawhide whip, knocking down horses and flinging off riders. The jaws crunched indiscriminately on men and animals. Blood and other bodily substances stained nearby rocks and trees and roadway. The dragon wasn't trying to feed, just to disable, so that the maximum amount of prey could be rendered helpless before fleeing. Then the feeding would be done at leisure.

"No! No! No! We've got to stand!" Lester called. "United, organized, disciplined——"

He was of course correct, and his military training helped him. But his words had all the effect of the proverbial cry down a dry well. Men, so eager to do battle earlier in the day, now fell over themselves and collided with one another following Keith Sanders' pusillanimous advice.

In that moment Kelvin realized that most men were just as cowardly as he knew himself to be. The difference between them was that he anticipated the things he feared, while others ignored them until it was too late. That didn't make him feel much better, but he did think his way was less foolish.

Meanwhile, the dragon was having a field day with cowards and bold men alike; it didn't care one way or the other about the social qualities of its prey.

Gaston Hayes brushed back gray hair from his face and raised his ancient crossbow. He aimed into the dust of the dragon's activity; his rheumy eyes squinted, and he squeezed the trigger.

The bolt went *thunk.* It had not even struck a dragon scale, but had lodged in a tree instead.

"Damn ye for cowards!" Morvin Crumb exclaimed angrily, addressing the running Knights. He moved out of the way of a horseman who seemed blind to his presence and all else but the way of escape. He adjusted the lance he carried. He had a polished, never-used lance that he had brought just for this unlikely situation.

Mor kneed his big plow horse out to meet the dragon. The lance lowered, aimed roughly at the creature's head. The whites of the horse's eyes showed, but he leaped a plow horse's ungainly leap at his master's urging. The dragon, who had been coming fast, wriggling almost comically from side to side, now put on its brakes. Its front feet locked and skidded. Its broad tail swished as it swung around and down, hard.

The tail caught Morvin Crumb across his chest. It struck the mailed vest he wore with a loud metallic clank. Crumb, big man that he was, went spinning like a child's tantrum-tossed toy. He lit in some nettle-bushes, wind gone and senses fled, on his broad back.

So much, Kelvin thought fleetingly, for courage.

"Help him," Les urged Kelvin. "If we go in fast, maybe we can save him!"

"Yeah!" said Jon.

Looking at his sister's eager young face, Kelvin did what he felt he had to, and pushed Jon off their horse.

"What are you doing!" Jon protested. But she knew. What he was doing was putting little sister out of the way of danger—or as nearly out of danger as was possible at the moment. This act infuriated her, but it was necessary.

He and Lester charged at the side of the dragon. Just as they reached it, its enormous head snapped around.

Les delivered a quick, slapping sword low to the snout, the monster's eyes being far out of reach. The creature's great clawed forefoot rose and swept him almost casually from his mount. Les flew, and lit down in the bushes not far from his father.

Kelvin felt his gauntlet pull the horse's reins. The animal responded by halting abruptly. Kelvin saved himself from going over the horse's head by a sudden grab at the bay's tossing mane. His sword slipped from his fingers, slid by the horse's neck without cutting, and clanked harmlessly on the roadway. Desperately he tried shifting his weight to keep his seat. Hero, indeed! He could hardly even keep his seat!

Morvin was up now. Shaking his big head, he looked for the lance.

Kelvin found it, or rather his left hand did. The gauntlet wrenched his shoulder, reaching he knew not for what. He saw the ground come up at him and he had to fling out both hands to avoid striking his head. He lit with a thump that at another time might have brought forth a cry of agony. Clouds of choking, gray road dust rose around him. His left hand fought him, finally closing on a smooth shaft.

Kelvin forced himself to his feet, the shaft of the lance smooth in his right hand and gripped clumsily and higher up by his left. He felt dizzy. Because of the dust he could see neither horse nor dragon.

A great chilling hiss froze him. Terrible, swordlike teeth flashed directly overhead. Hot and carrion-scented air blew sickeningly into his face.

Glunk!

He felt the shaft driven into the ground. His left arm remained steady as he tried but failed to retain his balance.

Dust swirled. Stench overpowered. Saliva and blood dripped down on his face. The ground shook, heaved, and rocked. A great hiss was followed by a bubbling noise, which in turn was followed by a loud, gusty, fading sigh.

Barely conscious, Kelvin saw figures emerge from the settling dust. Mor and Les Crumb came to stand over him. Jon, coming up behind, looked as if she were crying.

"Ye did it again, son," Morvin said.

"Huh?" What a brilliant retort, the cynical back of his mind remarked.

"Look, lad!"

Kelvin struggled to his elbow.

He was lying, he discovered, in a messy bubble of thick, sticky, steaming dragon blood.

While above him, staring with a single fading eye, held upright by the lance that impaled its mate and entered the hidden recesses behind the socket, swayed the dead, nightmarish head of the once unconquerable dragon.

CHAPTER 13
The Flaw

"SO THIS IS THE Kingdom of Throod," said Kelvin, sniffing the spicy smell of orlemon cakes that reached them from the beehive-shaped ovens. It was as hilly as Rud, but the trees and the crops were different, the trees running much to citrus.

"Good enough for me," Jon said from Mockery's back. She wiped some limfruit juice from her mouth, licked the rind, and then tossed the rind at a barking wolfox's pointed face. The wolfox promptly disappeared into the thicket of hazbert brush.

"You've got some treats in store," Lester Crumb said, riding up to their left. "I was here for nearly a month, once. Prettiest girls in the Seven Kingdoms."

"Girls, phooey!" Jon said.

Little sister, Kelvin thought, would soon enough be changing her attitude, once she got into a situation where boys behaved decently toward girls. Of course they always had behaved well toward certain girls. He wondered what Maybell Winterjohn, the prettiest and freckledest girl in school, had done since he left. If things had been different . . . but there had been no choice. But of course she would never have been interested in a roundear.

"A rudna for your thoughts," Heln murmured.

Kelvin jumped. He hadn't seen her ride up beside Jon. "I, uh, um, that is—"

"Why do you feel you have to blush every time the subject of women comes up?" she asked.

Heln, of course, was not turned off by round ears. That made her so obviously the girl for him that he wondered why he was unable to believe it. He blushed harder.

"I was only teasing you, Kel," she said. "I know it's hard for you to adjust to being a hero, just the way it's hard for me to live with the fact that I got—" But now she choked off.

"N-no difference!" he exclaimed.

"I think that's what I like about you—besides your burning red round ears—that you represent no threat to me," she continued after a pause. "You aren't like those beasts. You wouldn't ever—"

"Never!" he agreed fervently.

"Because I guess you know that it's likely to be a long time before I can—that is—you know."

And probably just as long a time for him. She had drawn a nice analogy, between his supposed heroism and her degradation. Both of them had had to do things for which they had been totally unprepared, and it remained difficult to adjust to the new realities. They were indeed well matched, in devious as well as the obvious ways.

He looked at her, and she smiled at him, and suddenly he wished he could just take her in his arms and do all the things with her that made him blush to think about but that he never had the nerve to take seriously. He felt his blush intensifying yet more. But then he saw that she was blushing, too, and that helped a great deal.

"Say—" Jon started.

"Quiet!" Kelvin and Heln said together.

"I hope I never get like that," Jon said, and rode on ahead, affronted.

"I hope she *does*!" Kelvin said.

"She's ready now—when she meets the right boy."

"Never!" Jon called back.

A blue and white bird different from any in Rud flew over, calling from its long beak: "Cau-sal-i-ty! Cau-sal-i-ty!" At least that was what it sounded like to Kelvin. That could only be the creature known as the primary bird. Rud's bluebins and robjays were so much more sensible; at home birds sounded like birds, not aged philosophers.

The road ran downhill, past a stone cairn dedicated to the memory of Throod's soldiery who had perished in the two-hundred-year-old war with Rud. It was discomfiting to imagine the shades of those soldiers out there on the grass in front of the cairn. What would they think, Kelvin mused, of the two Crumbs and two Hackleberries and one Flambeau come to their homeland for mercenaries to fight in a war that hadn't happened yet? Probably they would approve; after all, soldiers were soldiers. How many had ever fought in the name of a cause so noble or for pay so magnificent? Yes, they would have to approve.

Mockery made his mockery sound, and Lester looked over at him, and then at his father. Kelvin knew what the latter was thinking. They should have taken more men. With Mockery and the one pack horse loaded with scale, they could be in danger from highwaymen. But Throod for some strange reason was far more law-abiding than its neighboring kingdoms, especially Rud.

"Whoa," called Morvin suddenly.

They drew their mounts to a stop as the big man dismounted and crossed the road to a rough, wooden fence. He crossed the fence into a field filled with trellises supporting large yellow clusters of curapes. He spoke briefly to the farmer dressed in creaseless brownskins, paid him a full scale, and came back with his arms loaded. Kelvin took the fruit handed to him and popped and squirted the sweet tart ovoids into his mouth. Paradise, he thought, paradise. The most luscious fruit growing anywhere in the Seven Kingdoms, and yet the boys of Throod took up soldiering for the highest bidders in other lands. Strange, but then maybe Rud would look like paradise to someone who didn't know. Possibly the government here was not much different from Rud's, though all he knew was that they voted for officials and changed officials frequently. In civics class he had heard Throod's government described as "one weak step above anarchy." He hadn't understood that exactly, but then it had seemed probable that he would never need to.

"Recruitment House ahead," said Mor, wiping yellow juice from his mouth and pointing. "We'll order our men and supplies, show that we've got gold to pay for them, and then head back."

"By way of The Flaw," Lester said, verbally capitalizing. "Visitors have to see The Flaw while they're in Throod. Wouldn't be right if they didn't."

Mor made no reply other than a grunt as they rode on to the large, unadorned structure that was not unlike a barracks.

"I do hope Captain Mackay will be here as agreed," Mor said, worried. "He's supposed to have the men —experienced warriors *and* experienced officers —ready for us. But there's a saying that Throod mercenaries, though reliable, do get into scrapes. I remember last time I was here, back in the big conflict, when a third of the men were unavailable. Seems some of them had started a mercenaries' union to fix rates, and some liked the idea and some didn't. So add to the other reasons we lost and the Queen won the fact that we didn't get the right men."

Kelvin thought that if he had been a mercenary he would have wanted a union to fix rates. But then he hadn't been a paid soldier, wasn't now, and never would be. The mercenary's life of endless marches and battles until wounded too badly to function or continuing until either slain or too old to fight had no appeal. Better a farmer's life, or even the life of a tradesman.

They entered the door of Recruitment House and stood looking around at the scant furnishings and the dozen or so men. No one moved or spoke for a moment, and then the big, gray-haired man with one arm stood up from his table in the corner. He held out his hand, gray eyes meeting Morvin's blue.

"Morvin Crumb. I'm Captain Mackay. Welcome to Recruitment House and the Kingdom of Throod."

Morvin merely glanced at the empty sleeve. Good

officers, after all, were traditionally warriors who had lost something in a fight. There were officers with patches over eyes, or with wooden stumps for legs, or misshapen shoulders, or deformed backs. Experience was what counted, and that with the training and leading of more able men to fight.

"You know why we've come," Morvin said. "This here"—he indicated Kelvin with a thumb—"is the Roundear. Kelvin, take off your cap."

Hesitantly, Kelvin reached up and pulled the head-covering off his straw-colored hair. He didn't like being placed on display like this, but he knew it was necessary. Jon and Heln were both now wearing stockelcaps, for different reasons, and he was glad of that.

"Glad to meet you, Roundear," Captain Mackay said, gripping his hand. It was a rough hand callused by years of sword wielding and horse handling. It was a large hand, which all but engulfed his.

"I'm not certain I'm the right roundear," Kelvin confessed. "But I do have this gauntlet I found, and it's evidently the one of prophecy. With it on, I just can't lose in a sword fight."

"And the gauntlet great shall the tyrant take. The magician bad, by the gauntlet had," quoted the Throodian. "Yes, one of the interesting prophecies, clumsy as their wording tends to be. Don't worry about whether you're the one or not, son. As long as you've got the gauntlet and people *think* you're the one, it helps. What really counts of course is something else—military tactics and men trained to carry them out. How are you on tactics?"

"I, uh—"

"Don't worry. You'll learn. And you'll have good officers, I'll see to that. Well, sit down and we'll make our plans."

Kelvin took the proffered chair, as did the rest of the party. It seemed to him that though he was supposed to be the hero of the prophecy, he did little but let others move him around. Still, it was sensible to sit here in this quiet place and make plans. That was true even if he had little to do with making them.

"We brought scale to get things started," Morvin said, waving away the amber bottle the captain silently indicated. "We'll need everything—swords, lances, shields, body armor, war-horses, the works."

"I understand," the captain said, pouring himself a glass and not offering the refreshment to Kelvin or Lester or Jon or Heln. "You've come to the right place. But the terms—"

"When we win, each man gets a choice of citizenship and land, or a mercenary's top wages plus bonus."

"And if the fighting lasts and the men need gold to send to their families?"

"More scale. There are more dragons where the last two came from."

"Last two? You went on a hunting expedition into dragon country?"

Morvin nodded. "We did that. But I've got to tell you, this roundear here slew both of them."

The gray eyebrows raised. Kelvin felt the steely eyes going over him. "You don't look like a warrior," he said.

"I'm not," Kelvin said. "But the prophecy and the gauntlet—they made the difference."

"Tell me how."

Kelvin took a deep breath. He had told the tale so many times in recent days that it was almost like reciting a piece. "When Jon, my younger sibling here, and I arrived in dragon country the first time, we were all on our own. Just Jon and me and the deaf donkey outside. I had a sword, but it was an old sword. Jon's the best with a sling, of anyone I've seen. When Jon saw the dragon, Jon thought it dead, and—" On and on with the familiar tale.

Captain Mackay listened intently. His eyes turned to fix on Jon, and it was evident that he understood her nature quickly enough, but he gave no overt indication. He was the kind of soldier who could keep a secret. Silently he motioned to the grizzled officers drinking at the other tables. They rose and came across the room. All stood listening raptly, now and then one or another breaking his silence with a brief and appropriate curse.

"And I never even knew until I regained consciousness," Kelvin concluded. "There he was, skewered right through the eye, just as the first had been skewered by the tent pole."

"Wizard's Teeth!" cried a bearded man with one ear missing and an ugly scar across his cheek. "That was some adventure! You're either the Roundear of Prophecy or the luckiest roundear in any of the Seven Kingdoms!"

"Yes, I guess that's so," Kelvin said. "But I don't *feel* special, and without the gauntlet—"

"You'll do just fine until another contender comes along," the captain said. "Personally I don't think anyone could be that lucky. It has to be the prophecy."

"I agree with you," Morvin said. "He just don't realize what he is yet."

"He's learning, though!" Jon piped up.

Kelvin gave his sister his customary light kick. His sister, experienced in his ways, drew her foot back under the table, and the captain gave a slight jerk as the kick connected.

But the grim oldster was smiling. "I, too, had a sibling once, Roundear. And whether this one be your blood sibling or your friend sibling, I know what prompted that kick."

"Blood sibling," Kelvin said. "Our father was a roundear, our mother a pointear, so the chances were even, and that's the way it happened: one of each. Then our father was killed, and our mother remarried."

"Who was your father?"

"He called himself John Knight. He was from Earth."

"I know of him."

"You do?" Jon exclaimed eagerly.

"That is to say, I heard of him. That was all." But by the way his jaw tightened, Kelvin realized that the man knew more than he was telling. Was it something bad? It couldn't be! Yet—

"About our business," Morvin suggested.

"Eh," the captain agreed, switching his attention. "The business will be concluded satisfactorily. I know my trade, Crumb."

"Mor. Mor Crumb."

"Mor."

"Yes, I'm sure you do." Morvin stood up. "If it's agreed, then, two thousand men and at least thirty good officers. With your men and our men when our men get trained—"

"It will be a battle," the captain said. "That Queen of yours—I'm not sure we have any edge. We could take 'em in regular combat, but they've got a magician that's as slippery as a greased eelshark, and twice as mean. So don't be thinking this is any pushover."

"We have a secret weapon," Mor said.

"Eh? Where?"

"I can't tell you that in front of your men."

The captain nodded. "You aren't bluffing?"

"No."

"Then tell me when you're ready. If it's enough to make up for the edge their magic gives them—"

"It may be."

"Then I trust we'll have a satisfactory outcome. I'll have the men and supplies ready in half a day. Come back here and we'll all ride together for Rud."

"Agreed," Morvin said.

"Then why don't you take these young folk sight-seeing? Take them to see The Flaw."

"I had it in mind," Morvin agreed. "Come, Knights."

They trooped out. Kelvin, however, felt less than satisfactory. "You know we haven't tried using Heln for spying yet," he said. "It may not work."

"And then again, it may," the ruddy man responded. "If we can spy out their plans ahead of time, we can lick them every time. I'd call that a good edge."

"Still—" Kelvin said.

Heln put a fine fair hand on his arm. "It will be all right, Kel," she said. "Those berries didn't hurt me before, and now we have plenty of them. I'm sure I can do what needs to be done."

Kelvin was silent, still not liking the risk either to her or to their effort if this ploy failed. But again, what choice was there? He seemed to be fated to participate in things he didn't like or trust, again and again. Was this a hero's lot?

"The Flaw," Jon asked brightly. "It's near here?"

"Very near," Mor said.

"It's just a big old crack without a bottom," Jon said, giving Mockery's neck a pat as they walked past. "Who wants to see that?"

"You do," Lester said. "And so does your brother. Believe me, it's something you're never going to forget."

Jon snapped a rock from her sling into a tall oaple tree, disturbing a squirbet who was packing off a sugary nut high amid the branches. It was a for-fun shot, Kelvin knew, and not one that Jon intended to score.

"Schoolmaster used to tell us that when he brought out the strap," Jon said. "And you know, he was right: I never forgot. But maybe you're right. Maybe a dumb old hole in the ground is worth seeing."

"It's behind that high board fence over there," Mor said. "It's got slits you can see through. You can poke an arm and your head through if you've a mind to, but there's no sense in that. I've heard of women who've been jilted by soldiers dropping their engagement rings down there. Waste of good metal and precious stones."

In a moment they were at the barrier, some distance from others who had come to see The Flaw. Like the others, they approached the nearest openings in the fence. The sawn-out viewing place was chest-high on Morvin and Les, head-high on Kelvin, and chin-high on Jon. Heln was just the right height for it. Hesitantly and just a bit fearfully, on Kelvin's part, they looked.

Down, down at twinkling stars set amid velvety blackness. Now and then a bright object such as was seen in the night streaked through the black, trailing a long tail: a luminous tadpole in a froogpond of space.

Kelvin shifted his feet, half fearful that the solid ground would disappear beneath them. Then he looked over at open-mouthed Jon and Heln, and the big eyes of Mor and Les.

"The metaphysicians say it's a tear or a rip in the physical universe," Les said. "It's said that two universes, two realities, are here joined; that one bleeds or oozes into the other."

"And sometimes something or some*one* manages to cross," Heln murmured. "Like my mother—"

"Or my father," Kelvin finished, awed.

If the mood touched Jon, she flung it off. "I'm going to get a star," she said briskly. She hurled. The rock flew over the barrier and plummeted. A quick flash and it was gone.

"Didn't lead it enough," Jon said, and tried again. Again the flash in the adjoining starfield.

"You really think you'll hit a star?" Les asked, sounding amused.

"I will if I keep trying," Jon said.

"Not a star, Jon. They're too big and too distant. You haven't a chance."

"You sound like a schoolmaster," Jon said.

"I might have been," Les said. Then, giving Kelvin a nudge he felt in his back, he pointed to two dark-haired tourist girls a short distance away. "I bet those two are from the Kingdom of Aratex," he said. "Let's go talk to them."

Heln's hand clamped firmly on Kelvin's hand. She didn't say a word, but he received the message. "Some other time, maybe," he said.

Morvin laughed. "Maybe never, eh, son?"

But Kelvin didn't reply. He was too conscious of Heln's hand on his. He would be satisfied, he realized, if she never released it. But he couldn't say so. Maybe this was another flaw in his character—one that faintly echoed the amazing Flaw they had just experienced.

CHAPTER 14
Messages

"Now, I want," Morvin Crumb said, leaning over Kelvin at the writing table, "for this to be just right. Read what you've written."

Kelvin looked at Jon and Lester and the odd dozen or so Knights crowded around their outdoor table. He cleared his throat and read.

"To Her Imperial Majesty, Queen Zoanna of Rud. Your Majesty: Whereas you have seized power without popular mandate, and whereas your rule has become oppressive in the extreme, I, Kelvin Knight Hackleberry of Rud, the Roundear of Prophecy, call upon you to abdicate the throne and restore to it your rightful consort, King Rufurt, should he live, or someone of the people's choice, should Rufurt be presently slain or incapacitated beyond the ability to rule. You have seven days from the receipt of this message to announce your abdication. Should you not abdicate within that time, the Knights of the Roundear shall attack with all their magic-supported strength and fury, seize the imperial palace, and force your abdication, if need be, by sword point."

Morvin frowned. "It seems right, but—"

"It should be more insulting," Jon said. "Say, perhaps, 'Your Imperial Majesty, Usurper, Hag, and Meanie.'"

Les laughed, but his father seemed to consider it. "Perhaps," the elder said, "usurper might fit . . ."

"But we want her to agree!" Kelvin protested.

"Hmm, quite right. She won't, of course, but—oh, hang it, Hackleberry, just write 'In the Name of Freedom, I am.'"

"In the Name of Freedom, I am," Kelvin said, writing.

"There. Hold it. You got the wax ready, Les?"

"I have, Father."

"Then affix his signature."

Lester leaned over and deposited a drop of wax on the paper.

"No, no, not *there,* you idiot! Quick, scrape that off."

Lester scraped, using a knife blade. The wax came off cleanly.

"There, above where the wax was, write 'Kelvin Hackleberry, Roundear of Prophecy.'"

Kelvin did so, feeling uncomfortable about the prophecy part.

"Now date it. Anybody got the date?"

"It's June twenty-first of twenty twenty-four," Lester said.

Kelvin marked the date.

"Now fold in past the middle and overlap the edge."

Kelvin followed instructions.

"Now, Lester. Your wax."

Lester dripped wax, in a round, big circle. The wax made a small puddle across the overlapping edges.

Lester blew on it.

"Now, Hackleberry, your ear," Morvin ordered.

"You want me to—"

"Just *do* it, Hackleberry!"

With a sigh, Kelvin turned his head sideways and pressed his right ear in the wax.

"My, that looks like fun," Jon remarked.

"Hold it, hold it, hold it," Morvin snapped as Kelvin showed signs of bolting upright. "It has to set. All right, now up, carefully."

Kelvin raised his head. He looked at the paper. The impression was that of a round ear, more or less. That had been Morvin's idea, as had almost everything. He touched his ear. How smooth it now felt!

He glanced across the landscape, to the cabin where Heln was fixing food. He wished he could go feel *her* round and smooth ears, not to mention her round and smooth—

"Messenger!" Morvin shouted.

One of the Knights was almost instantly at his shoulder. Kelvin recognized him as one whose farm had been burned.

Morvin put the document in a message tube and capped it. "Deliver this to the imperial palace. Just call out, 'A message for the Queen,' and toss it to the gateman. Then ride out—fast."

"Aye, sir," said the Knight, giving them a faintly impudent smile. "I'm on my way."

As he left, Morvin remarked, "We have to get more discipline. Now, about these posters and handbills . . ."

All afternoon they were putting them up. They would ride to the edge of a village, find a likely tree, and while one of them kept a lookout for the Queen's minions, the other nailed poster to tree. All the posters read the same, and by now Kelvin, if not Jon, was thoroughly sick of them.

Each poster said:

> ATTENTION: A new day is coming and those who would help bring it about are invited to join with us in our demand that Queen Zoanna abdicate. Sign the petition and deposit it with your local representative Knight; he will tell you how you can help further by resisting oppression locally or by joining our ranks. We are all free people and will not long continue to suffer tyranny. Right and Prophecy is on our side!
>
> (*signed*) Knights of the Roundear

Kelvin sighed as he nailed up another one. He was growing so tired! No one had told him that revolution would have so much tedious labor.

The distribution of handbills was hard work that soon became a bore. After the posters came the handbills, freely thrown from horses and placed also in many reaching hands:

PEOPLE OF RUD: Should the Queen not abdicate her position by the end of this week, we are at war. To join the right side, the winning side, see your local recruiter. Give any snooping soldiery short shrift or the long shaft, as appropriate. Join now, today, while you still can.

Knights of the Roundear

Some job for a hero, Kelvin thought, tossing the last of the flyers to a boy he almost recognized. And now, back home to the tent, and then another day of doing Crumb's bidding.

Snap! Snap! Snap! Plunk! Plunk! Plunk!

They were getting a little better, Kelvin thought, as he watched the arrows hit the scarecrow targets the mercenaries had set up. Most farmers, and some townsmen, did after all hunt for game. But in a battle, with other men for targets? He shivered, just at the thought of it.

"You're sure it's safe?" Morvin Crumb demanded. "We've tested those berries on animals, and you know every one of them died. I can't see that the shape of the ear should make that much of a difference."

"It's not just the shape of the ear," Heln said. "It's the Earthly ancestry. Those of us with round ears must be breeding true to our heritage, so are not affected the same way as the natives are. Anyway, I survived it before."

"Could be a fluke," Mor said.

"I'll just take one berry this time," she promised. "If I make it to astral separation, I'll do something simple, like—"

"I don't trust this either," Kelvin said. "To gamble on poison—"

"Like visiting my folks—and yours," she continued brightly. "To be sure they're all right."

Kelvin's protests dried up. Of course he wanted to know that his folks were all right! So, reluctantly, he acceded to the experiment. After all, they did need to know whether it worked reliably.

Heln solemnly consumed a single berry, from the horde they had harvested from the dragon's garden. Again Kelvin wondered why a dragon should have tended it so carefully. Of course the ability to separate astrally could be an immense advantage—but were dragons smart enough to realize that? Or did they simply like the feeling of astral travel? Maybe that was it; they did for recreation what they could have done for phenomenal power over their environment —because they were stupid creatures. A man would never be that foolish!

Or would he? Kelvin thought about some of the people he knew, and remained disquieted.

Heln sank into sleep. Then she stopped breathing. "She's dying!" Kelvin cried, horrified. He leaped toward her, though there really wasn't anything he could do.

"No, don't touch her!" Jon said. "She was like that before. It's the astral separation!"

"But she's not even—"

"That's the way it is. She looks dead, but she's not, quite. When her spirit returns, she'll recover. I'm sure. I think."

With that note of confidence, Kelvin had to be satisfied.

After an hour there was a tremor at Heln's breast. She was recovering!

Soon she was able to talk. "I did it!" she said. "I traveled to my folks, and they're all right. Then to yours, and they're all right. Only—"

"Only they need gold to cover the taxes," Kelvin said, with a dark glance at Morvin Crumb.

"No, they aren't being bothered about that. But I saw guardsmen camped around their farm. Not doing anything, just watching. What does that mean?"

Morvin slapped his thigh. "It means confirmation!" he exclaimed. "Just as I suspected! Your folks and their farm are a trap for you, Kelvin! They're waiting for you to visit home; then they'll nab you. That's why I didn't want you to go, not even to take them money they might need. The Queen's guards won't bother your folks as long as they remain bait—but you can't go back there."

Kelvin felt weak in the knees. The big man had been right all along, saving him from a horrendous mistake!

"I didn't know how much time I had," Heln continued. "So I looked around, and I found I could orient on people who were thinking of you, Kelvin. There were a lot of them, all friendly, but one was very unfriendly. So I went to that one, and it was Zatanas."

"Zatanas!" Morvin exclaimed. "The Queen's evil sorcerer!"

"Yes. He was talking with the dwarf, the one who bought Jon—"

"What did he say?" Morvin asked, almost drooling in his excitement.

"Something about how he had brought the round-ears here—"

"*He* did it?" Kelvin asked, amazed.

"And something about lizards. Then my time ended, and my spirit was hauled back to my body. I'm sorry I couldn't have stayed a little longer. Maybe I should have eaten two berries . . ."

Then, exhausted, she slept again, but this time her breathing did not stop. It seemed to Kelvin that one berry had been quite risky enough; probably the new ones were more potent than the ones Jon had carried around squashed in her pocket, and then soaked in her mouth. Three full-strength dragonberries might very well have killed Heln!

Morvin looked at Kelvin. "That was a message we didn't expect!" the big man said. "Why should Zatanas make a claim like that? About bringing the roundears here?"

"And what does he want with lizards?" Kelvin added.

"It's beyond me! I only hope we don't find out the hard way!"

Heln slept the rest of that day, and on into the night. Obviously astral separation took a lot from her! Kelvin sat beside her for hours, finally working up the courage to take her hand. What a lot of information she had gathered, in that one brief hour of astral travel! But he remained worried about its effect on her health.

Mainly, though, he just liked holding her hand.

CHAPTER 15
Zatanas

THE LABORATORY WHERE ZATANAS performed his miracles was a veritable rat's nest of stacked caldrons, rolled-up pentagrams and other magical charts, old books of spells and sciences, and other traditional tools of the trade. The place smelled of a thousand herbs, intermixed with the scent of burned incense and charred bones. In the center of the room an owlhawk perched on a human skull held upright by a dagger stuck in the remaining neck vertebra. Another skull had been sawn lengthwise, one-half serving as an incense burner, the other as a receptacle for some vile-smelling unguent. Light streamed in from the high windows, and yet the place was dark, as though the interior drank the light, or forbade its passage.

Zatanas, dark of visage, long of face and nose and claw, hummed contentedly to himself as he sat at a table and munched the simple repast that Queeto, his dwarf, had set out for him. Unlike Queeto, he still sometimes ate when the physical act of eating pleased him, as it did now. The meat tasted like dragon, he thought, though actually it was axoglatter, a particularly ugly lizard with a green skin that in the right light shone like the scales of a dragon.

"A little less strong and a little more rancid," Zatanas said, musing as much to himself as to the hovering dwarf.

"What, Master?"

Zatanas belched loudly and reached for the flagon of good orange wine on his table. The wine was specially spiced, as was most of the magician's fare. A little dried blood from the right sources added greatly to taste.

129

"I said," Zatanas said, "that the meat is aged to perfection. A little less aging and it would be tough. A little more and it would be leather."

"Thank you, Master," the dwarf said, widening his already wide mouth. He frequently responded like that, no matter what Zatanas said. That was one of his more endearing traits, and made it slightly harder to punish him properly when he erred. Zatanas had been furious at Queeto's recent loss of his purchase at the Girl Mart, but had elected for the time being to withhold action. When Queeto began to think of becoming impudent, then Zatanas would punish him for that error, restoring appropriate equilibrium to their relationship. The dwarf, knowing this, was meanwhile being extremely well behaved, as servile as he had ever been. That was good.

However, this matter of the abduction of the girl could not remain unattended. He would have to locate the culprits and deal with them in a manner that would discourage any repetitions. That meant that simple extinction was not enough; their deaths had to be public and horrible beyond any reasonable expectation. He knew their identities, of course; that wasn't the problem. The problem was bringing them down in precisely the right manner, an object lesson for all time in all the land.

First, however, he had to get hold of them. As long as they remained hidden in the wilderness, moving constantly about, he was unable to pin them down.

So Zatanas watched, and waited, unwilling to act until he could accomplish his full purpose in his own exacting way. He had patience; his ire, once incited, never cooled. Sooner or later the stupid round-eared boy would seek to visit his home farm, and walk into the trap, and the idiotic would-be revolutionist Crumb would try to rescue him, and then—ah, then it might begin.

Meanwhile, he had a rebellion to quell. He trusted that Crumb would not risk either himself or the roundear boy in a direct conflict. That was important, because he didn't want anything to happen to either, prematurely. It wouldn't make much of an impression if they both died coincidentally in battle.

Zatanas picked daintily at a foreleg with its three toes still attached and crunchy. "I have decided to hold a conference with my daughter the Queen."

"Will I attend, Master?"

"No. She doesn't wish for you to be in her sight."

Queeto frowned, his toad mouth and swine eyes making a face. "Why, Master?"

"Because you frighten her. She still thinks you're a demon from another world. I don't see any reason to enlighten her, do you?"

Queeto grinned more broadly than ever. He, as Zatanas well knew, liked being feared by royalty. In fact, he liked being feared by anyone.

"You tell her about the lizards, Master?"

Zatanas tossed the leg bone to the owlhawk. The owlhawk caught it in its strong beak with a snap and immediately set to pulverizing it. Zatanas swallowed more wine.

"Just what do you think you know about the lizards?"

The dwarf answered promptly, almost as though rehearsed: "That they are little brothers to the dragons, Master."

"Right. Most fortunately."

Zatanas rose and crossed the dimly lit room to the worktable. On it he had set up and molded hills and valleys of clay and dirt and sand. It was a perfect miniature landscape of the terrain for leagues about the castle. A carved palace occupied the same position in the miniature landscape as the castle they were in did the real landscape. There were miniature houses and even a miniature river that had to be continuously fed from a small spigot and a bucket behind the scene of distant hills and houses. All in order, a work of incredible delicacy that had taken many pains and much time.

"You see, Queeto, bringing roundears to this world was a mistake on my part."

"You, Master?" Queeto was properly incredulous that Zatanas could make any mistake, let alone admit to it, even in complete privacy.

"Yes, a possibly serious mistake," Zatanas continued, enjoying the effect on his minion. "You might call it a grotesque flaw." He smiled, appreciating a private joke. "I reckoned not with Mouvar and the force of his prophecies. But no matter," he said, waving the dwarf's concern away. "It's a mistake that my daughter and I will soon rectify."

"With lizards, Master?"

"With dragons, small friend. In this very place."

Queeto looked at him, baffled. "You and the Queen, your daughter—here?"

Zatanas rubbed at a speck of lizard dung on the tabletop. "She out there. You and I in here."

"Ah."

Just as if he understood. Remarkable animal, this. Almost as remarkable as dragons. Not quite as large, not quite as stupid.

"Queeto, little brother, remember what I told you about the magic that can be performed with miniatures?"

"Yes, Master. The doll that looks like an enemy and that you break so that the enemy breaks."

"Exactly. Well, here we have a small copy of the land and the palace and the houses and the river. Over there"—he pointed at the lush growth of transplanted shrubs forming a forest—"is where in our actuality is dragon country. If little brothers emerge from here, they will appear to us to be the size of real dragons in relation to the palace and the farms."

"I—understand, Master."

"Do you? Well, watch."

Taking a lizard from a cage, Zatanas set it among the plants. He then took a clay figure molded to look like a mounted knight with tiny sword and placed it in an open field. From a jar he took a bit of honey on a knife blade and applied it to the figure. He stood back, and soon a large fly was buzzing at the honey.

"Now!" he said, and dropped a pinch of herbal powder on the lizard.

The lizard raised its dragon head, sniffing. Its green scales seemed to flash gold; it raised its small hood. Suddenly it was running full tilt, wriggling from side to side.

The lizard reached the knight, pulled it down, and licked it with its long tongue. The fly, buzzing loudly, disappeared down the creature's throat.

"Now, what," the magician asked rhetorically, "do you suppose the real knight will look like when a real dragon steps on him?"

Queeto looked at the squashed clay. "Gooey," he said happily. "Blood making a crimson puddle, bones all white and broken, brains a pulpy pink mess."

"Exactly. And that's why I am going to hold a conference with the Queen. Her spies will locate the enemy, and there's where I'll have a dragon—or several dragons." He made an expansive gesture. "And that," he finished dramatically, "is how dragons doing my magical bidding will win the war."

Queeto's exclamation of servile appreciation of genius seemed almost genuine.

The Knights and the Queen's guardsmen were met in battle. Horses neighed or screamed, men cried challenges or curses or groans, swords clanged, crossbows twanged, blades and missiles made meaty clunking sounds. Dust rose in clouds beneath the horse's hooves and obscured everything that wasn't happening over a horse's length away.

War, Kelvin realized, was no more glamorous in practice than was dragon-fighting. It seemed to consist of flowing blood, billowing dust, and endless confusion. Where was the glory and the honor men spoke of? All he saw was phenomenal wasted effort.

He had trained for days to try to use his gauntleted left hand with his sword, but it was all but hopeless. In order to stay mounted he needed at least his right hand on the reins, and the left, even with practice, could hardly counter a sword swung with a good right arm.

Except, he discovered, under actual battle conditions. Then as in previous encounters, the gauntlet knew the threat, and countered sword blows, darting in to stab or disarm attackers. There was blood on the sword and the gauntlet, and Kelvin didn't want to look at either. Fortunately it made little difference. When a guardsman was close, the gauntlet knew before Kelvin did.

"Gods, but you're a fighter, Hackleberry!" Morvin Crumb said at his right. "Reminds me of me when I was your age."

Kelvin wondered what it would do to his image if he vomited—again. Taking lives, even the lives of evil men who wanted to kill him, just wasn't the way it was presented in storybooks. At least, not for him. He was appalled by this whole business.

"Just got me another, Dad!" Lester said to the far side of his father. "Makes three."

"Four for me," Morvin said. "The lad here polished off half a dozen. Without, I think, a sweat."

Kelvin wondered whether Mor was being kind. Kelvin was sure he was bathed in cold sweat. If he had to think about more than guiding the horse and ducking an occasional blow, he would soon be exhausted. His left arm was beginning to ache. Without the gauntlet, he would have been finished long before.

"Bet this whole pass looks like one big rolling cloud," Morvin said with gusto.

Reminded of the dust, Kelvin tasted it. He spat, and the spittle didn't quite clear his chin. His left hand tingled and he knew another enemy approached.

"Gods!" Morvin exclaimed. "There's something —Gods!"

Kelvin's blade met an enemy's, deflected it, and lunged, nearly unseating Kelvin. He saw the guardsman, no older than himself, give him a stricken look, then drop his sword, slump forward, and slide from the saddle under their horses' feet.

"Seven," Lester said. He had moved past his father to Kelvin's back.

"Gods! Oh, Gods!" repeated the elder Crumb, delighted.

But Kelvin knew that it was little of his own doing. He had tried to intercept the enemy's blade, true, but his aim had been bad. He would have been skewered had not his gauntleted left hand shoved him over so that, losing balance, he had whipped his other arm about—so that the sword had made a completely unplanned and unexpected trick motion, deflecting the other blade and continuing with horrible force into the other man's body. Certainly it had looked clever, but the cleverness had all been in the self-willed gauntlet, which seemed determined to make a deadly fighter of him despite his ineptitude. This had been happening all along.

What would the gauntlet do if he threatened to vomit on it? Cut off his head?

"Kel! Kel! Wait!"

Kelvin's head snapped around. It couldn't be! But it was. Coming full tilt down the hill, Mockery, and on his back—

"Jon! Jon! Over here!"

Guardsmen started for the girl. Three of them.

Kelvin needed no gauntlet to put his steed into motion. He kneed the horse, turned its head, was yanked down by the gauntlet and thereby ducked a blow from his right. His horse made a leap over a crawling guardsman and a wounded Knight, and detoured around others not identified. Kelvin yanked the reins, bringing it back on course. Then he was there on the hillside, and his sword was flashing and his reins lifted with his buckler as a blow almost took him across the face. It was amazing, the precision with which that gauntlet yanked him about, just so, so that every move was right.

A Knight on a black stallion flashed to his right, and then that Knight was confronting his attacker on his right hand as Kelvin lurched, pulled about yet again by the gauntlet, and his wildly flailing sword dealt with the man to his left.

Two bodies fell.

Kelvin sighed. Lester sighed, for what he was sure was a different reason. The bodies of their late foes lay unmoving in the dirt.

"Watch out, Kel!"

Jon's warning saved him just in time. He ducked, even as his left arm unsheathed the sword from its gory grip in the throat of a third foe and swung around to counter and disarm this fourth.

But the fourth attacker was no fool. He whirled his horse and fled.

"Jon, you idiot!" Kelvin exclaimed. "Why did you come here?"

"Heln remembered!" the girl cried.

"What's this?" Mor Crumb asked gruffly.

"She remembered about the lizards!" Jon said. "From when she saw Zatanas! So I had to come warn you!"

"What *about* the lizards?" Mor demanded.

"They're dragons!"

"What?" Kelvin was having trouble following this.

"And I saw them! 'Cause I knew to look! The dragons!"

"You saw dragons?" Mor cried.

"Three of them! Big brutes! Coming here!"

"I don't understand," Kelvin said, understating the case.

But suddenly Morvin Crumb did. "Sympathetic magic! Lizards are like miniature dragons! That evil sorcerer must've enchanted dragons by working through lizards!"

"I could see them from above," Jon continued. "Coming up the pass."

"You sure?" Kelvin asked, somewhat dully.

"I saw them!" Jon repeated. "Just as Heln said.

Three lizards. 'Cause Zatanas didn't think you'd be fool enough to go into battle yourself!"

Kelvin turned to Morvin, baffled. "Does that make any sense?"

"It must, in some twisted way," the ruddy man said. "Gods! Nothing can face three dragons!"

"That's why Heln was so worried!" Jon said. "She'd been trying to remember all these days, and just couldn't, and then she saw a lizard and it clicked. So she told me, and I—"

"You did right," Kelvin said. "If those monsters catch us—"

"We'd better retreat, fast!" Lester said.

"Son, I think you're right. Kelvin, you get that horn to your lips and you blow the way I told you you never would!" Shaking in spite of himself, Kelvin lifted the polished ox horn Morvin Crumb had hung about his neck. Three long notes meant retreat, and would give the other Knights their location.

He blew. The sound came out and carried. *Whoomp! Whoomp! Whhhoooommmmp!*

Blowing it made his head swim. So did the heat. So did the action he had just seen.

"Come on, now," Morvin cried. "Uphill and fast! Dragons don't like heights, everyone knows that!"

Kelvin hadn't known that, however. Still, it probably made sense. Flying creatures liked heights, and the local dragons were landbound.

They turned their mounts uphill, donkey and Jon just ahead of them. Looking back, Kelvin saw other Knights, some of them barely holding on to their horses, coming at a gallop. Behind them a cheer sounded as guardsmen thought they had won.

"We were beating them!" a Knight exclaimed. "Why did you sound retreat? Now we're in disarray, and soon's they regroup they'll come after us and destroy us on the run!"

"Maybe, maybe not," Morvin said. "We got word there's—"

"*Ahhhh!*" someone screamed behind.

And there it was: a dragon riding out of the dust, with a man in its mouth. Then another dragon and another, shimmering gold and deadly.

"Run for your lives!" Lester cried.

They ran, all of them, including the donkey. Now no one questioned the wisdom of their sudden disengagement from the fray.

Panting, standing at the top of the steep hill and looking down into the pass where the dust roiled and men and horses were being slain and rapidly devoured, the Knights knew they had made their escape just in time. The pursuing guardsmen hadn't been that fortunate, for the dragons had come up behind them.

"The girl saved us!" Morvin exclaimed. "That division of the Queen's guardsmen—they'll never be the same!"

"But if Zatanas sent the dragons," Kelvin asked, musing it out, "wouldn't he have known that his own side would be in the way? Why would he do that?"

Morvin nodded. "Something doesn't add up. We'd better get right back, and your girl will have to eat another berry. We'd better spy on the evil magician, and find out what's he really up to."

Kelvin hated having Heln risk her life again, but realized that it was necessary. The dragon attack had been too near a thing.

CHAPTER 16
Doubts

"I DON'T UNDERSTAND IT," Heln agreed. "Maybe that's why I couldn't remember about the dragons—I mean, how they related to the lizards Zatanas had. It seemed impossible that they could be the same, or that he would send dragons to ravage his own side as well as the enemy. So I suppose I just didn't believe it, until almost too late."

"Better take another berry and find out," Morvin said gruffly. "We can't afford many more surprises like dragons coming into the fray! I never guessed the evil sorcerer could control dragons!"

"But it's been only a few days since she had a berry," Kelvin protested. "We don't know whether it's safe for her to—"

"It isn't safe to go into battle against dragons!" Mor exclaimed vehemently. "Those could have been our boys as well as theirs getting chomped!"

Heln put her hand on Kelvin's. "I'm sure it's all right," she said. "I do feel woozy after a berry, but a good night's sleep helps, and I recover strength next day."

"I don't know," Jon put in. "You're losing weight."

Morvin's great fists clenched, but his voice was controlled. "Why don't you go outside and play, child?" he said to Jon.

"I'll try to eat better," Heln said, smiling tolerantly.

"You look just fine to me!" Kelvin said without thinking, distracted as he always was when she took his hand. Then, of course, he started blushing.

Heln smiled at him. "You're getting better at expressing yourself, I think," she remarked.

"Here's the situation," Mor said. "Our camp is

closer to the site of the battle than Zatanas' den is, and we hurried, so I'm sure we got home first. But the evil sorcerer will be getting the news about the battle within the hour. If we can spy on his reaction when he learns, we may find out what we need to know. It's the best possible time; we know that it's no use wearing you out spying when Zatanas is asleep or eating or not doing anything special. We have to catch him when he's plotting against us; then we can counter his plots."

It did make sense, Kelvin had to agree. He hated to see Heln seem to die, but she did recover, and they did need the information. That business with the dragons had been entirely too close!

Heln settled on her bed and swallowed a dragonberry. Soon she sank into her coma. The others left, but Kelvin remained beside her, ill at ease. If only she didn't have to risk her life this way, to help their cause!

And if only he *could* express himself adequately to her! Instead of always being so confounded tongue-tied. She had made it plain that she would be receptive to his advances, within reasonable limits. He felt so silly, bumbling about; but every time he tried to do something about it, he wound up blushing again.

"Gods, Heln, I wish I weren't such an ass with you!" he exclaimed aloud. She, of course, could not hear him; she had just stopped breathing. Her hand in his was growing cool; that had alarmed him before, and it troubled him now. It was so like death, this astral separation!

"I wish I could just take you in my arms," he said, venting his frustration aloud, because that made him feel marginally better. "I wish I could kiss you, and say, 'Heln, I think I love you, and I want to be always with you!' But I just can't! I know I'm a jackass, and I hate it, but my stupid tongue just tangles in my mouth and I blush—Gods, I wish I didn't blush!"

He looked at her, so deathly still. "How I would curse myself if you didn't wake!" he continued. "If somehow the berries—if the worst happened, and you—if I'd never even said to you—" Then everything clouded up, and he found himself bent over her cold hand, his tears flowing as he kissed it. "Damn, damn, damn!" he muttered brokenly. "If I'm a hero, they just don't make them the way they used to!"

Then, embarrassed anew, he pulled out his shirt tail and used it to dry off her hand. If she should ever suspect he had made a scene like this—!

Heln recovered consciousness as her spirit separated from her body. This was the third time she had traveled astrally, and she was learning its pattern. The first time she had been trying to die, and had thought her spirit was going to the afterlife. She had been amazed when she discovered otherwise, and then intrigued. Separation was actually an exhilarating experience; she was so free, with no body to drag after her or worry about! Of course she paid for it when she became physical again; Jon was right about her losing weight. She just couldn't seem to force herself to eat enough to make up for the energy she lost. Perhaps astral separation was part of the process of dying, and it was easier to die than to live. She had wanted to die, that first time; maybe that had made the whole experience easier. But the experience itself had gone far to restore her will to live, and, indeed, to participate in life as the woman she was, rather than as the object of degradation the guards of the Girl Mart had made of her. How glad she was that Kelvin was not at all like that! Every time he stammered and blushed, she liked him better.

She hovered above her body, gathering her presence, getting ready to make the jump to the evil magician's lair. Her vision cleared, and then her hearing. Kelvin was with her body, as he had been the last time; she really appreciated his loyalty. He was holding her hand.

"Gods, Heln, I wish I weren't such an ass with you!" he exclaimed abruptly.

What was this? He hadn't spoken before, as far as she knew. She decided to wait a moment more, and see what this led to.

"I wish I could just take you in my arms," he said.

Well! Apparently Kelvin could be much more expressive when he thought he was alone!

"I wish I could kiss you," he exclaimed. "And say, 'Heln, I think I love you, and I want to be always with you!'" he continued.

"Well, why don't you?" she asked, but of course he couldn't hear, because she had no voice in this state.

"But I just can't!" he added, sounding tortured.

Heln continued to listen and watch, until he completed his statement. When it was evident that he would say no more, she gathered herself for the jump to the other place. But she was thoughtful. She understood Kelvin better now; how could she make the best use of this explanation of his puzzling behavior?

Because of her delay, she arrived at Zatanas' residence just after the messenger left. She hoped she hadn't missed anything critical. She phased into the dusky chamber where the evil sorcerer and his dwarf henchman were.

"I don't like it! I don't like it at all!" Zatanas stormed, startling the owlhawk into flopping its great wings as it perched atop its human-skull pedestal. Queeto, too, looked scared.

"That messenger just now said we lost nearly two hundred guardsmen! To dragons. Dragons! What incredible, astounding luck! Black Star curses on the witless beasts!"

"But Master, didn't they attack the Knights? Didn't they get some of them, at least?"

"No!" The sorcerer looked as if he felt like taking out his anger on the dwarf, but managed to refrain.

"But why, Master?" the dwarf asked plaintively.

Zatanas chewed his lower lip, perhaps deliberately making himself hurt. "Because, stupid dwarf, dragons destroy all men without natural discrimination. They have very small brains. Even smaller than yours."

"But you directed them with lizards. The images were dressed as Knights."

So that was it, Heln realized. The dragons had been guided to attack the Knights first—and of course the guardsmen would have quickly gotten out of the way. Heln knew that Morvin and Kelvin would be glad to know that explanation. Costumes were the key!

"Quite right," the sorcerer was saying. "But the infernal Knights were not present. Somehow they got out of the pass before the dragons came. And the guardsmen were still there, luxuriating in the Knights' rout."

"Then they *were* defeated, Master! The guardsmen had the ruffians beat!"

"That's what the guardsmen want to think. But not I. I think that somehow one of the Knights must have been above the pass and seen the dragons and called retreat."

Heln held her breath, before remembering that she wasn't breathing in this state. If the evil magician ever realized exactly how the Knights had known the dragons were coming—

"But—" the dwarf protested.

"Exactly. It shouldn't have happened. Next time it will *not* happen. Next time the dragons will see Knights and not be tempted by guardsmen."

"How, Master?"

Yes, how? Heln echoed. Morvin had been right: this was exactly the time to spy on the sorcerer!

"Through sensible intelligence. I intend to make good use of my daughter's spies. Her *official* spies."

"But your magic, Master. Can't you see ahead without—"

"No. The ingredients are missing for the spells. Anyway, you are confusing precognition with clair-voyance."

"What?"

"Seeing ahead is precognition. That magic I can do, when I have the right ingredients for the magic, which ingredients are so devious and perishable that I am chronically short of them. Seeing *around* is clairvoyance—knowing what is happening elsewhere without going there. That magic I lack. How I wish I had an astral propensity!"

"Master?"

"Oh, never mind! Mouvar, cursed be his memory, was precognitive, and he believed that there would be clairvoyance among men someday. But he was mistaken; only the dragons have it, and they're too stupid to take advantage of it, fortunately. What a waste it was, for Mouvar to have precognition, when *I* could have used it to conquer the planet! And the dragons—"

"Master, will the dragons do your bidding?"

"They will," Zatanas said grimly. "Everything will. In time."

"And the Queen's guardsmen will defeat the Knights?"

"They will be defeated," Zatanas said, "as surely as I am the supreme sorcerer."

Then Heln's time was running out, and she had to return to her body. She hoped she had learned enough; certainly she now had explanations for some mysteries. So the dragons *did* use the berries for astral separation, and Zatanas knew it—but didn't know about Heln's own ability to do it, too. And Mouvar had had precognition! That suggested that the prophecy Mouvar had made was valid. Still, why, then, did Zatanas have such confidence of his own victory?

Kelvin paced the outside length of the tent, the side farthest from the campfire. His mind was not on the scent of woodsmoke or the calling hoots and wails of wild things in the forest. Rather his concern was the sour bile taste in his mouth left by continual efforts to vomit.

It wasn't fear that caused his stomach to revolt. Not exactly. It was doubts. They formed and re-formed like the long, grotesque shadows of the Crumbs and two of the Knights on the other side of the tent wall.

What he was doing was right and just. He had to believe that. But the killing was as unheroic as slaughtering a farm animal. His gauntlet did it, and each time he felt sick. He wanted to escape the destiny the prophecy claimed for him, but that was according to all accounts impossible.

He sat down under a tree and looked at the moon peering like a yellow goblin face through the twisty dark branches. By and by he raised his hands to his eyes, and quietly, so as not to be heard and discovered, he wept.

It's hell being the victim of prophecy, he thought.

"Kelvin." He jumped; it was Heln's voice.

He tried to clean up his face, but it was way too late for that; she had seen. "You should be resting," he muttered.

"There is something more important," she said.

"The revolution," he agreed, and his stomach gave another twinge.

"That, too." She came close. "You don't look well, Kelvin; I'm concerned about you."

He shrugged. "I'm just not much of a hero, for sure!"

"I suppose the only thing harder than being brutalized is having to be brutal yourself."

He stared at her. Could she understand?

"I was raped," she reminded him. "I wanted to die. I tried to die. I think I felt as bad as you do now."

Surely so! "I guess I really don't have much to complain about," he said. "I guess I wasn't thinking."

She reached out and took his limp hand. "No, Kel, no! That's not what I mean at all! I mean I do understand! You're in a horribly difficult situation, having to do things you don't like at all, like going out into battle and killing people. You're a gentle person, you don't like to fight, and I see it tearing you up, just the way it would tear me up if I had to do it. And I wish I could make it easier for you."

"I—" But as usual he froze up, and couldn't have said what he wanted to say even if he had known what it was.

"Kel, I like you the way you are," she continued earnestly. "It's not just your round ears, and it's certainly not the prophecy. I liked you when I first saw you, in my first astral separation, when everyone else was hustling you along and you didn't know what to do, you just wanted to save your sister from the Mart. You gave me reason to want to live, because you were like me in the ears, and that helped a lot, but I think I would have liked you anyway. And I liked you even more when I just saw you, in my last astral journey."

"What?"

"Kel, I didn't go right away. I heard you talking to me—"

Oh, no! Kelvin felt the blush rising so hot and fierce that it threatened to make his face blister. He tried to retreat, but she hung on to his hand.

"Do you know what I have to say to that?" she asked softly. Her eyes in the shadow seemed huge, their brown turning black.

"If I'd known—I'm so sorry—" he stumbled.

She reached around him, embracing him, drawing him in close. "Kel, I think I love you," she said. Then she drew him in closer yet, and lifted her face, and kissed him.

It seemed almost as though he had separated astrally himself. Part of him looked down at the embracing figures from above, while another part of him simply floated in a tide of sheer bliss. What he had always wanted—and *she* had brought it to *him*!

At last she broke the kiss and gazed at him. "Now you may slap my face, if you wish," she said.

Caught off guard, he started to laugh. Then they were both laughing helplessly, clinging to each other for support. She felt phenomenally good that way, too.

"But there is a condition," she said as it ebbed.

"No difference!" he exclaimed.

"And that is that if I'm going to be close to you, I want you more like the hero you are supposed to be."

Now he felt dread. "I just *can't* enjoy killing!"

"Nor should you. I want you to assert yourself. *You*, not Morvin Crumb, are the Roundear of Prophecy! *You* should make the key decisions."

"But—he's the only one who knows—"

"Listen to him, certainly, but don't be governed by him."

"Uh, I suppose—"

"Make up your mind, hero, or I'll kiss you again."

"I, I just doubt that I can—"

She kissed him again.

When it was over, he felt pleasantly giddy. "I'll try," he said.

"See that you do," she said, smiling.

"Now we'll attack this guardsmen's barracks," said Morvin Crumb, pointing at the map. The heads of all those who had been designated officers nodded agreeably.

Kelvin swallowed. He thought of Heln's kisses. "Yes!" he exclaimed. "I mean no!" Even so, he surprised himself. *It's now or never,* he thought, knowing that Heln was right. *Now is the time for me to make my stand.*

The eyes of all the six strong men in the tent were turned to him. Morvin seemed amused; the others were either surprised or openly incredulous. They all knew that Kelvin was a mere figurehead.

"I don't understand, youngster," Pete Palmweaver said. He was the youngest and in many ways the most likable of the graybeards who had fought guardsmen before Kelvin's birth.

Now he had committed himself to an opinion; he

had to follow through. "I may be a youngster to you," he said, "but I'm also the Roundear of Prophecy. I feel that I should decide what is done in my name."

They watched him, not indicating whether they were taking him seriously. He found that unnerving, but again he thought of Heln's kisses, and knew that they were rewards, not punishments, and he wanted to be worthy of such rewards. "I feel strongly that we should *not* attack there."

"Where, then?" asked Morvin, setting down his pointer, now looking less amused and sounding it.

Where? He had thought this out before, and decided, but now his mind threatened to go blank. He wrestled it back into focus. "We must move as close to the palace as possible. Bypass the barracks and attack here," he said, pointing with his finger to the area in front of the palace.

"That will be hard to do," Morvin said. "It will mean going over Craggy Mountain."

"We will do it," Kelvin said. "Instead of attacking Heenning, we bypass Heenning, and Dawlding, and Kencis. We move directly to Gorshen."

"I don't know, youngster. That's a pretty illogical move, seems to me."

"Maybe," Kelvin said, feeling inspired in this moment, "that's exactly what the Queen's strategists will think. They could have ambushes at any of those places. We can't afford to take the chance."

Morvin considered. "Just could be. Too bad we don't have any way to know for sure."

"Yes, too bad," Kelvin agreed, feeling on firmer ground. They had not spread the news of Heln's ability, because that would make her a high-priority target, and she was completely helpless while in astral separation. They had made it a policy not to send her on such missions unless they had reason to believe there was something significant to be learned, so she was not spying out the locations of the guardsmen this time. Morvin had declared that they could not afford to become too dependent on her information, and with that Kelvin heartily agreed.

"Hmm, you think they will expect us to attack the barracks at Heenning."

"I do." *And I, after all, am the Roundear,* he reminded himself.

"Well, I suppose we could give out the story that we planned an attack on Heenning, with subsequent ones in mind for the others," Morvin said. "Then we could do as you suggest. Just in case there are any spies."

"There aren't any spies," Palmweaver said.

But Kelvin wondered. He did not always trust the faces he saw turned to follow his every move when he strolled around camp. It occurred to him that Morvin didn't either. Maybe it was Morvin's notion to test for spies in this manner, to rout them out before they found out about Heln. Certainly he had the impression that Morvin didn't really mind Kelvin's assumption of power. Still, his doubts, about both their situation and his ability to lead, were not fading out.

CHAPTER 17
Queen's Ire

KELVIN LOOKED BACK AT the column of Knights following him and Jon and the Crumbs and Palmweaver. They had gone about two leagues and already the horses were noticing the steep ascent. No road here, only the paths made by deoose, meer, and other large game. The footing was rough; broken shale and fallen boulders made it hard on men and horses. The sky was overcast, threatening rain. Ozone made the air sharp, as did the needletrees' scent of aromatic green spice. Owlhawks hooted in the woods. A bearver lumbered across their path, its dark red coat blending subtly with the reddish moss that grew on the tree trunks and boulders.

"It's a long, long way to Gorshen, as I told you," Morvin said. "By now we could be at Heenning."

Yes, Kelvin thought, and an hour from now we could all be dead. But he did not say such to Morvin, mainly because he knew it wouldn't be expected of a tool of prophecy.

"What say, Kel?" Lester asked jovially.

"I say that we will take them by surprise at Gorshen."

"I sure hope you're right, brother mine," Jon gasped. She had insisted on coming along, but her enthusiasm was waning as she got tired.

At Heenning, a huge dragon reared its golden head, smacked its enormous mouth, and looked about the deserted barracks. Where were the brownberry shirts and greenbriar pantaloons of the morsels it had been driven here to find? It stepped on a fence, squashed a roof, and bit in two a large timber that had formed part of a now ruined catapult. The dragon always knew hunger and rage, but now it knew more. It also knew the growing frustration of having come so far and finding not the tasty bits that had somehow beckoned. How much better it would have been to dream with some dragonberries, and range across the world and down into The Flaw with complete abandon!

Behind the big dragon were four lesser dragons that came barely above the rooftops of the barracks. They reacted as strongly. Dragons liked feasting and dreaming and mating, in that order, and combinations of the three when they could work it. They did not like hunger or boredom.

Tails lashed. Walls smashed. Timbers splintered. The strong smell of dragon urine and excrement mingled with the lesser odor of human beings. The smell of food. But where was it? The buildings were being demolished, but they were empty.

Then the breeze changed. The big dragon raised his snout, sniffing.

There, hiding on the hillside: *food*

As appetites sharpened, the dragons rushed for the blue-and-gold-clad men hiding behind bushes and trees and rocks. They brushed aside the little sticks that rained off their scales, and the larger sticks leveled at them by men astride horses. The dragons slapped their tails, gnashed their teeth, chomped, squashed, and ate.

There was food here after all.

The Queen's guardsman arrived on a lathered horse at the gate of the palace. He called to the gateman and was admitted, then was taken by a guard directly to the audience chamber.

Watching from the window of his quarters, Zatanas half guessed the meaning of the man's appearance. He took time only to clap on his pointed wizard's cap—an affectation that had once impressed his daughter—and then ran. He hurried down the three

winding staircases to the little antechamber beside the
room where the Queen held a hurried audience.

The Queen, of course, would know he was there,
though he was hidden behind a curtain. He listened as
the messenger told his disturbing story.

"O Queen, we deserted the barracks and waited, as
commanded, but the enemy did not appear. The
dragons *did* appear. They destroyed Heenning, as we
expected they would, and then—then they found
us."

"Do you mean to say," exclaimed the Queen, "that
the dragons attacked guardsmen *again*?"

"Yes, Your Majesty. The enemy was not about. The
dragons attacked. They destroyed us! There's not a
guardsman alive who can stand up to a dragon!"

"Father!" the Queen called abruptly. "Father, come
in here now and explain why you have done this to
me!"

Zatanas took a deep breath, cursed himself for the
foolishness of ever having a child, and went through
the velvet curtain.

The Queen was a sight he would rather have
missed. She sat on her golden throne, her skin red as
dragon-sheen hair, and her eyes the color of dark
green feline magic alight with the cometing yellow
lights of intense anger. Her fingers gripped the carved
arms of her throne like talons, and she looked more
like a witch than a monarch. A witch from some land
deep down through The Flaw, more inhuman than
human. In short, his daughter in her natural state.

"My dear daughter and proudest materialization,"
he said in a suitably placating fashion, though he
knew that little but dripping flesh would placate a
dragoness, "the enemy is using magic. Mouvar's
magic, cursed be his name. How else than by magic
could they have known—"

"The question is, Father, why didn't *you* know? Are
you a sorcerer or are you not?"

That again. Well, he wasn't about to plead lack of
expertise! If she ever guessed that he wasn't all-

powerful, she might decide to destroy him. She was his flesh, after all.

"I was depending on your spies," he said. "Why haven't they—"

"Foolish old fraud! My spies gathered their intelligence. The Roundear's Knights were supposed to have attacked Heenning. You stood here when they reported. You knew—"

"I knew what they said. But the Knights were not there, Your Majesty, as this man has just testified."

"Don't belabor the obvious! Then I suppose they are somewhere else?"

"Undoubtedly," he agreed with a certain irony. "The question is where."

"The question is why there should be a question at all!" she flared. "If you can't—"

They were interrupted by a second guardsman who burst into the audience chamber in the company of a guard. "Your Majesty!" the man cried, falling to his knees. "I beg to report that the Roundear Knights have attacked Gorshen! Caught unprepared, we were outnumbered, and—"

"Beaten?" the Queen supplied with deceptive calm. The man hung his head.

After brief questioning that established the extent of the disaster, the Queen dismissed the others, remaining alone with her father. She inhaled.

Zatanas felt the Queen's eyes. "You—you unmitigated wretch!" she exclaimed. "I should have you castrated in the public square! *Why didn't you know of this?*"

"Think carefully before you threaten me, daughter," Zatanas said grimly, knowing that she was not given to bluffing. There was a time for placation, and a time for self-defense, and this was the latter. "It was my magic that made you Queen."

"Yes, magic made me Queen. *Roundear* magic! I used it then and I'll use it again."

"No, no, you mustn't." Now he felt desperate. "You must never use roundear magic again."

"Mustn't I?" The threat sounded in her tone.

"No, it's . . . risky. Better to destroy all roundears and all tools brought by roundears. Better my magic than—"

"Father," she said severely, "would you have me destroy my own magic?"

"No. No, of course not." What *had* he been thinking of? There would be no talking her out of this now. They faced horrible danger—all because he had slipped.

Looking very much his daughter, which was to say much like a dragon, she said, "I intend to use all tools and all persons to secure my throne."

"Of course, daughter. But with care, due care! Otherwise—"

"It's this roundear stripling who claims to represent the prophecy!" she exclaimed. "I'm going to use my spy in their camp to eradicate him once and for all. Then this nuisance will fade out."

"But you shouldn't waste an emplaced spy!" Zatanas protested.

"What good has he been to me so far? If he can't get word about the enemy's movements to me in time, I might as well use him in a manner that counts."

She was making a certain amount of sense, but Zatanas didn't trust this. It would be almost impossible to get another spy placed, once this one was exposed, and if he failed in his mission, as was quite possible considering the way the breaks had been going—

Still, this was better than risking the wrong kind of magic. It was true that the elimination of the enemy figurehead could have considerable impact, and perhaps so demoralize the upstarts that their effort would fall apart. "What do you have in mind, daughter?"

"I was always apt at poisons," she said briskly. "It will be nice to get my hand in again."

"Very good, daughter," Zatanas agreed.

* * *

Jon skipped a rock on the smooth stretch of creek. It hopped three times, as a well-skipped rock was supposed to. The circles formed and raced outward.

"I'll bet there's fish in here," Jon said aloud.

A Knight heard her and smiled. "You're probably right."

"If I had some equipment," Jon told him, "I could catch us some!"

"Not enough for the whole camp, you couldn't," the man said, coming over. His hair color was brick, and his name, appropriately, was Appleton. She had seen him around often enough. He was, she guessed, about three years older than Kelvin, and halfway handsome.

"But I'd enjoy trying," Jon said. "I get tired of just running errands for you fellows. I'd like to be doing something besides polishing boots and fetching firewood and spring water."

"I don't blame you," Appleton said, his hands still occupied with the rope he was braiding. He stood close to her, gazing out over the stream. "It does get dull here."

"I wish *I* had some magic!" she exclaimed. "I wish I was a Knight!"

"You're useful enough," Appleton said, abandoning his rope braiding. "But you know, you should try dressing your own way."

"How's that?" Jon asked, not understanding.

"Like a woman. You'd be a really pretty girl if you ever let yourself."

"I don't want to be a girl!" she said vehemently.

"Well, I could see your point if you were an ordinary girl. But even though you try to cover them up, I can see the lines of you. You would be no ordinary girl."

Something strange overtook her certainty. "I wouldn't?"

"Not at all! I tell you, you could start smiting hearts right here in this camp if you tried."

"Me!" she exclaimed derisively.

"You," he agreed, with no derision. "You've got the face, you've got the lines. Look at the way that roundear girl took over your brother. You're as pretty as she is."

"Never!" But she felt herself flushing.

"I'll make you a bet that if you borrowed one of her dresses, and walked out in the camp, you could beckon to any man here, and he would come to you."

This was beyond belief. "You're teasing me!"

"Am I? Then laugh this off."

And he took her by the shoulders, brought her into him, and kissed her on the mouth.

She was too amazed to react. She felt the pressure of his hands on her, so strong and firm, and his lips on hers, and she felt as if she were floating.

Then he drew his head back, and released her. "There," he said. "I'd be lying if I said that wasn't fun. But I suppose you'd better slap me."

"Wh-what?" Her knees felt like sodden reeds.

"I just made a pass at you," he said. "Because you're an attractive young woman. Now you slap me, because I shouldn't have done it. That's the way it is."

"I couldn't do that," she said, feeling faint. She had to sit down on the bank, before she fell down.

He sat beside her. "Well, maybe next time," he said. "A girl can't be too free, is all. Bad for her reputation."

"When I was at the Boy Mart, they found out and tried to, to—" she said, starting to babble and quickly stalling. She didn't know how she felt.

"Like Miz Flambeau," he said. "That's different. They do it to anything they can get their hands on. But among civilized folk, it's different. You're in no danger here."

"I don't know," Jon said. "It's a whole different realm. It's like magic." Indeed, the notion of being an attractive young woman was like being a changeling, becoming something she had never thought to be.

"Magic is what you make it. I know the feeling. My granny was a witchwoman and spell-maker."

"Really?" Jon asked, impressed, and glad enough to change the subject. "She turned people into froogs and batbirds?"

"Hardly!" he said, laughing. He found a dry bed of red moss and sprawled on it. "She could mend a broken arm, ease the pangs of childbirth, cure barrenness, that sort of thing."

"Oh. No real magic."

"I wouldn't say that. She knew a thing or two, Gran did."

"About what?" Her attention was drifting back to the kiss, and her feelings associated with it, that still hovered about her like little vague clouds. Could she really be a girl—and like it?

"Oh, about our name fruits, for instance—oaples and appleberries."

"What did she do with them?" Really borrow a dress from Heln? How well would it fit her?

"Put magic into them. She could make a weak man strong or a strong man weak, and I learned from her."

"You did, huh? Magic?" Magic: beckoning any man, and making him respond.

"That's what I said, Hackleberry."

That brought her attention back to reality. She *wasn't* a girl, not any way it counted. Just as her brother wasn't a hero. "Could you help Kelvin?"

"Help him? In what way?"

Jon thought about the night she had seen Kelvin crying. "I don't think he's as brave as he could be. Or as strong."

"Hmmm. I could probably help him there, if that's true."

"You could?" And if it was possible to help her brother become brave, then it might be possible to help her become a proper girl.

"I think so. I know the spells. Let me fix him a stockelcap full of appleberries, and you take them to him. Only don't tell him they're magicked. If you do, they won't work."

"I won't tell," she agreed. "And he'll eat them. Kelvin never could resist a stockelcap full of fresh wild appleberries."

Kelvin was sitting on a log, staring glumly at a map and picking at a scab on his hand where a knife had slipped. Jon rode up on Mockery. Wordlessly Jon held out a stockelcap filled with ripe red and white appleberries.

"For me, Jon?" he asked, sounding surprised.

"Got lucky," she said. "Found a whole patch of them. Maybe not as sweet as you can make them when you do the picking, but pretty good anyway."

Kelvin eyed the berries. "It's awfully soon after lunch and my stomach's been bothering me."

"Appleberries should fix that right up," she said eagerly.

"You never brought me appleberries before. Usually I had trouble keeping you out of those I picked."

"I'm reformed," Jon said, "and you're important. Gol' dang it, Kel, can't I do something nice for my own brother?"

"Of course you can, Jon! Of course. But climb on down and we'll eat them together."

"They're all for you," Jon said. "I ate my fill where I found them."

"I should have known." But he hesitated.

"What's the matter, Kel?" she asked, concerned.

"This fool gauntlet. All of a sudden it feels warm. Matter of fact, it tingles. There aren't any of the Queen's own around, are there?"

"I d-don't think so, Kel." What was bothering him?

"Well—" Kelvin took the stockelcap with his right hand and placed it at the end of his log. But as he set it down, his left hand shot out and sent the stockelcap flying. The berries rolled into the dust under Mockery's snorting nose.

"Now, why did it do that?" Kelvin asked, annoyed. "That gauntlet ruined the treat you brought me!"

Jon wondered, too. Could the gauntlet object to Kelvin becoming brave? So that maybe he wouldn't need it so much?

Mockery didn't wonder. His nostrils flared. He lowered his head and began to eat appleberries.

Kelvin watched, frowning more deeply. "Jon, is there something different about these berries?"

"Different?" Jon felt apprehensive. If Kelvin knew, the magic wouldn't work, Appleton had said. But of course it made no difference now, because the berries had been spilled.

Mockery gave a jerk. His eyes rolled until the whites showed. He trembled from nose to tail and then, to Jon's complete horror, he slowly sank downward.

"Jon, what's going on?" Kelvin demanded. "What's the matter with Mockery? What—where did you get those berries? What's wrong with them, anyway?"

Jon was scrambling to get off the donkey's back. Then, sitting in the dust and looking at Mockery's closed eyes and protruding tongue, a horrible suspicion came over her. Mockery, she felt certain, was either dying or dead. She let that sink in until she not only believed it, she understood the cause. Then, painfully, she answered Kelvin:

"He said the berries were magicked—that they would help make you brave."

"Jon, your donkey's been poisoned," Kelvin said, looking into the animal's mouth. Then he looked from Jon to the donkey and back, a new expression sweeping his face.

"I didn't know!" Jon protested, starting to cry. "I didn't, Kel. Honest! I thought—oh, I was a fool!" Poor Mockery, she thought. Poor dear, deaf, faithful, brave, true Mockery. What had she done to him? What might she have done to her brother? The tears flowed faster.

"I believe you, Brother Wart," Kelvin said. "No need to cry."

"Yes, there is!" she cried. "He—he sweet-talked me, told me I'd make a pretty girl, and I believed everything!"

"Well, he was right about that much," Kelvin said. "You'd be as pretty as Heln is, if you tried."

"But it was only to fool me, so I'd bring you p-poison!" she said. "Oh, Kel, I'm so ashamed!"

"No need, no need, Jon! Anyone would have been fooled. We'll find him and—" His face turned grim. "Question him. Who was it?"

"Appleton. Oh, I hate him! I hate him!"

Kelvin blew on his horn, and every Knight within hearing dropped what he was doing and came.

But Appleton, of course, was not among them.

CHAPTER 18
Roundear

"I'VE GOT TO DO it, Kel," Heln said. "You know that! After what happened—"

Kelvin nodded. "After they tried to poison me. That means that Appleton was a spy for the Queen, and we'd better find out if there are any others."

"Yes. I can scout around, astrally, and see if I can locate Appleton. But mainly, I'd better spy on Zatanas, and try to learn what mischief he's cooking up next."

"Better wait a bit," Morvin said. "They have scouts out, and we can spot those, but let them go. When the first one reports to the Queen, that's when we'll likely learn something from her or Zatanas. Timing is everything, in spying as in battle."

Kelvin had to agree with the logic of that. He certainly didn't want Heln taking such a risk for nothing. Also, it meant she could wait another day or two before eating a berry. He still hated to have her go into that temporary death.

Zatanas scowled his blackest and tried his best to look the part of the menacing warlock. His daughter, unfortunately, did not seem impressed.

"I want you to drain his blood," she said.

"But why? His blood is worthless to me. Only the blood of some truly innocent person, or a virgin of either sex, has the potency required for my magic."

"Never mind that. I want revenge. He was supposed to have destroyed the upstart, claimed he did, and what had he done but send a girl on a man's mission? No wonder it failed! Let him now take the place of the girl."

"Better I work on my invincibility spell. Your agent failed, and that is unfortunate, but then the Roundear was protected by magic."

"You think so?"

"I know it," he said. "Just as I know that no part of your agent—Applebee, was that his name?—is of any worth. Perhaps my lizards can feed on him. That should cause him some reasonable agony."

"You won't take his blood?"

"No. If you want him bled, use your royal torturer. That pig likes to waste flesh."

"But it's you he fears. He knows the royal torturer will harm only his body, whereas you—"

"I gave you my final word, daughter. I won't waste my time on worthless flesh."

"Stubborn old man!" she snapped, but she did not seem displeased.

"Bothersome witch!"

Perhaps they would not have talked that way if they had thought anyone could be overhearing.

The messenger arrived covered with dust and sweat, smelling of blood and horse. He was quickly ushered by the palace guards directly into the Queen's audience chamber.

"O Queen," the messenger cried, falling to his knees before her throne. "I beg to inform you that the Roundear's Knights are nearing Skagmore, but one day's ride from this palace!"

The Queen scowled at the messenger and then at Peter Flick, her latest, and weakest-chinned, consort. She liked her men servile.

"What do you think of that, Peter? The old man's magic isn't helping us."

"I say," Peter said with the high squeak that designated his excitement, "that now is the time! Use *roundear* magic against your roundear enemy. Do it now, Your Majesty, while there is yet time!"

He was saying exactly what she already wanted to

do. She liked that in a man. If only her father weren't such a curmudgeon!

Nevertheless, she argued the other side of the case, hoping this would provoke a truly convincing refutation. "Prophecy," she said. "How can mortals, or even immortals, fight against it? Prophecy always works out."

"Not always as expected," Peter piped. "There's a roundear who is your enemy, but is he the only roundear? No, certainly not! You have one. One of your own, my Queen."

"Yes, so you've reminded me." Casually she tweaked one of Peter's very pointed ears. "So why do I hesitate?"

Peter looked at her with that abject lustful longing that was his prime attraction; he existed to treasure her mind and body as fully as was possible. So intense was his stare that she found her own passion responding; perhaps she would take him to her private chambers soon, and have her way with him. "Dare I remind you, O Queen? Dare I say that you have a, shall we say, an intimate relationship?" He licked his lips, being eager for intimacy himself.

"There is that," she agreed in an offhand manner. "But if the prophecy doesn't apply, then we lose."

"Well, maybe," he said, reluctant to concede such a possibility.

"If my best guardsmen and my father's magic don't stop the enemy, I will use roundear magic. But—"

"Queen, you *must* have a roundear fighting on your side. Only in that way can the prophecy be fulfilled to our—to your—satisfaction."

"Yes," she said. "There will indeed be a roundear fighting on our side. In the next battle. And he, dear Peter, will go equipped with the strongest possible kind of ages-old magic."

He licked his lips again, his desire for her causing him to flush and fidget. "Which is?"

"A mother's love."

"Uh, yes," he agreed, disgruntled.

She decided it was time. She reached out to stroke him in a sensitive region. "Come to my chambers now," she murmured, turning away.

"Yes, Your Majesty!" He was practically slavering with anticipation.

"They know we're near Skagmore," Heln reported as she recovered. She was still woozy, as she tended to be after astral separation, but knew she had to report quickly.

"Of course they do," Morvin agreed. "We let their spy go through. But what are they going to do about it?"

"They're going to use roundear magic," she said.

"But I'm the Roundear of Prophecy!" Kelvin objected.

"The Queen said she would have a roundear fighting on her side, at Skagmore, and that he would have the strongest possible magic—a mother's love."

"What does that mean?" Kelvin asked querulously.

"I don't know. She didn't say any more about it. She had this—this courtier, who, well, dotes on her, and they—well, it's not relevant. But it certainly seems as though they have another roundear."

"I don't know anything about any other roundear," Morvin growled. "But I do know of that palace flunky. The Queen's latest in a long line of panderers. She beds them until she tires of them, and then gets rid of them. There's a name for men like that."

"And for women like that," Les put in.

"I'm sure I wouldn't know it," Heln said delicately. "But that's all I got. They're worried about the prophecy, but think they can nullify it with this roundear. The Queen certainly didn't seem to be joking or bluffing."

"What of Zatanas?" Morvin asked. "He's the dangerous one."

"He's against it. He doesn't like the use of roundear

magic, and tried to talk the Queen out of it. But if his magic doesn't stop us, then she'll use what she's got. Whatever that is. I wish I could have learned more, but I have no way to question them."

"You learned enough, girl," Morvin said gruffly. "We're well warned to be alert for the unexpected. Better rest now."

Heln made a tired smile and sank back on the bed, sinking immediately into a normal slumber.

Kelvin felt his stomach burn as they left the tent. Tomorrow—Skagmore, and the battle that would decide if they were about to push on for Sceptor and the palace. Heln had required him to assert himself, and he had done so, and saved the Knights much misery as a result, but still he hated this warfare. He just wasn't cut out to be a soldier!

"Fortune come a-callin'; and I did hide. Little devils at my side."

Kelvin jumped. Morvin was singing! This was uncharacteristic and unmusical, but the big man was definitely doing it.

Then the man laughed, seeing Kelvin's wonder. "Just making a point, maybe," he said. "I can see you don't much like this business, Hackleberry."

Kelvin could only nod agreement.

"Come to my tent. We've got some talking to do."

Kelvin followed him into his tent, feeling uneasy. When they passed the tent flap, he half expected to see Crumb's son or some of the designated officers, set up for a briefing. Instead there was only a large amber bottle.

Morvin picked it up and waved it at him. "Drink, youngster?"

"No," Kelvin said uneasily. He had tasted liquor and hated it. Whether this was a conditioned response because of what he had seen it do to others, or whether it simply tasted awful, he wasn't sure. It probably didn't matter exactly why the stuff was vile.

He had learned that Heln felt the same way about it, so perhaps the stuff affected roundears differently than it did natives.

"You ever hear me tell about the old days?" Morvin inquired. "About fighting with the loyalists and the upstarts? We were winning, youngster, and make no mistake. Got about as far as Skagmore, and then—"

Kelvin felt a chill. Skagmore was to be the site of tomorrow's battle. Obviously Morvin was not just rambling. "Magic?" he asked, dreading the answer he knew was coming.

"*Roundear* magic, son. Took us by surprise. The roundears—not as the Gods intended, Hackleberry. Not as the Gods intended."

"Tell me about it," Kelvin said, abruptly twice as interested. If the big man knows about the roundears of the past . . .

"It was 'fore your time, but I remember it as though it were this afternoon. I killed roundears with my sword—did you know that?"

"I—I think I guessed it," Kelvin said. He sat down on the stool Morvin kept for visitors, and his hand reached out almost of its own volition to touch the battered map case. He knew that Morvin Crumb had been a good soldier, like his father before him and his son after him.

"Hard to kill, they were. Great fighters. But the worst of it was, they had magic. Weapons such as no sane mind ever imagined. Not swords and crossbows, no. Magical."

"Tell me," Kelvin repeated, eager to hear everything.

Morvin took a drink. He wiped his mouth on the hairy back of his hand and said: "Explosive thunders that blew apart men and horses. Lightning that struck with a red bolt and went right through men and war-horses and good solid armor. Oh, I tell you, Hackleberry, it was awful! And some of them flew —flew overhead, but not as birds fly. I saw two of them high in the sky pierced by crossbow bolts. I saw them fall to their deaths, Hackleberry. But then I saw another, equally high. This one controlled the lightnings. I saw men, horses, trees—just smoking red holes where the lightning struck. We ran and we ran. We had to. There was no fighting that."

"I understand," Kelvin said, and thought that perhaps he did.

"Do you? Do you really?" Morvin took hold of his arms and looked drunkenly into his face. "It was as if we were weeds and grass before a fiery scythe. Do you understand what it is to face such beings?"

"You say I'm one of them," Kelvin reminded him. It was the sharpest retort he had ever given Crumb.

Morvin looked at him hard and shook his head. "You may be one of 'em, son, but you haven't their magic. Not that I've seen, anyway."

"No," Kelvin admitted. Why did he feel that Morvin saw to his depths? Saw the fear he knew was there, however hard he tried to bury it? He swallowed a lump. "Not now, I haven't. Just a little plant-charming, and I guess that isn't the same. But—"

"But you will have, won't you?"

"I—I don't know." Tearing himself away, Kelvin pushed through the tent flap to the outside and the good, clean night air. It occurred to him in a rare flash of fancy that all he faced now were the uncaring and unknowing eyes of distant, unreachable stars.

CHAPTER 19

Skagmore

"How BAD DO YOU think it'll be?" Jon asked.

"It gives me a deep chill," Heln answered. "They know we're coming, and when and where, so they'll be ready. They aren't bringing in the dragons this time, because we've been able to turn the dragons against the Queen's guardsmen too often, but they've got a lot of troops. I wish—"

"Me, too," Jon said. "But Morvin's determined to fight and win, and he's convinced Kelvin, so I guess it just has to happen. Men are such fools!"

"You're finally seeing the light!"

"I'm finally seeing the light," Jon agreed morosely. "What good can it be, to be a man, if you just go out and get yourself killed?"

"Not much. That's why there are women. To catch the men and make them settle down on farms and live decent lives."

"You like farm life? It bores me!"

"I like it a lot better than warfare or the Girl Mart!"

Jon nodded, seeing the point. "Still—"

"But it has to be with the right man."

"I don't have a man, right or wrong."

"But you're young yet, Jon! *I'm* young! We have time."

"Not if all the men get killed fighting!" Jon retorted.

"We just have to hope that the Knights win this battle, and don't get killed, and that then the Queen will abdicate and there won't be war anymore. Then I'll capture your brother, and you—you can find someone."

"Do you really think I—?"

168

"Of course! You're a pretty girl, if you'd just let yourself be!"

"When I tried to—to let myself be, I almost got my brother poisoned!" Jon said bitterly.

"He was a bad man. He was using you. But if you really went looking, you could find a good one."

"If any good ones survive the fighting."

Heln smiled. "I'll make you a deal, Jon. If we win this battle, then good men will survive. If we win, I'll help you all I can to be a completely female girl, and you'll give it a really honest try."

"I don't know—"

"You'd rather have the Queen win?"

That brought home the horror of the alternative. "If my being a girl-type girl can encourage our side to win, then it's a deal!"

"Every little bit of magic helps," Heln said. They shook hands.

Skagmore was particularly ugly. Faded army barracks, stripped paint, unrepaired fences, scattered refuse piles. Appalling. The place smelled, as only an army town could, of horse dung and latrines and unhauled garbage. Altogether unbeautiful.

The place was so still that one could hear the rustle of a bird's wing. Kelvin looked from Morvin to Lester Crumb and then at the rest of the accompanying Knights, their main force, and wondered. It was remarkable that this place, so near to their ultimate goal, was deserted. The enemy *knew* that the Knights were coming; Heln had spied on the messenger's delivery of word to the evil Queen. But the enemy didn't know that the Knights knew they knew. So this apparent vacancy could only be a trap.

And were they to walk right into it? Yes, they were, for that was the only way to spring their countertrap. They had drilled for this. To lure the enemy into open battle in a seemingly advantageous position, so that they would attack with confidence, and carelessly. Then—

Kelvin felt his stomach twist. They had planned so carefully, but it was risky. Suppose their surprise didn't work? Suppose something went wrong? Then what?

There was only one answer: they had to make sure that nothing did go wrong.

So they moved down into the town, seemingly innocently, commenting loudly about the marvel of its emptiness. "We scared them off!" "They knew they couldn't win!" "See if there's any food left in the storehouse!" That sort of thing, also rehearsed.

They rode all the way into the town square. Then the trap sprang. Horsemen were suddenly racing down each alley, pikes ready, swords drawn. The enemy plainly outnumbered the Knights, and were now closing in for the quick kill.

Kelvin raised the signaling horn and blew the blast that signaled the formation of the phalanx. Now his fear was dissipating into excitement. *This had to work!*

The Knights formed a close living fence with shields joined at the edges and spears raised and ready to stab. They had never separated far; a formation had been maintained, of its special loose kind, so that each man had only a few feet to step to reach his key position. In the center the horses waited, secure until the line should burst. Archers and crossbowmen formed a line between the horses and the spearmen. In practice it had seemed impenetrable; now it seemed less so, but it was ready.

They had picked up many recruits in the past few weeks. Many of them were without horses, and a few without even swords. But their mercenaries had taught the recruits well, and the knowledge that it was their land they fought for gave even the least experienced men courage. The Queen, obviously, had no respect for farm boys turned fighters, and the guardsmen evidently proposed to cut them down without mercy.

Arrows rained from the advancing foe, as the Queen's archers stepped from their concealment behind the horsemen and aimed their shafts over their vanguard. Almost casually, because of the practice they had had, the Knights raised shields and stopped the missiles that sought their blood. The rattle sounded like hail. The barrage that should have cut down as much as a third of the force at one stroke, and demoralized the rest, brought no casualties and no demoralization. The phalanx remained tight and strong.

With a great cry that rose like a wave at sea, the men in blue and gold uniforms threw themselves hard against the waiting phalanx. They met much fiercer resistance than they had anticipated. Men cried out as waiting spears stabbed through their bodies. More came, for they could not stop their impetus. These were met by the strokes of swords. The enemy formation was crashing against the wall of shields and breaking like a wave across a rocky shore. Still they came, seemingly maddened beyond reason, still not believing that the Knights were fighting back so effectively.

Bows twanged. Missiles flew. Blue and gold uniforms sprouted feathered barbs. But the sheer mass of the charge had its effect, and the phalanx lost cohesion. Brown-and-green-clad Knights cried out here and there, dropping their arms, dying as bravely as any soldier.

The phalanx had done its work. The thrust of the charge had been broken, and three or four guardsmen were down for every Knight lost. Still they came, and came. The guardsmen outnumbered the Knights by as much as ten to one. This was worse than Morvin's worst projections! The Queen had thrown all her reserves into this effort, holding nothing back, and that threatened to make the trap effective after all.

Now Kelvin and the Crumbs were fighting from their steeds. Kelvin was glad that Jon had been banned from this engagement; it would have been terrible to have his little sister see their end! Immediately he condemned himself for thinking so quickly of defeat. They were supposed to win!

Kelvin's left hand, with the gauntlet, knew what to do. He had learned how to make it hold a sword, and it was now fighting with that sword so expertly that any surviving observer would have thought him left-handed. But gradually his left arm grew tired. The hand was powered by the gauntlet, but the arm was not; it obeyed the imperatives of the hand, but at the cost of increasing fatigue.

In a brief lull, realizing that even the gauntlet could not save him if his left arm became too tired to follow its dictates, Kelvin changed sword for shield in his left hand, and took the sword in his right. He had no magic there, but did have some training, and at least that arm was relatively fresh.

Now, you devils, come on, he thought, maneuvering his horse away from corpses. His stomach had no qualms now, despite the bleakness of the likely outcome of this encounter; he was ready for the next stage of the fray.

Suddenly there were three guardsmen before him, each mounted. They were charging him as if he were a magnet.

Mor Crumb saw the situation and angled across to engage one of the attackers. Les Crumb moved too slowly, and was knocked off his mount by a lucky blow from the second. The third reached Kelvin, striking at him.

Kelvin's sword blade missed as his gauntlet raised the shield and deflected the enemy's sword. Now they fought, and steel clanged against steel. Each blow and counter shook Kelvin's whole arm and shoulder and the shock seemed to reach right through to his mind, dulling it.

Kelvin was tiring. Now it was not merely his left arm; it was his whole body. Battle was hard work! He wished he could get out of this, just quit fighting and go home to the farm, but of course he could not.

There was something else bothering him. His opponent's face—young, determined, and somehow enormously familiar. He racked his brain in the midst of the fight, but all he could think of was that the stranger bore a slight resemblance to Jon. That was impossible, of course; Jon was a girl, and this one was a man, several years older than Kelvin himself.

Then the other made a deft move, and Kelvin was unhorsed. He landed hard, twisting about, and saw the enemy sword swishing down at his unprotected face. His shield was pinned partly under him, no help now.

His incredible gauntlet let loose of the shield and snapped across to grab the naked blade.

The stranger did not release his weapon. Kelvin's left hand jerked.

Crash! The stranger hit the dust beside him, his sword flung wide. Now neither combatant was armed with a blade.

The stranger raised his head, as jarred by his fall as Kelvin was. For a moment they sat face-to-face, staring at each other. There *was* a resemblance to Jon, or somebody like her, a resemblance that bothered Kelvin as much as the notion of imminent defeat and death.

Now, in his fatigue, he saw something else. It had failed to register before, but on the right hand of the stranger was a gauntlet identical to his own.

The other man moved—and Kelvin's left arm jerked up. His gauntlet met the opposite gauntlet and grasped it. He felt the effort down the length of his worn-out arm. The two gauntlets were struggling against each other—the two that should be a pair!

Back and forth, up and down and around, the gauntlets and the trapped hands struggled, stirring up sweat and dirt. Kelvin saw exhaustion on the other man's face, and fear. The stranger felt the same exhaustion and fear Kelvin did, but was a similar captive to his gauntlet!

The other gauntlet pulled his down, as if seeking to pin it to the ground. Kelvin reached with his right hand to help, and met the left hand of the stranger.

Their two bare hands grasped and squeezed and struggled and fought, exactly like the two gauntlets, but more weakly.

Suddenly there was a noise close at hand. Horsemen—but of which side? Kelvin was too weary to raise his head. Too weary to really think. So, it seemed, was the stranger. The battle had devolved to their four struggling hands; little elsewhere seemed important.

Their bare hands weakened, and fell apart. Human flesh had met its limit; they could fight no more.

But the gauntlets still fought like scorpiocrabs in a bottle.

Other figures came to stand by the combatants. One person or the other was about to be struck down. Which one would that be? It hardly seemed to matter.

It seemed to Kelvin that there would never be, could never be, an end.

Mor Crumb maneuvered his war-horse as close to his son as he could. Les, on the ground, guarded somewhat by his well-trained horse, was either dead or unconscious.

"Oh, please, Gods, if Gods there be, let him be only unconscious," Mor mumbled as he simultaneously fought off two attackers.

Neither Les nor the gods made a sound.

Mor finished the attacker on his left with a well-aimed thrust. The guardsman on his right got through his guard, to the side of his shield, and sliced his left forearm.

Mor felt the sharp sting and the wetness and knew he was wounded. But the mailed vest he wore was still doing its duty and the shield remained strapped securely to his now bleeding arm. "Oh, ye would, would ye? Well—"

He barely got his sword around, saving his face and possibly his head by the slimmest margin. He felt the swish of the enemy's sword and felt his left ear sting. He had lost part of the ear from that blow. How much, he couldn't now be concerned about.

Somehow his sword deflected the guardsman's, and then, with less science than he felt he usually commanded, he got his blade under the other's helmet and drove upward.

"Ahhhh!" The man fell, pierced to the brain. Part of his nose had been lobbed off by the blade's keen edge.

Now to see to his son.

Lester was still lying there, his face turned upward.

"Damn ye, you've got to be all right!" Mor shouted. It was a foolish thing to say, and he realized it. Where was help? There had to be help for them. For *him*, Morvin mentally amended. For Lester. For his precious son. If Les didn't live, then all of this was for nought. It was for Lester and Lester's future children, if any, that this war was being fought.

A horse wheeled to his left. Mor jerked on the reins.

A brownberry shirt and greenbriar pantaloons, much dusted and a little smeared with blood. A freckle-faced boy who should be out working his father's fields and whom Mor remembered they had left with the main force at the edge of town.

"We have to retreat," the boy said. "There's too many for us!"

"Greenleaf, is that you?"

"Yes, sir."

"Yes, *Mor.* Show a little respect!"

The boy managed a faint smile. A good lad, this. Mor recognized him from their training sessions. Greenleaf had been as clumsy as Kelvin Hackleberry without his gauntlet, but then had learned. As they all had to learn.

"Les," Mor said, indicating his fallen son. "I'd like

to get him out of here. He got clubbed by the flat of a blade. He will live, I think. If we can take him to safety."

"I—I'll see what I can do, s—Mor." Then, turning his head slightly, Greenleaf called, "Broughtner! Over here!"

A dapple gray war-horse joined them. This one was ridden by a craggy-faced, ruddy-complexioned fellow who had some months ago been working hard to be a Franklin's ne'er-do-well.

"You called, Greenleaf?"

"Les, he's down."

Broughtner arrived. "Um, I see."

"Can we take him back?"

"Can try."

"You'll do more than try!" Mor told them. Then, simply because it seemed the appropriate thing to do, he began to swear.

"Look out!" Broughtner cried. In the same instant, Mor's horse gave a terrible scream and started to collapse under him.

Mor got his head twisted around as he fell. He saw the big guardsman who had ridden in at them and the pike that had been deflected downward by Broughtner's blade. The pike had gotten his mount right behind the rib cage.

He had allowed himself to forget that they were still amidst the battle!

Mor hit the ground and rolled over as a war-horse's big hooves tried hard to trample him. Then the big guardsman was coming down to join him and Les. As he fell with flailing arms, Mor saw that his intestines had been split.

"Good work, Greenleaf!" Broughtner called.

"Uh, uh, uh," Greenleaf said, shuddering at his own act.

Saved by a boy and a man whose previous destiny had been to drink himself to death. The ignominy of it! But better alive, better alive than dead.

"You look a bit battered, Mor," Broughtner said.

Mor stood up, shaking his head. It did have a buzz in it, he discovered.

"You'll need Les's horse," Broughtner said. "Better cut the throat of this one."

Mor reluctantly had to recognize the man's good sense. Better do it now, he thought, before the animal suffered more.

He placed his sword tip against the horse's neck, drew back, and mentally called upon whatever gods there were for strength. "Sorry, old friend," he said, and swung hard at the vein he knew was pulsing just beneath the slick hide.

The horse gave a very loud sigh. Blood spurted, catching Mor's face and sword arm. He moved back, wiping at it, refraining from cursing because it wouldn't do to curse his dying equine friend.

"You certain he's alive?" Broughtner asked.

Mor gave him a hard look. "Can't you see that I just killed him?"

"Your son. Not your horse."

Gods! For a moment he had actually forgotten.

Moving as swiftly as his wounds and weariness permitted, he knelt by Lester as Broughtner caught and held the horse. The mount neighed, but steadied under Broughtner's hand.

"Lester, Les, speak to me, speak to me!" But there was no response.

He raised the head a little, and there was blood. Not a lot, not as much as soaked his own clothing, but some. Internal bleeding—how bad was it?

He drew off a gauntlet, wishing again that he might wear the gauntlet the Roundear had. *That* glove was—

The Roundear! Where was he? Mor lurched up, gazing across the battle. There was no sign of Kelvin Hackleberry!

"Find the Roundear!" he panted. "We can't lose *him*!"

"Yes, Mor." Greenleaf cast about, searching.

Mor returned his attention to his son. He felt under the brownberry shirt, trying to find a heartbeat.

"If he's dead, we'll have to leave him," Broughtner said.

Damn the man! "He's alive!" he snapped.

"Then get him on the horse. This horse. You take his."

It took almost all Mor's strength, but he placed his hands underneath Les's arms and hoisted his body up to Broughtner. He had never before felt so incredibly weak! It must be the bleeding, and the drinking last night and the fact that he hadn't really slept. *I've gotten old,* he thought sadly. *But I recognize it.*

Broughtner took Les and positioned him in front of him on the horse. Meanwhile, Greenleaf returned, spreading his hands: he had been unable to locate the Roundear.

"I can't fight this way," Mor complained. "You two will have to watch out for me."

"We will," Greenleaf said.

Mor wished that he could feel as confident.

"The Roundear!" Broughtner cried. "There he is!" He wheeled his horse, almost knocking Mor down.

Mor strained his eyes. He counted six guardsmen riding hard. Slung over the neck of the leading horseman's mount was a slight figure wearing the green and brown. No wonder Greenleaf hadn't spotted Kelvin; he had been draped across an enemy horse!

"After them!" Greenleaf cried, his own dismay sounding.

"No! No, they've got him," Broughtner said. "We can't even catch them, let alone overcome them. Best we get back to the others with the word. Best we get back alive."

Mor grabbed hold of the mane on his son's warhorse and levered himself up to a mounted position. His head whirled. He all but slid off. Any notion he had of pursuing was obviously futile.

"Yes," he said reluctantly. "Too many guardsmen. Too many for us to fight anymore."

"We've got to retreat, regroup," Broughtner said.

"Yes. Regroup," Mor gasped. But he was thinking, even as he spoke, mostly of Les.

CHAPTER 20

Nurse

IT WAS A SAD party that straggled back to the camp. Morvin Crumb was wounded, his son was unconscious, and more than half the Knights were missing.

Jon and Heln ran out together. "Where's Kelvin?" Jon cried, horrified as she failed to spot her brother in the group.

"Captured," Mor said wearily. Then he fell over in his saddle, and others had to catch him before he dropped from his horse.

Jon turned to look at Heln, and found the other's face a reflection of her own horror. Kelvin— captured! What would become of him?

Quickly they learned the details of Kelvin's loss. He had been carried off by several guardsmen, after apparently fighting against one with another gauntlet like his own. "That other—he had round ears!" a Knight said. "I caught one glimpse of him, before I had to defend myself from another charge."

"Roundear magic!" Heln said. "A roundear with a magic gauntlet! That's what the Queen meant!"

"If only we had understood better!" Jon said, her heart gripped by the horror and grief of her brother's fate.

"I must find him!" Heln cried.

Mor, now standing on the ground, propped by two other Knights, responded. "Girl, get that notion from your head! You can't go after him!"

"I meant—my way," she said.

"It's too soon, girl! You haven't recovered from the last time!"

"I love him!" she exclaimed. "I must find him!"

Mor glanced across at the stretcher on which his

son lay. "I know how that is. Then do what ye must, girl—but only this once. It won't do him any good if you die from overdosing."

"I'll watch over her," Jon said quickly.

Morvin turned away. "Les—got to get a nurse for him—"

But there was nobody to tend the unconscious man. All the survivors were tired, many of them wounded; it was all they could do to take care of their own.

"Put him in our tent," Jon said. "I can watch two as well as one."

No one argued; they were glad to have her assume this burden, so that the others could collapse. They hauled the stretcher in and got the unconscious young man on Jon's bunk.

Then Heln ate a berry and lay down, and Jon watched both: the unconscious woman and the unconscious man. Both were so still it was as if they were dead. One should recover; the other—

Jon went to Lester Crumb and checked him more closely. There was a trace of blood on his lips, and more in his mouth; something had ruptured inside him and this was the only evidence. How bad was it? She had no way to know, but the fact that he remained unconscious did not bode well.

She decided to do the job right. There was no one else to do it, after all. She got a basin of water and a cloth and washed off his face. Then she stripped his clothing, discovering numerous cuts and bruises, and cleaned these off. She tied bandages around the bad ones, so that no further blood leaked, and formed a more comprehensive bandage for his head, because the whole side of it was one massive purple bruise. It looked as though the blow to his head had caused him to bite his cheek and tongue, and that was the source of the blood in his mouth; that suggested that he had no bad bleeding deeper in his body. That same blow had put him in a coma, and she could do nothing for that except make him comfortable. She covered him over with all the blankets she had, trying to keep his cold body warm, and hoped. Lester Crumb was a decent man, who had helped Kelvin and had always been courteous to Jon herself. It would be awful to have him die.

Heln was normal for this stage, lying as still as a statue, her breathing stopped or was so slight it wasn't evident. There was nothing more for Jon to do except wait.

After half an hour, Les groaned. Jon hurried across and took his hand. Was he pulling out of it?

He turned his head, choked, and spluttered out some saliva and blood. Jon grabbed his shoulders and helped him sit up so that he could cough and get his throat clear. He retched, and spat, and then sank back. She washed off his face again, and found that now it was hot: he was running a fever. But he sank back into a more natural sleep, and that meant that he was recovering. His color was better now, despite (or maybe because of) the fever; he was a handsome man.

Not long later he stirred again, and again she helped him sit up and retch. This time his eyes opened. "Thanks," he said, and slept again.

Then Heln began to recover, and Jon went to attend to her. By this time she was feeling very much the nurse; both her patients were improving!

For the next hour she shuttled between the two, doing her best to keep each comfortable. Heln woke and reported:

"I found him!" she said weakly. "They took him to the dungeon under the Queen's palace and dumped him there with two older men. I think they drugged him, because he never woke up, and somebody said something about how he would sleep for at least another day. He didn't look injured. So I think he'll be all right, and maybe the long sleep will even do him good. But we've got to get him out of that dungeon!"

"That's for sure," Les said, startling them.

Jon turned to him. "I thought you were sleeping."

He smiled. "I was, until I heard you two talking. I seem to be in the wrong tent."

"No, they brought you here so I could watch you," Jon said. "You were unconscious, and your father was wounded, and over half the Knights are gone and the rest in bad state, so—"

"I thank you. But now I had better get out. What happened to my clothes?"

"But you're feverish!"

"Not anymore, I'm sure. We Crumbs heal quickly."

Jon went and put her hand on his forehead. Sure enough, the fever was down. Maybe that was his little bit of magic. She explained about the clothes, and brought them back to him, then turned her back while he dressed.

He stood, and wavered, and she had to run to provide support before he fell. "I think you'd better lie down again," she said.

"No, I've got to consult with my father, plan strategy," he said. "With Kelvin captive—"

Jon could hardly argue with that. "Then I'd better help you walk."

"Ooo, my head!" he said. "I'm dizzy! I think you'd better."

"I'll be all right," Heln said. "Get him to Morvin. If there's any way to rescue Kel—"

Jon supported Les as he staggered out, and got him to Morvin's tent. There a strategy meeting was already in progress. The generals had the war map unrolled and were fretting over it.

"Son!" Mor exclaimed, lurching up to embrace Les. "How are you?"

"Some fool is still slashing about with a sword inside my head," Les said with a pained smile. "But Jon here got me patched up, and Heln has found out that Kelvin's in the Queen's dungeon, so I had to come here."

"The Queen's dungeon!" Mor said. "They haven't killed him?"

"Drugged him. They say he'll sleep for another day. So they can't be planning anything sooner than that."

"They've got their own wounds to lick," Mor said

grimly. He looked terrible; the top part of his left ear had been sliced away so that he looked like half a roundear. His left arm was in a sling.

"There's not much we can do but surrender," General Jeffreys said. "The Queen's terms, total and unconditional surrender, aren't to my liking, but—"

"Ye talk like a fool!" Mor snapped. "Surrender unconditionally and she'll hang or imprison the lot of us!"

"She might not," Jeffreys said, looking sheepish and as though he wished he could be back on his farm.

"And I say she will! The officers, at least!"

"I—I agree with my father," Les said. His eyes did not quite focus, but his mind seemed sound. "I gather a messenger arrived while I was sleeping. That means the Queen knows our location, and this may just be stalling for time while she gets together another army to destroy the last of us. If we surrender now, we have to be prepared to flee Rud. Maybe some of us can survive in the Sadlands, a few can venture into dragon country, but most of us will have to get all the way out. I'm hoping that most of us can find our way to Throod. But—"

"You can be sure you'll be taken in," said Captain MacKay. "We Throodians don't abandon our friends."

"I appreciate that, Captain," Les said with dignity. "But my point is, that we could be better off *not* surrendering and being dispersed, with many of us executed out of hand. We might best stick together and fight on. The worst that could happen is that we'd get killed."

"When most of us could live, if we surrender," General Jeffreys said. "Understand, the word is gall in my mouth, but I'm trying to be practical. We have scant resources remaining to fight, and—"

"Har-rumph," said Mor, drawing attention back to himself. "I'm not prepared to say we surrender unconditionally."

"Why not?" General Saunders demanded.

"Because of the Roundear."

"He's captured. Imprisoned in her dungeon. He'll be killed, probably publicly. Even if we had the manpower to raid the dungeon, they'd just kill him before we could fight our way in. They'd like nothing better than to have us present our remaining troops for slaughter like that."

Mor nodded. "Hmm, I hate to agree with you, but I fear you're right. There's little we can do to save him."

"Yes, there is!" Jon exclaimed before she thought. Abruptly all eyes turned to her.

"Jon!" Mor snapped. "Why are you still here? This is a strategy conference! Go outside and—"

"Play?" Jon suggested, knowing that that was not what he had been about to say. "The Roundear you talk about is my brother! He didn't want to be a hero and fight this war. You, Mor, and you, Les, you forced it on him! He'd be back on the farm now, if you hadn't interfered!"

"She's got a point, Father," Les said. "She has a right to be here, and—"

"She doesn't know what she's saying!" Mor said. "She's only a girl!"

"Yes, a girl!" Jon agreed hotly. "And Kel's only a boy. But then, who else are you fighting the war for?"

There was a stunned silence. Jon leaped into it, determined to express her thought. "You told us over and over, Mr. Crumb. 'It's for the young, it's not for the old, that we're fighting this.' Everyone here heard you say it. Everyone in the camp!"

"She's right," Les said.

"Youngster," Mor said, looking sad, "if I could help your brother through direct action—"

"But you can! You can! He fought for you, and now you talk of abandoning him. What kind of people are you? What kind—"

"The realistic kind," Mor said. "We know the difference between fact and fancy. We can't—"

Without giving herself a chance to think, Jon ran at

Mor, fists raised. She wanted to punch him into some kind of agreement, crazy as that was.

But Saunders caught her and held her. "What kind of respect is this, you gamin?" His face, normally so calm and solemn, was now fierce.

Jon felt all her madness go. Here she was trying to act like a man again, and succeeding only in childishness. She would be lucky if the general didn't shake her in humiliating fashion.

"Let her go, Saunders," Les said. "She has reason to react. It's her *brother* we're writing off. My father would react much the same if I were the one being deserted."

Mor started to speak, then paused thoughtfully. "Gods," he muttered. "It's true. When I saw you down, son, I couldn't think of anything but—"

Saunders' grip tightened briefly. Then he let go.

"You got anything to say, Jon?" Mor asked. "Anything we need to know?"

"I think we should fight," Jon said. "That's all I have to say."

"We?"

"We patriots. We who care about Rud."

"You're only fourteen, Jon, and female, but you may be right," Les said. "Maybe we should make an all-out effort. Tell the Knights we're making one last effort to take the capital, defeat the Queen, and rescue the Roundear."

"Are you daft?" Mor demanded of his son. "After all you've been through, you still want to fight? I wasn't going to suggest attack, merely that we not surrender."

"I don't want to fight at all," Les said. "But you've convinced me time after time, Father. We have to defeat this tyrant. We have to rid this land of its ugly sore so that it will heal and become fair and free once more. How many times have you said it, Father? How many?"

Mor looked away. "I don't want you to be killed, son. You came too close today! I don't want any more deaths. I don't want to surrender, but if we surrender now and get us to—"

"She'll never let us out. She'll want a formal surrender, with you and me and the main officers. Then you know what will happen? Then she will send us to the dungeons. If we ever get out from there, it won't be in any condition to fight anybody, and more likely just for execution. There's no reprieve in surrender!"

"I—"

"You know it's so!" his son said challengingly.

Jon kept her mouth shut. What a beautiful job Les Crumb was doing, arguing her case! She was glad she had helped him recover.

Mor swallowed, his big throat producing a gurgling sound. "You may be right, son. You may—"

"I say he *is* right!" Saunders said suddenly. "I say we'd *better* fight another battle and make it an all-out one. Even if we don't win, maybe we can force surrender terms."

"How can we win?" Mor asked, his face rigid. "They've got magic."

"No more than we had! Father, we've got *arms*."

"Um, maybe so. One all-out attack on the capital."

"She won't be expecting it now. Not after that last defeat. And she doesn't have that many guardsmen in good shape right now."

Mor turned to the map. As the big man traced a possible route of march and attack, Jon noticed that the river ran all the way into the capital. Why not go by the river, she wondered? But Mor was talking.

"We've lost a lot of ground, and a lot of lives. But if we start our march tomorrow and we're not stopped before we get there, four days will see us there."

"Four days?" Jon asked. "I thought it was only one day's ride from Skagmore to the capital."

"One day's ride for a messenger on a fast horse," Les explained. "Four days for a tired army, hauling supplies, foraging for food. The Queen's guardsmen will take longer than that, because they're licking their wounds and don't believe there is any need to return rapidly to the capital. That's our advantage: striking by surprise, at their weak spot: the capital whose reserves have been expended for the battle just past."

"I'll come along!" Jon said.

"No, you won't, girl," Mor said, turning on her. "Your mother needs to be sure of at least one child. If we fail, that's you. Before we leave, you are starting your march home. The same goes for the roundear girl."

Jon started to protest, but Les made a warning signal. She understood: Les knew that his father had gone as far as he would go, and that it was best to settle for that. And, she realized, Mor was probably right; this tough march and battle, using the remnants of their army, would be no place for two young women. She had to quit while she was ahead.

CHAPTER 21
Travel

JON WAVED AT THE Knights who had brought them to the road and were now riding back to the camp. *They didn't even give us horses!* she thought angrily. *They could at least have spared us two of the lame ones.* But then, of course, they would have had to lead the animals, and move slow, and find grain and water for them. Besides which, all the animals were needed by the army for this final effort. So they could travel faster than the guardsmen would, and fall upon the capital when its defenses were minimal. She didn't question that; it was her brother who stood to benefit.

Except that the Queen would surely have him killed the moment the attack materialized. What would they gain then, even if they won?

She brushed at some perspiration on her forehead, squinting into the morning mists, wondering why it had to be so hot, hoping the mists would soon rise. They had a long walk ahead.

Maybe, just maybe, they should go back, she thought. But she knew that no girls would be allowed along. Mor had made that absolutely plain.

"Are you thinking what I'm thinking?" Heln inquired.

"Yes, but they'd never let us do it."

"How could they stop us, if we went by a separate route?"

"Separate route?"

"Maybe you didn't know that my folks' farm is between here and the capital."

The capital! If they could get there ahead of the army and rescue Kelvin, so that the Queen *couldn't* kill him—!

189

Then Jon sobered. "I might sneak in, in the guise of a boy; I've had a lot of practice. But you could never pass for anything but a beautiful girl, and besides that, your ears—"

"But I want to save Kelvin as much as you do!"

"And how do you think you'll help him, if they catch you and rape you again?"

Heln was silent, and Jon was immediately sorry. She was sounding just like Morvin Crumb!

"I mean—" she started awkwardly.

"No, no, you're right," Heln said. "I really can't help him directly. But maybe I can help you to help him. If I eat a dragonberry, and spy out the terrain for you, so that you'll know exactly where to look and what to avoid—"

"Yes!" Jon exclaimed. "Then I could sneak in and free him, before the attack, and then when the attack started it would be easier to get out in the confusion!"

"But first you have to get there," Heln pointed out. "I know my folks would help, if we asked them—"

"Let's go!" Jon exclaimed.

But they were afoot, and that made the distance to Heln's folks' farm stretch out. They plodded step by step, resting when they had to, and gradually the mists lifted.

Ahead was the bridge. She remembered crossing it on the way to dragon country and adventure. How long ago that seemed! Why then, just weeks ago, she had been a child!

She touched the top of her pantaloons and her sling. At least Mor had left her that, she thought. It was a wonder it hadn't been confiscated for the war effort!

They walked on, this time not toward the Hackleberry farm, but toward the Flambeau farm. And by dusk, weary, dirty, and hungry, they reached it.

There was a flurry of amazed greetings as Heln made herself known. She explained how Morvin Crumb had purchased her, and freed her, but that she hadn't been able to communicate with them because that could have alerted the Queen's guardsmen to the whereabouts of the Knights.

"We wondered why they had guardsmen camped nearby, watching us," her father said. "They never did anything, just watched. Until they were called away a few days ago—"

"To fight at Skagmore," Heln finished. "And that's why we're here. This is Jon Hackleberry—"

"Hackleberry! You mean—?"

"His sibling. Jon needs to get quickly to the capital, to help rescue Kelvin, who is the Roundear of Prophecy. I said you'd help—"

"Certainly we'll help. The river flows right down there. We have a raft—"

"A raft!" Jon exclaimed. "Of course!"

So it was arranged. They had a great supper, and then Jon slept while Heln ate another berry. This was risky, because it was the third in as many days, but the need was great.

In the morning, Heln told Jon what she had spied. Kelvin was still asleep, but was supposed to wake soon. The two other prisoners were friendly, and would take care of him. She had studied the layout of the dungeons as well as she could, with all their approaches, and the city around, so was able to make a fair map. Jon now knew where the guards marched, and where the river bypassed their observation.

Heln's point-eared father took her down to the raft tied at the river's edge. "It isn't the fanciest craft," he said apologetically. "We made it to carry firewood down from the forest, and we just lashed the larger logs together with what vines we could find. I think it will hold, but—"

"It's great, sir!" Jon exclaimed. "Much better than I could make!"

"Then the Gods be with ye, lad, and may you rescue your brother just as he rescued our daughter." He set a bag of supplies on the raft.

"Thank you, sir." She didn't like deceiving these

good folk about her nature, but feared they would not have let her go if they knew. She scrambled on and took up the heavy pole.

Flambeau untied the raft and shoved it out into the channel. The current caught it and bore it on, slowly rotating, until Jon managed to steady it by poling. She was on her way!

The novelty of it palled soon enough. All she had to do was keep the raft in the channel where the current was strongest, using the pole to push it away from the banks and shallows. Every so often it snagged, but all it took was work to free it. At this rate, she would arrive well before the Knights! She hoped.

A wave rippled up beside the raft. It didn't look natural. She hefted the pole, watching.

There was a great splash, and a sheet of water drenched her. Something the size of a small colt dived underneath the raft. The craft rocked, dipped, and swirled.

A bearver, Jon realized. Probably just playing, but maybe—

A shaggy red head broke the surface. The bearver looked at her, large ears laid back, seemingly considering.

This game was not nearly as much fun for Jon as for the animal. "Go 'way!" Jon called, splashing with the pole.

The bearver seemed not to notice. It dived.

Jon grabbed hold of the edge of her raft just as a loud thump sounded on the bottom, and the whole craft lifted. The thing bowed, the logs sinking down at the edges. "Hold, vines, hold!" Jon prayed. This was a sturdy raft, but it wasn't constructed for this kind of stress!

The support dropped out. The raft smacked the water. The vines parted. Jon found herself in the water with floating logs. She struggled, kicking out.

Then something grabbed her leg.

Now I'm finished, she thought as her head dipped under. All her grand notions of rescuing her brother, and she couldn't even get there without drowning! She inhaled water, and then her head was above water again, and she was choking and spitting it out.

The bearver's head broke water right beside her. It was a cub. An infernal brat!

"Shoo! Scram!" Jon said. She didn't think it intended to eat her. At least, she hoped it didn't.

The bearver blinked muddy-orange eyes. "Ooompth?" it inquired.

"I don't talk bearver," Jon said. "Beat it!"

The animal paddled along beside, far more comfortable in the water than she was.

Jon grabbed a floating log. She was a good swimmer, but the water was swift. She could tire quickly enough even if the bearver let her alone.

She had her sling tucked into the top of her pantaloons. She slid a hand down and got it. But she didn't have any ammunition.

"Shoo, bearver!" she cried, and smacked the creature right across the face.

The bearver looked surprised. Then it opened a large mouth, displaying sharp yellow teeth.

What have I done? What have I done? She wished she could undo what she had done, but of course it was too late.

The bearver shook its head, splashed water on her with a paw, and swam away.

Jon sighed, amazed at her luck. Apparently she had hurt its feelings more than its body, and it had retreated in a pique instead of advancing in a rage. A mature one might have reacted otherwise. She grabbed at a new log, and determined that she would rebuild the raft if she possibly could, adding new and stronger vines.

She was in luck. The main part of the raft remained tangled together; not all the vines had broken. Her bag of supplies was bobbing nearby. She clambered aboard the remnant, got the pole, used it to snag the bag, and then pushed for shore.

Landing the craft proved to be no problem. Repairing it was more difficult. Here there were no decent vines; she had to use the ones she had come with, and she didn't trust them.

She sat on the shore and opened the bag, pondering what to do. Inside she discovered really nice food: nuts, fruits, and bread, now sodden but still good. Heln's folks had been kinder to her than she had known!

She finally gave up on the notion of rebuilding the raft; she just didn't have the time to go in search of the necessary vines. At last, regretfully, she tied the bag of supplies to her waist, and launched out from the shore with a floating log with a vine looped around it.

The log promptly dunked her. When she climbed back on, it dunked her again. It wasn't nearly as easy to stay on a single log as she had supposed!

It's a long, long way, she thought. Could she make it? Could she make it there ever, let alone on time? She began, not for the first time this day, to feel really sorry for herself.

A stinging fly flew down and lit on her nose. Jon struck at it. She missed the fly but scored on her face. Her hand came loose from the vine she was holding, and then she was at pains to get hold of it again.

Was it going to be this way all the way, she wondered? She was very much afraid that it was. Still, she intended to get there, no matter what. She clung to the log and let the central current carry her. This wasn't much fun, but it was getting her in the right direction.

As it grew dark she found a sandbar, landed, ate some more from the bag—bless the Flambeaus! —stretched herself out, and lapsed into a fully exhausted sleep.

CHAPTER 22
Tommy

JON WOKE FOR THE second morning in a row feeling stiffer and sorer than she had ever felt before. How she wished that the bearver hadn't broken up her raft! She had managed to lash two logs together so that she could lie on them and float with some efficiency, but then the sun beat down on her back, and she had to spend much of the time in the water anyway. She had made, by her best estimate, adequate time, staying constantly in the swiftest current, but it was one wearing effort!

She crawled out from behind the log where she had slept, stretched, yawned, and rubbed her eyes. Blearily she walked to the nearest appleberry bush and proceeded methodically to eat her breakfast. She lacked her brother's finesse with ripening the fruits being plucked, but these were pretty good anyway. She was fortunate that these bushes grew all along the river, and even more fortunate that the bag of supplies the Flambeaus had provided had enabled her to remain all day in the river, not having to break to forage for food while traveling. That was perhaps the major reason for her moderate progress.

She discovered a few rounded stones near the bushes. She picked them up; they were just right for her sling. She didn't want to encounter a bearver again without ammunition.

As she made ready for yet another siege of log-clinging, her spirits dampened. *This is turning out to be one miserable adventure,* she thought. She chewed the last of the appleberries, relishing the taste less than she had on the first morning. *I'll never get to the*

capital, and if I do, what can I do? I haven't an army.
All I've got is my sling.

She felt sorrier for herself and more discouraged than ever before in her life. Why was she even bothering to try to be a stupid male-type hero? She wasn't even a male! The very notion of getting there in time, and then being able to sneak past the guards into the dungeon, and then get her brother out—what had ever made her think she could manage all that? The guardsmen would surely catch her, and discover what she was, and she knew what they would do then. Maybe she should admit that her mission was impossible, and quit right now.

She wiped appleberry juice from her mouth and looked across the river. And her heart made a leap like that of a fly-snaring fish.

There was a boat. A small boat, containing one man. The man was hunched over, rowing, and two fishing poles stuck out of the back of the craft. As it drew near, Jon could see the man's gray hair and seasoned face. Soon he had pulled almost abreast of her.

Could she somehow wangle a ride? That would be an enormous help! Maybe she could, after all, make it in time. Then—well, she would worry about the rest when the time came. After all, she did know the layout, thanks to Heln's astral visit. What had seemed doubtful now seemed promising.

"Catching any?" she called.

The boatman paused in his rowing, tugging a large ear with freckled spots on it. "Eh?"

He couldn't hear well, Jon realized. She should have kept still and let him row right past. But curse it, she hadn't seen other than bearvers and mooear for the past two days, and she didn't know how far she had still to go. She was anxious for information and any help she could beg.

The boat's oarlocks squeaked as the old man resumed rowing, drawing closer. He was coming in to meet her. Jon waited, working out what she would say. She stepped a little nearer to the bank.

The boat bumped shore and the old boatman raised rheumy eyes to look at her. "Eh?" he repeated.

"I said, sir, I was wondering how far to the capital?"

"The capital's right over there, lad," he said, pointing a trembly hand at the opposite shore.

Jon blinked. The morning fog still hid the other bank. It might have been possible for her to float right by the capital and not know it!

"Uh, thanks," she said. Now she was uncertain again, because she had decided to worry about getting past the guards when she arrived, and here she was already! Did she really want to risk this? Did she have any chance, realistically?

The old man was looking at her speculatively, his forehead furrowed and his hand on his chin. "You wouldn't be one of the bound boys, would you?"

"Bound boy!" Jon kicked herself mentally. She had all but forgotten both her situation and her masquerade. She had indeed been sold in the Mart, and remained technically the property of the dwarf who had bought her, and of course the old boatman had taken her for the boy she pretended to be. "I'm not bound to anyone," she said, deciding it was true. Her delivery to the Boy Mart had been illegal, so nothing that had followed was legal, and anyway, she had been rescued. Certainly she had never been a bound *boy*!

"Not with the maintenance crew, then?"

"What maintenance crew?"

"What maintenance crew? My, you are a stranger, aren't you! The maintenance crew at the palace. The grounds maintenance crew. Never less than a dozen boys, cutting grass, trimming trees, repairing walks. You say you're not one?"

"I'm not," Jon said, wondering if he was an agent for the Queen. No, that was unlikely; the old man could hardly row his boat, let alone recapture a bound boy.

"Well, if ye are, I'm not blaming you. Dirty business, this bound boy business. Dirty business!"

"Yes, it is," Jon said. *Glad you think so, oldster! You could be my big break!*

"I've got a grandson got bound. Little skinny fellow. You know him? His name's Tommy. Tommy Yokes."

Jon felt her mouth open. Tommy? Here? The boy who had kept her secret at the Boy Mart, then summoned the guards so as to stop her from getting raped? She could hardly think of a person she would rather encounter, if she needed help getting into the dungeon undiscovered.

"I—I know him," she said.

"You do? Really?"

Jon nodded. "We went to school together after he moved to our village. I'm—" No, better not give her name, she realized; the old man just might recognize it, and know her for a girl. "A friend of his."

"Ye are! Why, that's something, that is!"

"Yes, it is. It really is. Is Tommy working with the maintenance crew?"

"He is. Has to. You see, he has no choice."

"I know. Once a boy's been sold into slavery—I mean, legally bound—"

"Ye had it right the first time, lad! The way the Queen squeezes the common workingman—"

"Could you row me across the river, Mr. Yokes? I haven't anything to pay you with, but—"

"I can row you. But ye'd best not go. Many a greedy hand in the capital would have you impressed, bound, and sold. You'd be working with Tommy, then, but you wouldn't like it much."

"I'm sure I wouldn't like it!" Jon agreed. "But I—I've business."

"But no money?"

Jon shook her head. "I'm sorry, Mr. Yokes. I'd pay you if I could."

Yokes scratched an ear again. "Maybe I can lend

you a wee coin until you've seen Tommy from a distance. That what you want to do?"

"That's part of it."

"Yes, I can lend you a rudna. And if one of the guardsmen grabs you, tell him I'm your employer. Tell him you're checking on my grandson for me."

"I'll do that!" Jon agreed.

"Well, get in the boat."

Jon got in and pushed them free of the bank. The old man rowed. Straining her eyes, Jon could make out the piled-box affair that was the royal palace. She wondered if she would actually get there, and if she did, would she see Tommy and maybe find out a little more about Kelvin? It had now been three days since Heln had checked, and anything could have happened. Her brother might even have been moved to some other prison. At the moment she just couldn't be sure of anything. That was part of what made it such nervous business.

"Well, here we are," the old man called as their boat bumped the opposite shore.

Jon scrambled to get out. "Thanks, Mr. Yokes, and—"

"Here. Here's the rudna. Now, you be sure and look me up and tell me you've seen Tommy."

"I will, Mr. Yokes." The grandfather was as decent a man as the grandson!

"I'll be fishing all day. I fish all day every day. But I've a house over there. Just a shack, with a couple goeep staked out front. If you need a place to stay, you can stay with me and fish."

"Thank you. Thank you, Mr. Yokes. I've a brother—"

"Oh, then you're not alone in the world."

"No. Not quite."

"You're lucky, then. But if you need help keeping out of the Boy Mart, come to me. I'll help any young fellow I can."

"Thank you. Thank you," Jon repeated. She had

never felt more grateful to anyone, or more guilty. This old man was giving her trust and help, and she was deceiving him about her nature and her mission. Yet, if he knew either, would he let her go into that danger? She couldn't risk it. She took the rudna, pocketed it, and prepared to climb out of the boat.

"One thing more," the old man said. "This being so early, the grounds maintenance crew will be at their camp back of the orchard. That's along the palace wall and then right. Just follow that big wall, but keep away from guardsmen and anyone else you see. Some of those fellows are real eager to 'press; they get a bonus for anything they bring in, you know."

"I'll remember," Jon said. She hardly needed that particular warning! She wondered whether her greenbriar pantaloons and brownberry shirt would identify her as from the country. Well, it was way too late to change.

She climbed out, bending over to hold on to the rim of the boat while she stepped to shore.

"Hold on, that won't do at all," the man said. "Not at all."

"What?" she asked, pausing with one foot out and one in.

"Got to patch up that tear in your shirt, or the whole world'll know."

Jon looked down. Indeed, her shirt was torn, and at the moment, the tear was gaping open, showing her bosom quite clearly. She had never worn an undergarment in that region, considering it unmasculine. "Oops." The material must have snagged on a sharp branch when she got dunked, because no normal stress would damage the tough fabric.

"I have needle and thread," he said. "I patch my own, you know, these days." He fumbled in a small chest, and brought them out.

Jon climbed back into the boat. It occurred to her that the man didn't seem surprised. "You knew?"

"I'm halfway deaf, but I'm not blind, child. I raised

a son and a daughter, and I still know the difference atween them. You were doing such a good job of being a boy, I figured you might pass if you wanted to, so I let it be. I know a girl wouldn't dare go where you're going. But that tear's worse'n I thought. Here, I'll get it."

Jon sat still in the boat while he worked on her front, carefully sewing the tear closed. It wasn't the neatest job, but it was adequate, and it made it impossible to see through to her body. Though his hands had to brush her front frequently to complete the job, he took no liberties; he was just making sure the job was done right. He was like his grandson in this respect too: he could keep a secret, and offered help only when it was warranted.

"I—I don't know how to thank you, Mr. Yokes," she said as he finished and knotted and broke off the thread.

"Just make sure nobody else catches on," he said. "You're playing a dangerous game, girl."

She stood, leaned forward, and kissed him on his weathered cheek. Then, quickly, she stepped out.

"And she said she didn't know how to thank me," the old man muttered as she shoved his boat out into deeper water. He touched his cheek, then grabbed the oars. Jon had to smile.

Following the wall as the old man had instructed, she soon came to a squalid series of tents. Heln had not described these, which meant that they must have been set up in the last two or three days. Probably the boys pitched their tents in whatever section of the palace grounds they had to work on that day. As she looked out from behind a tree, she saw a large boy belaboring another with a stick.

"You going to work today, Tommy Yokes? Or are you going to hang back again and pretend you're sick?"

"I'll work," Tommy said, cringing back from the stick. "I know you're the foreman, Bustskin, but I can't work when I'm sick."

"You can try," Bustskin said, and poked his stick in the thinner boy's stomach.

Then the big boy turned—and saw Jon.

Suddenly Jon felt enraged. After all she had been through, after facing a bearver at very close range, Bustskin held little terror for her. She knew he would recognize her in a moment, and she knew what he would do then. She had a vision of Heln, huddled in her cell, the victim of rape. That enraged her further. What right did any male have to—

Bustskin's mouth opened. Tommy, spying her himself, reached for him, as if to stop him from going after her. Bustskin swung his fist backhanded, not even looking, and smacked him hard on the chest.

Then Jon's sling was in her hand, and she was putting a stone in it, and her arm was swinging forward, seemingly all in the same motion. Bustskin was wide open, because of his strike at Tommy.

The rock flung true. It struck Bustskin in the stomach, hurled with all the force Jon could muster. He doubled over, dropping the stick and clutching himself in surprise and pain.

"Get him!" Jon said, starting forward herself. She knew that if Bustskin got away, or even got a chance to yell, her effort would be all over.

The younger boy leaped on Bustskin's back and bore him to the ground. Tommy began pummeling him, as Bustskin tried futilely to defend himself. Jon picked up the stick, ready to knock the big boy on the head. But now Tommy seemed to require little help. He was raining blows on Bustskin, smashing into his chest, neck, and face.

"Stop! Stop!" Jon cried. "He's unconscious!"

"I want him that way!" Tommy gasped. "I want him never to wake up!"

Such fury! Now that Tommy had a chance to get even, he was almost uncontrollable. But she had a more important task than beating up the bully.

"We have to tie him up and get him out of sight."

"Why? A lot of kids'll be glad he got what's been coming to him!"

"And a lot of guardsmen won't! I want to take his place."

"What?" He was dumbfounded.

"So that I can go with you through the palace gate, onto the palace grounds, and get inside the building. So that I can rescue my brother from whatever dungeon he's in."

Tommy looked at her, freshly amazed. "You're crazy! The guardsmen will kill you!"

"Not," Jon said evenly, "if I have your help. *Do* I have your help?"

Tommy grinned sickly. He looked at his enemy on the ground. "You've got more than that," he said. "You have my friendship—right up until a guardsman takes your life, and mine. Because once they find out what we've done here—"

That, Jon thought, feeling the chill of what she had gotten into, could be all too soon. But she shrugged it off. "Your grandfather sends his greeting," she said, as they got to work tying and hauling Bustskin. "I promised to tell him how you're doing, but now I think I'd better deliver you personally to him. There'll be no life for you here, after this."

"That's for sure!" he agreed.

CHAPTER 23
Kian

THE FIRST THING KELVIN was aware of was the smell:
stale and musty. Then he heard the drip, drip, drip of
moisture. His mouth tasted bad and his head ached.
He placed a hand on the back of his skull and felt a
lump, but he did not remember being hit. Slowly,
hating the necessity, he opened his eyes.

Rock walls. Chains. Two faces, bearded and dirty,
looking down at him. He felt around and discovered
he was lying on straw. High overhead a barred window let in a little light that illuminated only this end
of the cell.

"Welcome to the Queen's dungeon, lad," the man
with the grayer beard said.

His gauntlet was gone, Kelvin discovered. That
other fellow probably had the pair, assuming the two
gloves hadn't destroyed each other.

"I'm the former King of this land," said the gray-
beard. "Not that it makes any difference now. Who,
lad, might you be?"

Kelvin took a deep breath. So this was the rightful
King of this land—King Rufurt! Somehow he had the
impression that the King already knew Kelvin's identity.

And the other man—Kelvin's head whirled when
he looked at him. The man's eyes were as blue as his
own. That was what had caught his attention about
his enemy, the one wearing the right-hand magic
gauntlet. The enemy's eyes had been dark and blue,
too.

And—this man had round ears!

"Recognize me, Kelvin?" the man asked in a husky
voice. His voice seemed to choke as he said it.

"F-father?" Kelvin gasped.

Then, suddenly, he and his father were hugging each other. "I thought you were dead!" Kelvin said.

"It's a long story," John Knight said. "A long, long story. But we have plenty of time. Tell me how you come to be here. All we know is that you've been unconscious from the drug for two days; we were concerned that you would suffer amnesia or something."

Kelvin did not have amnesia. He told them everything. It took some time.

His father listened to all his adventures without comment. He did flinch when told of his wife's remarriage, but relaxed when reassured that Hal Hackleberry was a good man who had taken excellent care of all members of the family. He swore briefly and colorfully when told of Cheeky Jack's stealing the gold and kidnaping Jon. He was skeptical about the magic gauntlet at first, but then seemed to accept it. He was interested to learn of Heln, the female roundear. The forming of the Knights of the Roundear, and the subsequent battles, fascinated him.

John Knight asked many questions when Kelvin was done. Kelvin answered patiently. Finally his father began to talk himself, and then it was Kelvin's turn to be fascinated.

"Son, I've long hoped to talk to you this way, but I thought it unlikely that the chance would ever come. It's high time! You see, I was born in another—I suppose you could call it another existence. Things are different there. Not better, necessarily, just different. Many of the things that are here regarded as make-believe are normal there. Flying machines, horseless carriages, talking boxes, moving pictures, thinking machines, nuclear bombs. Fantasy here, but reality there. And in my world much of what is taken for granted here is regarded as fantasy. Magicians, prophecies, magic gauntlets, astral separation—I never believed in these things until too late. I suppose there's a leakage between the universes, somehow, so that the visions, if not the reality, cross over. People in this world imagine horseless carriages, while people in my original world imagine magic gauntlets.''

The man paused, rubbing his eyes. "It is better in my world in some ways; many of us have conveniences that you can only dream about, literally. But it is also worse in some ways. We have pollution, crime, inflation—these become complex to explain, but they are nevertheless pervasive evils. So when I came here, I thought this world a paradise. It seemed so peaceful, so safe from such things as bombs—"

Kelvin could keep silent no longer. "How did you get here?" he asked. "To this world. Zatanas claims he brought the roundears here—"

''Zatanas! That old fraud? He had nothing to do with it! He just pretends he did, so that others will think him more powerful than he is. He's strictly a magic man, not an alternate-worlds man."

"I thought as much," Kelvin said. "But if it wasn't him, then—"

"How?" His father seemed to look backward into time, sorting it all out behind his suddenly closed eyelids. "They called it a 'clean atomic artillery shell,'" he said. "They said we were in no danger. Just testing, as they'd tested other weapons on other human sacrifices. We were soldiers, but not one of us wanted to be there, any more than the boys and girls sold at the Marts want to be there. I was a platoon leader. There were twelve men in my squad, counting Mary Limbeck and Jeanne Donovan. The girls were the only ones who tried to pretend it was a lark. The shells were supposed to whiz overhead, but one of them didn't. I saw it coming in, yelled 'Hit the dirt!' and then . . . I suppose the other squad escaped, but us, we were right under. Somehow, someway, we ended up—"

"In Rud?" Kelvin asked excitedly. Now at last he was getting answers to questions he had had all his life, and he could hardly contain himself. The miseries of his bruised head and body, and his confinement in this dungeon, were for the moment forgotten.

"In Throod. At the lip of what you call The Flaw —that big, incredible tear right through the center of . . . existence. Anyway, we were there, wearing combat equipment. All twelve of us. We had on our uniforms. We each had a laser pistol and hand grenades. Four of us had jet-propulsion backpacks. None of us had radiation sickness, though at first we feared—"

"Radiation sickness?"

"Forget it. Or think of it as a hostile type of magic that causes people to bleed from unbroken skin and waste away and die, with no cure. Just let me tell you that we were all right. *All right!* That was our miracle, perhaps our first taste of magic. We set about living, and we found that we were in the one land where mercenaries were commonly recruited. We heard of some fighting in Rud. The two women, wouldn't you know, married locals and settled in Throod—"

"Heln's mother!" Kelvin exclaimed.

"I don't think so," John Knight said. "Every one of their children I know of had pointed ears. Round ears seems to be a patrilineal trait, here."

"But—"

"What was her mother's name?"

"Helen."

He nodded. "I may have an alternative explanation for you, in a moment. To continue: we brave ten men were out to get our fortunes."

"Fortune came a-callin'," Kelvin said.

"Right! Fortune came a-calling, and only the women hid—we thought. We ten went to Rud and to Rud's contemptible would-be Queen. Queen Zoanna, she calls herself, and I can well believe her father is the legendary sorcerer. She bewitched us, I tell you. Every one of us, but especially me."

"What did you do, Father?" Kelvin was breathless.

"What did I do? What weak men have ever done

when confronted with the likes of her. She convinced me that the King here"—he jerked a finger at Rufurt —"was dead. I didn't know different. I fought for her, with my nine men. She got her kingdom and four of the men got their deaths, pierced by arrows or spears or lances. The six of us roundears who survived the campaign thought we'd lead rich and idle lives."

He shook his head. "Ha! We were fools. She distrusted us too much. She was devilishly clever in the manner she first divided us, then eliminated us. Me, she married; the others she imprisoned one by one. I, befuddled by her wiles, didn't catch on until it was too late, and I realized that I alone remained free—and I was in fact captive in the palace. I tried to leave, and could not. Then I knew what I should have known at the outset. I stormed at her, threatened to kill her. But I was a fool even then, for she had deprived me of my weapons. Before I knew it, guards had hold of me and were dragging me to the dungeon on her orders."

"But the Queen—" Kelvin started.

"The Queen. Yes, the Queen. She took a new consort, the first of a long line of them. She never made the mistake of choosing a strong-willed one again; each was a marvel of spinelessness. The latest is a jellyfish by the name of Peter Flick, a coward and a sniveler of the worst sort. Perhaps that's why she fell under the spell of her father, who claims responsibility for our being here. He was the only strong man remaining in her life. He gave her advice, and she killed—I call it murder, but she called it execution —my remaining men, one by one. You see, she still wanted something from me, and each time she asked for my cooperation and I told her to go to hell, she killed one of my men, and made sure I knew it. Finally, to save the last of the five, I agreed to do part of what she asked. It wasn't totally against my will, I confess. In that manner I bought his freedom; she swore to me that she would let him go, let him out of Rud unharmed, and I think she honored that. I never knew what happened to him after that, though I think I can guess now."

"I don't understand! What did you agree to do, and why do you think the Queen honored the agreement?"

"The two are linked, Kelvin. The Queen keeps me alive because she—we—have a son. It's not that she has any particular affection or loyalty to either of us, but her magician father advises her to maintain us both in health. Again, I never knew why—until I heard your story. The favor she wanted was for me to train our son in the way of roundear magic, as she puts it, and I think she honored her agreement to free my last man because she was afraid that if she didn't, and I found out, I would take it out on the boy. So she offered a life for a life—my man's life against our son's life. I did train our boy, and I did not try to turn him against his mother. I kept my part of the bargain, and now I am glad I did, because I see that she kept hers."

"But how can you know that?"

"Your roundear girlfriend—who do you think was her natural father?"

"Heln!" Kelvin exclaimed. "She—had a roundear mother, who had to give her up, and—"

But John Knight was shaking his head. "My surviving man was nicknamed St. Helens, after a volcano, because his temper—well, that's irrelevant."

"Helens?" There was the name, all right! "But—"

"Think it through, son. If you married a pointear and wanted to protect her from possible malice by the Queen, what would you do?"

Then it came to him. "They put out the story that it was the *woman* who was the roundear! So that the Queen's guards would not realize that the man had a child, or where he was—"

"And when things got too hot anyway, then he just disappeared, drawing away the pursuit—"

"And Heln's *pointear* mother remarried—just as my mother did! And Heln herself never knew—"

"That's the way it goes," John Knight agreed. "Surely St. Helens knew that his daughter would be safer in a point-eared family, and that her mother would take care of her, just as I knew that your mother would do the right thing. Surely it was painful for him, as it was for me, but necessary."

"Yes, Mr. Flambeau is a fine man," Kelvin agreed. "He protected her, but when the taxes got too bad, she volunteered to go to the Mart—and I guess I'm glad she did, even though she got—"

"There are aspects of the life of the good folk of Rud that none of us like," John Knight said gravely. "That's why the prophecy is so important, about the overthrow of the tyranny. I never believed that prophecy, but now I think I do. If you really are the one—"

"But you—how did you get free to—?"

"To sire you and Jon? Kelvin, I escaped once. My other son helped me, though I didn't ask him to. Apparently even the Queen could not eradicate all decency from him. He was only three at the time, but he managed to distract a guard so that my cell gate didn't get properly locked, and 'accidentally' let me get out. I'm proud to say that I destroyed every weapon that remained from my own world, with the exception of one flying unit, which I couldn't find but know the Queen has hidden away somewhere. And a few grenades and laser pistols. Your mother was —now, there is a *real* queen! She knew where I had come from, what I had been doing, and accepted me anyway. She was—*is*—the most beautiful woman I know, outside and inside. There, on that land with her, and with you and Jon, that was *really* paradise. But it couldn't last. I knew it couldn't. I heard of the spies coming, and I left you and my only true wife, and I took with me the grenades and the pistols. I used those weapons to defend myself. I left fragments of guardsmen, and suspect that those were found and identified as me. That's why the word went out that I was dead. Well, long life to Charlain! She deserves better than an otherworld roundear!" He paused, wiping his eyes.

Kelvin considered what he had learned. Now at last he knew the full story of his father's origin, and his own! But there was one other matter. He took a deep breath. "About your son—yours and the Queen's."

"Kian. Yes, fine boy, Kian. Or he could be. You met him under unfortunate circumstances. Perhaps when he visits you—"

"Visits me?" Kelvin could not conceal his surprise. "Here, in this dungeon?"

"Turn around and look," his father advised.

Kelvin turned, startled. There stood his opponent of the battlefield, the one he had fought gauntlet-to-gauntlet. Kian, blue eyes, blond hair, a light blond mustache, and round ears. Four years older than Kelvin himself. How had he failed to recognize him immediately as his half brother? Because he hadn't known he *had* a half brother!

Kian was now wearing the gauntlets as a pair. Did they work as well for him? If they did, he must be truly invincible, immune to anything short of a projectile. No swordsman alive could fight as well as those gauntlets could!

"Kelvin, brother," Kian said. His voice, too, was a little high-pitched, much like Kelvin's own.

Kelvin stood up from the bed of straw that served as furniture. He felt woozy, and his head hurt, but in a moment he steadied. "We are brothers," he agreed. No use denying it, and he really couldn't bear Kian a grudge.

"I'm glad you were not killed," Kian said. "You could never be my brother, dead, or my friend."

"Yes," Kelvin said. Was Kian as lonely as he, deep inside?

"You know about the prophecy," Kian said. "It refers to me. I'm to rid the land of Rud of a sore: your band of Knights, Kelvin. Now that the confusion engendered by the separation of the gauntlets has been abated."

Kelvin choked back an exclamation of astonishment. That was one enormously interesting interpretation! What would his mother Charlain have made of it? What had John Knight and King Rufurt made of it?

"We both have round ears, Kelvin," Kian continued. "My mother, the Queen, explained it to me."

Kelvin looked at his father, and his father shrugged. Then, seemingly taking pity on him, John Knight spoke.

"If prophecy isn't all nonsense, he could be right, Kelvin. But of course it could refer to you, too, or to Heln Flambeau. Who knows, where prophecy is concerned?"

"I did defeat you in battle," Kian said.

"No, you didn't!" Kelvin said hotly. "I fought you to a standstill!"

"He's got you there, Kian," their father said. "I think it has to be called a draw."

"Without the gauntlet you were wearing—" Kian started.

"And without the one *you* were wearing—"

Both broke off, and Kelvin had half an impulse to laugh. If the situation had not been so serious—

"You see, Kelvin," their father said, "Peter Flick has been after Zoanna to get Kian trained to the jet-propulsion backpack unit and the laser pistols —all the otherworld weapons left. I trained him in the background of our world, its philosophies and politics and technology, so he understands the principles, but not the specifics. He knows enough to know that if he tries to use that jet unit he's likely to break it or get himself killed in an accident, and of course he doesn't know how to charge the pistols. So my input remains necessary; that was one safeguard I kept. Kian's loyalty is to his mother, and he thinks he can't have it for an alien creature such as me. Right, Kian?"

Kian shook his head. "No. I would be loyal to you, Father, were you not the sworn enemy of my mother."

John Knight turned away, and Kelvin realized that

he had hoped for a more positive answer. He had
challenged Kian to agree that his own father was an
alien creature unworthy of loyalty, or to disagree and
to change sides; instead Kian had steered a careful
course between the extremes. Kelvin had to respect
that.

But Kian's face was stricken for a moment. Kelvin
realized that Kian wished he did not have to choose
between his father and his mother, and felt bad about
doing it. Kian was free, and in the Queen's favor, but
his course was not easy.

"We may be on different sides," Kelvin said, "but
we're still brothers."

Kian flashed him a look of gratitude, then covered
that, too. Obviously he could not afford much emo-
tional attachment to the enemies of his mother,
whatever his private inclinations might be.

"Well, isn't this cozy?" a new voice came. A man
virtually pranced in, like a high-spirited pony. He
came to stand beside Kian, his right hand on his
sword. "The roundears united. Unnatural father and
two unnatural sons."

"You scum!" John Knight exclaimed. He was suddenly at the bars, reaching through them like an
enraged animal.

"What are you doing here, Peter Flick?" Kian
inquired coldly. "Did my mother get tired of spank-
ing your fanny and dump you in the dungeon with
your betters?"

Kelvin saw the expression of wild fury pass from
the face of his father to the face of the Queen's consort
without losing anything in transition. A backhand
across the face could not have been more effective.
Flick's right hand went for his sword—but Kian's left
hand shot out to intercept it halfway there. The
gauntlet must have squeezed cruelly, for Flick
clenched his teeth.

"One day you will go too far, alien spawn!" Flick
gritted.

"I doubt you'll ever see it, rear-kisser," Kian re-

torted. "Now state your foolish business and get out;
you're making the cell stink." He released the man's
wrist and turned his back.

Kelvin couldn't help himself; he was getting to like
his half brother. Naturally Kian didn't like the man
who was taking his father's place in the Queen's
bedroom, and because Kian was of the Queen's own
flesh, he had immunity to the threats of the other. So
he really wasn't being brave. But he had a very pretty
turn of the phrase.

"I'm here to lay out the facts," Flick said. "Either
you, John, cooperate in teaching Kian to use the
magic flying harness and the magic lightning-makers,
or your Rud brat here will pay. Neither Zoanna nor I
have love for that one—Zoanna least of all. I remind
you that the torturer's coals are hot. The chains are
oiled. The spikes are very sharp. Finally, should all
that fail, there is her dear old father and the use he has
for youthful blood. For the boy's sake, you had really
better cooperate."

Kelvin looked at his father and felt great fear.
Would this man whom he hardly knew help his enemy
in order to save him? Would John Knight let him be
tortured? And what was that about the magician and
his need for blood?

"You disgust me, you dragon dropping," Kian said,
flashing a look of pure ire at Flick. "That is my
brother you're threatening with torture!"

"Then you'd better help convince your father to
cooperate," Flick said with satisfied malice. "You are
the one who will benefit, you know."

"How can you trust me?" John asked. He seemed
genuinely curious.

"Why, the usual way, of course. There will be
expert crossbowmen watching. And of course you
won't be allowed to touch the otherworld artifacts.
You will stand back and direct Kian with your voice.
And you will direct correctly, or—" He looked at
Kelvin significantly.

Kelvin wondered if he could stand torture. He

doubted it. The very thought made him ill. Looking at his father's clenched fist, seeing how much it was costing him, he still wished him to agree.

"All right!" John said. "All right! Tell her I'll do what she wants, but to keep her father out of it."

"Agreed," Peter Flick said, smirking. He danced on out.

"I want you to know I had no part of this ugly ploy," Kian said, his gauntleted fists clenching.

"I know it, son," John Knight said.

Kian turned abruptly and strode from the dungeon. Kelvin knew this was not anger but his effort to conceal his flush of pleasure at the term their father had used. Kian might hate Flick and the Queen's methods, but he was on the Queen's side, and had to maintain his composure.

CHAPTER 24
Irony

HELN COULDN'T STAND THE suspense any longer. It was now the fourth day since Jon's departure; had she made it in time? Were the Knights attacking as they had planned? And, most important, what about Kelvin? Was he still in the dungeon with the two older men, or had something worse happened to him? She had to know, even if she couldn't do anything about any of it!

She had explained to her folks about the dragonberries, and how they had helped the Knights fight. Her mother was concerned, but agreed that if the berries had worked several times before, they should be safe enough to try again. She promised not to panic when Heln seemed to go into a coma or even to die. She understood about youth and love. "After all, I loved your roundear father," she said gently. "I was grief-stricken when he had to go."

"What?" Heln asked, thinking she had misheard.

"It is time for you to know, dear. You were not completely adopted. Your father, not your mother, was the roundear. I always was your mother. I did not want to burden you with this knowledge before, but now that you have found a roundear of your own—"

"But *why*?" Heln asked. She had no memory of the one she had been told was her original mother. Now, abruptly, she had learned that the parent she thought adoptive was genuine, while the one she thought genuine was adoptive. Her mother, not her father, was natural. She had never suspected!

"The Queen's guardsmen were searching for a grown roundear man," she said. "I believe now, from what you have told me, that it was your friend

216

Kelvin's father. But they would have killed any roundear man they found. It was just too risky for my husband to stay; too many people knew him, knew he was of foreign origin. So I moved with you to Rud, where they would never expect the family of a round-ear to go, and he went the opposite way. I never heard from him again, and fear he is dead. But if they had caught him with us, they would have killed us too, just to be sure. Your father saved us by deserting us, just as Kelvin's father did. I remarried for the same reason Kelvin's mother did: to complete the concealment. We hid your ears, and I married Frond Flambeau, and that is the way it has been ever since. I'm afraid I rather threw myself at him; he was a good man, but plain, a widower, and it seemed to me he would be a decent provider. So I promised him everything he might wish in a woman, if he would keep the secret and treat you as his own. He agreed, and he did that, and I don't regret my decision, though I never really loved him. He even protected me by claiming that he was your natural father, from an affair with a round-ear woman, so that no one would suspect you were the child of a hunted man."

"You—you made yourself a plaything of a man you didn't love—just to protect me?" Heln asked, horrified.

"For myself, too, dear," her mother said. "I needed the security. This land is not necessarily kind to a woman without protection. I never deceived Frond about my motives, and as it turned out, he needed a woman to manage the farm, and I think perhaps I was a more attractive woman than he might otherwise have had. Not all marriages are made in paradise, but they can work well enough when their basic aspects are understood. If you marry another roundear, you may face similar realities."

Heln thought about her ravishment at the Girl Mart. She had not told her mother of that aspect of her experience, but perhaps she suspected. Sometimes desperate measures were required to keep body and sanity together. Heln had pretty much thrown herself at Kelvin similarly, wanting a man who would understand about her ears and who would not try to do to her what the guards had. How could she blame her mother for choosing rationally and doing what was necessary to secure her situation? Frond Flambeau *was* a good man, just as Hal Hackleberry was, and it seemed that in each case attractive women had used them for their own purposes but rewarded them too. Heln knew that Frond Flambeau had loved her mother deeply from the outset, and had taken excellent care of Heln herself in order to be sure that her mother would never wish to leave him. It had been no choice of his to send her to the Mart! But Heln, feeling guilty for the extra burden her existence placed on him and the family, had insisted, and had paid a worse price than she ever expected, and received a better reward than she had dreamed of, in encountering Jon and Kelvin.

"I think I am ready for those realities," Heln said. "I always believed Frond was my father, and I see no reason to change my opinion now."

"I am pleased to hear you say that," her mother said. Her words were mild, but there were tears streaming down her face.

Then Heln took a dragonberry, and sank into her sleep of astral separation.

Soon she drew free of her body, and saw her mother sitting nervously beside that body, trusting that what Heln had told her was true, but nevertheless afraid of her seeming death. She was sorry her mother had to suffer this concern, but there was no other way.

She willed herself to the capital, and to the dungeon where she had found Kelvin before. She was horrified when she found the cell empty; where had they taken him? But a quick search located Kelvin and an older man: they were going up a dark, hidden flight of stairs. They were escaping!

But would they succeed in getting out of the palace and off the grounds? Heln moved about some more, scouting the vicinity. She found few guards; they seemed to have been sent elsewhere.

She lifted up above the palace—and froze in horror. She saw dragons—many, many dragons, huge and ugly, converging on the grounds. And beyond them she spied the Knights of Morvin Crumb's force; the Queen was evidently sending the dragons against them! That would be disaster!

Yet she could do nothing except hope that the Knights would realize their danger in time, and flee.

Where was Jon? Heln zeroed in on her essence, and found her in a field near the palace. She was with a boy Heln recognized: one who had been sold that day at the Mart. And with several others, marching in together. They were heading in toward the palace —and toward the dragons.

Finally Heln saw the strangest sight of all: a man flying through the air! She knew that was impossible, but there he was doing it! He was flying toward Jon. What would happen when they met?

Then Heln's time was up, and she was drawn rapidly back into her body. She had seen much, but she understood little of it, and she still didn't know what would happen. But with all those dragons rampaging, she very much feared the worst. She hoped that Jon would succeed in helping Kelvin, and not in getting herself chewed up by a dragon. What an irony, to have Jon getting so close, only to be walking into so many unexpected dangers!

Tommy fitted her out in a pair of bound-boy coveralls and a large floppy straw hat. On the back of the coveralls were the letters BB. The clothing smelled of sweat from the boy who had worn it previously, but fit as well as any was likely to. She was getting entirely too broad across the hips! She pretended that Tommy wasn't trying not to stare, feeling perversely flattered. If she managed to get through this mission alive, she might have more to say to him. Tommy was a nice boy, and he had helped her a lot.

Jon stretched her legs and arms. Snug only around the rear, and fortunately loose around the chest. Reasonably comfortable.

"I'll want to get in with my sling and some rocks," she said.

Tommy shook his head. "You think you can defeat guardsmen?"

"I can avoid them," Jon said, wishing she were more confident. "The sling and the rocks are for getting my brother out."

"You think you'll just knock a few guards out and then unlock a door? Assuming you can find a door?"

"I can find a door." She remembered the layout Heln had described well enough; that was not her problem.

Jon checked over the river rocks in the bucket Tommy had brought her. A couple she discarded, but most were of the right weight and size.

"I think," Jon said, "that if I carry the rocks and sling in the bucket and you push the wheelbarrow ahead of me and everyone else just goes in as usual—"

"The guards will notice you."

"You said that new bound boys come and go all the time."

"Yes, but the gate guards probably know when new boys are with us."

"Just let Jerry," she said, referring to the boy whose clothes she wore, "stay here and—"

"We'd be one short. They count, I'm sure."

Jon pondered. To be so close, and yet to be kept from entering! "Bustskin has to lead us," she said.

"He does if we're to get through the gate. The guards know him already. He struts."

"Hmmm. Leave Jerry here, and have Bustskin lead as usual."

"Can't be done."

"Why not?"

"He won't cooperate."

"We'll make him," Jon said.

"How?"

Jon looked at Bustskin's hard, somewhat battered face. Even if the boy would lead, the bruises and black eye might make the guards suspicious. If the guards questioned them, that meant she would be caught, and she didn't care to be caught. Not at all!

"The guards," she said seriously, "will have to be distracted."

"Take off your clothes," he suggested with a fleeting smile.

"Not distracted that much," she said, with as brief a return smile. She liked Tommy.

"I know. But how?"

Yes, how? How would a great hero handle this? "Um, maybe we could start a fire."

"They'd look, but they'd look back again."

Yes, he was probably right. The shift was about to change, and they would soon have to move. She looked over at sullen Bustskin, and an inspiration struck. "Bustskin will have to escape, and Jerry with him!"

"What!" Tommy and bound Bustskin exclaimed in unison.

"We get all lined up to go through the gate. Then Bustskin starts running and Jerry right after him."

"I won't!" Bustskin said.

"Yes, you will," Jon said, "because there's going to be a slip noose around your neck, and Jerry running right behind you with the end of the rope."

"I'm not afraid of him," Bustskin said.

"And your hands will be tied."

"I'll yell," Bustskin said.

"And choke?"

"If I have to."

He probably would, she realized. The problem with Bustskin was that he was a terrible person but no coward.

She looked at the noose she had been making in the

leather thong that had been part of the tent lashings. There had to be a way! But if they couldn't make Bustskin cooperate . . .

Then Jon, desperate for an answer, thought she saw one. "Jerry will have to run and get the guards to chase him. Bustskin will stay with us, with a knife at his back."

"It will never work," Tommy said realistically. "He'll yell the moment the guards are close enough to hear."

Jon faced Bustskin. "Listen, jerk. Remember what you tried to do to me, at the Boy Mart?"

"Yeah, and I'll do it again," he said. "The moment I—"

"So can you guess where my knife is going to strike first, the moment you make a peep? So that even if you get me caught, *you* won't be the one to do that thing, to me or anyone, ever again?"

Bustskin gulped.

"You doubt me?" she asked, fingering the blade of the knife and eyeing his crotch. "You think I'll have anything more to lose, the moment you squeal?"

"Uh—"

"Do you think it will be worth it?" she persisted.

He was silent. He knew she had a score to settle with him, and that the main thing holding her back was the fact that she needed his cooperation.

"I think Bustskin will cooperate," she said. "Maybe I hope he won't. Meanwhile, I'll carry this knife low, like this." She held the blade down flat against her thigh. "And move it like this." She brought it up suddenly to crotch level, the point spearing forward. "If I don't score the first time, I'll just try again. Even from behind, I should manage to skewer something." She lowered the knife, then repeated her motion, this time stabbing upward with full strength. The odd thing was, she was absolutely serious; her memory of what Bustskin had tried to do to her was very clear, and it was mixed up with the memory of Heln huddled on the floor. There was a vengeance owing!

"I'll do it," Bustskin said, sweating.

"You bet you will," she agreed. She turned to Jerry. "You can do your part?"

"I—I think so," said the pale boy with smaller than average ears. "They won't kill me. They'll just beat me and bring me back."

"Good," Jon said. Then, looking at the sun, "We'd better go."

Jerry walked with them as far as the gate. Bustskin led the troupe, Jon close behind, actually touching his rear every so often, which made him jump. Indeed, her knife was ready!

But when they got there, the gate was wide open and there were no guards. The sound of fighting rose from some distance away, and with it clouds of dust Jon now associated with a proper fight.

The battle, she thought, *has begun!*

With no other thought than rescuing her brother before the dungeon guards realized what was happening and killed him, she ran through the gate, across the lawn, and into the flower garden. She knew her way from here; Heln had described it.

Glancing back, she saw bound boys scattering in every direction. One, who just had to be Tommy, hesitated for a moment and then ran with the others.

Jon heaved a sigh. Of course Tommy had to try to save himself. But it would have been nice if he had decided to help her first, just to get her on down into the dungeons.

She paused. What was that? That roaring sound? That wasn't regular battle!

A figure hung in the air, then began moving slowly as she watched. It moved at treetop height—an otherworld sky demon such as the Knights had talked about.

No, no, no, she thought. They couldn't have discovered her presence. They couldn't have!

The figure kept coming, heading right for her.

There was only one thing to do. She would have to bring down the sky demon.

Jon hefted her sling, fitting a rock. She waited, teeth clenched, determined not to let the sky person close.

The figure came nearer, and with it a whooshing noise like a great wind from the nostrils of a gigantic flying dragon. Jon was terrified, but she knew that if this demon got her, her brother could be doomed.

CHAPTER 25
Interpretation

As soon as the guards had left, taking John Knight with them, Kelvin had set about trying to think of a way that he and King Rufurt might escape. It was obvious to him that his father was really powerless to resist Queen Zoanna. Certainly that was the case while he, Kelvin, remained hostage for his father's cooperation.

"I think," he said to the King when they were alone, "that we'd better act fast. Is there any decent soil here?"

"There's manure from rats, and slops," the King said. "But—"

"That will do. Gather a pile of it and wet it down."

"Look, young man, I may be a prisoner, but I'm still a king! I don't do that sort of work!"

Kelvin had forgotten the man's rank for the moment. "Okay, I'll do it myself. But time is of the essence."

"You have something in mind?"

"I have a few seeds I saved," Kelvin said, fishing them out of his pocket. "Some of them seem to respond better to roundears than to natives. If I can grow something special, it might help us escape."

"Impossible," the King said. "It would take weeks to grow anything, and there's no decent daylight here."

"Um, yes." Then Kelvin's questing fingers found the shriveled husk of the flower he had plucked. It had lain for weeks in his pocket, forgotten. He drew it carefully out. It was battered but intact: a desiccated spicerose. "But maybe I can revive this."

225

"You can speak to flowers?" the King asked, amazed.

"Oh, sure. Flowers and fruits like me, I don't know why."

"I recognize that species," the King said, excited. "That's the shade-blooming spicerose—one of the most prized flowers! I used to grow them in my chambers, but they would respond to only one gardener."

"Yes, that's why I saved it," Kelvin agreed. "A mooear trampled the plant and broke the stem, so I thought I might restore it when there was someone who could appreciate it. But then things got complicated, and I forgot."

"You can restore that rose?"

"Yes, I think so. They prefer shade, and we have that here, so—"

"I'll get the damp manure!" the King exclaimed. He busied himself, scraping the stuff up from the edges of the cell, while Kelvin cradled the dry rose in his hands, breathing on it. Already it was beginning to revive.

The King brought a double handful of fairly foul stuff. "Hold it there," Kelvin said. "I'll just put the stem in, and then talk to it . . ."

This time the King did as he was bid without protest. He held the manure, while Kelvin planted the rose in it, then cupped the faded blossom with his hands and whispered to it. "Oh, lovely spicerose, bloom again for me, if you please," he said to it. "I long for your rare fragrance."

"It's working!" the King exclaimed. "The petals are filling out!"

"Yes. But it won't last; it's been dry too long."

"Careful! When the fragrance comes, a single sniff can put you out."

"No, it doesn't affect me that way," Kelvin said. "I like the smell, but it doesn't put me into a dream."

"The glory and penalty of being a roundear," the

King remarked sagely. "To have the power to restore a rare flower, but to be unable to reap its proffered reward."

"That seems to be the nature of heroism," Kelvin agreed with a shrug. "If I had my choice—"

They heard the steps of the guard returning. "But a native—" the King said.

"Yes. Pretend you want it, so he notices."

"I understand. Tell me when the rose is ready. I don't dare smell it myself."

The guard returned to his station outside the cell. He was bored, of course, just waiting until his shift changed.

Kelvin nursed the rose along. The petals filled out and pale red color came. The smell manifested. "Ready," Kelvin murmured.

"Hey, boy," the King said abruptly. "Save some of that for me!"

"No, it's mine!" Kelvin replied, playing the game.

"But I'm the King! I am entitled to the first sniff!"

The guard came alert. "What's that?"

"He's got a spicerose, and he won't share," the King said indignantly.

"A spicerose!" the guard exclaimed. "I don't believe it!"

"You fool," Kelvin said. "Don't tell *him*! He'll just take it for himself!"

"You bet I will!" the guard said, spying the rose. "Give it here!"

"But it's mine!" Kelvin protested.

"Give it here, or I'll club you on the head!" the guard said.

With obvious regret, the King brought the handful of manure and the rose to the bars. The guard leaned forward and took a deep sniff of the rose. His eyes glazed, his mouth curved into an idiotic smile, and he fell against the bars.

"Get his keys!" the King said urgently, holding the rose to the man's descending nose.

Kelvin reached through and grabbed the keys. Then he unlocked the gate, stepped out, and unlooped the rope he kept coiled beneath the waistband of his pantaloons. Made of lightweight thistlehemp fiber, it had gone unnoticed by his captors. He passed it around the body of the slumped guard and tied him securely.

"But we may need that rope," the King said, setting manure and flower down.

Kelvin agreed. So they tied the guard again, this time using strips torn from his own uniform. They hurried, because the blissful sleep produced by a spicerose lasted only a minute or two. This rose had been good for about two sniffs; now its petals were shriveling again. Its moment of glory was over, and there would be no reviving it again.

"You did well, rose," Kelvin said, and it almost seemed that the petals gave a final quiver before they curled up in death.

"Too bad it did not have a worthier subject for its joy," the King remarked.

"Now," Kelvin said, "maybe we can get out of here."

"Follow me," the King said, and started running full tilt up the stairs. The guard was stirring, but would be unable to free himself in time to do them any harm.

Kelvin followed, surprised at how fast the old King could run after months, no, *years,* of confinement. Perhaps all those exercises the King and his father did each day had kept them in better condition than even they could have hoped.

"This way," said the King, taking a branching flight of stairs. "This leads to the secret passage I had constructed. Even the Queen doesn't know."

The stairs took them to an apparent dead end. The King threw his weight against what appeared to be solid rock. At first nothing happened, but then as the King continued to push, his groans were answered by a louder groan. Slowly, protestingly, a heavy stone door swung in. It opened, at long last, on an empty room with dust and cobwebs and only a little light.

"But this isn't out!" Kelvin said, looking at the dirt-encrusted windows with dismay.

The King touched his elbow. "Follow me."

This time he led the way through a door he uncovered behind a worn tapestry hanging on the wall. This passage led outside, emerging at a solid clump of shrubbery. They had to force their way through it, and when Kelvin looked back, there was no sign of the exit they had used. This was a concealed escape the King had thoughtfully provided for himself back before Kelvin was born. Just in case events should make it necessary.

After a determined struggle, they stood outside in the strong sunlight. Kelvin took a breath of fresh air, untainted with dungeon odors, and smelled the spicy sweet scent of appleberries and other fruit. Then, as the song of a bird broke off in the nearby orchard, a strange roaring noise took its place.

Kelvin's first thought was a dragon. But then he realized what it was, even as he heard the King say, "He's teaching him!"

So they would see Kian fly, Kelvin thought. But should they risk it? Maybe they should just get away. By the time the practice session was over, they could be all the way off the palace grounds. But what would happen to John Knight, then? They couldn't desert him!

The roar became a whooshing sound as they suddenly saw Kian moving slowly across the grounds at treetop height. He looked thrilled but scared, his gauntleted hands clutching tightly to the harness.

Kelvin stared, hardly believing his eyes. The King, beside him, seemed as enraptured. This was true roundear magic!

As they watched, a small missile looped from the garden to their left. It was headed right for Kian's face. The gauntlets ripped the harness in their effort to intercept the missile, and caught it, but now the apparatus was out of control. The noise coming from Kian's back increased to a tortured whine. He shot up toward the palace's roof.

There was a sickening meaty smack when he struck.

Kian fell, his backpack unit smashed and smoking, twisting and turning in the air, until he landed on the hard cobblestones below.

Then there was silence, and a streamer of oily smoke.

Kelvin and the King reached Kian a few steps ahead of John Knight and his pursuing guards.

Kian looked up at Kelvin. Blood ran from the corners of his mouth. He made a wheezing sound. He tried to move, to sit up, but could not. His gauntleted right hand reached Kelvin's bare hand and held it, not squeezing.

"You're the one, Kelvin," Kian gasped. "The prophecy refers to you, not to me. I know that now."

"Don't try to talk, Kian," Kelvin said. He knew this was foolish; he should have run in the other direction. He could have escaped, and now he would be recaptured. Yet he could not desert his half brother in this time of tragedy.

The gauntlet seemed to grow warm in his hand. "I'm glad it's you, Kelvin," Kian gasped. "Take the gauntlets. Take them and . . ."

The eyes, so much like Kelvin's own, took on a glassy look. The hurt face relaxed. A sigh, ever so gentle, escaped the thin lips.

"Kian, Kian," Kelvin said, finding his eyes wet.

"Kian, son," said John Knight. He was there on the ground beside them, his fingers stripping off a gauntlet and feeling the wrist.

"Is he—?"

"There's a pulse," John Knight said. "He's not gone yet. If we can get help for him—"

From outside the palace grounds there was the clang of swords, the neighing of horses, and the shouts of men: the sounds of a wild battle just beyond the garden walls.

"I should never have let you use that harness, Kian," John Knight said brokenly. "They made me show you before you were ready. *She* made me. Your reactions were wrong! Those gauntlets tried to save you, but they aren't attuned to roundear science. They did exactly the wrong thing!" He seemed not to hear the battle sounds.

"Now I'll have to use these myself," John Knight said. With scarcely any comprehension, Kelvin saw his father remove the two otherworld weapons from short scabbards belted around Kian's waist.

What did any of this matter? The roundear magic had come close to killing Kian, and it was uncertain whether he would live or die. The prophecy had turned out to be purely a matter of interpretation, not anything to be counted on. Here they were, stuck in the middle of the palace grounds, surrounded by the Queen's guardsmen. What hope remained?

CHAPTER 26
Dragon Slayer

KELVIN RAISED HIS HEAD and saw a guardsman aiming a crossbow at him. He had allowed himself to be distracted far too long with Kian; now he was helpless before the enemy. He didn't even have the gauntlet to defend him.

He reached for the left gauntlet, the one John Knight had removed from Kian's hand, the one Kelvin had used before. But he knew it was too late; already the guardsman's finger was squeezing the trigger. He couldn't possibly don the gauntlet before that arrow pierced him.

Perhaps, then, Kian had been right in his interpretation: he, not Kelvin, was the Roundear of Prophecy. Because Kelvin was about to be dead, while Kian still lived. If that was the way it was, then so be it; Kelvin had no time for fright or anger, just for regret. Heln would be sad . . .

A ruby beam hit the crossbowman in the chest and went right on through him, stabbing on out the other side. The man dropped, a smoking hole in his chest. His shaft fired into the ground.

Dazed, Kelvin watched, his hand still reaching for the gauntlet. What was happening?

A second guardsman started to raise his crossbow. Another red ray appeared, transfixing him. The man never uttered a sound as he dropped backward onto the grass.

Kelvin saw his father lower one of the weapons he had taken from Kian. His face was grim. Astonished, Kelvin realized that the magic lightning weapons—or laser pistols, as his father called them—were really as deadly as the legends portrayed them.

"Come," said his father, and raced for a flight of stairs that led to a balcony at the front of the palace.

Kelvin lurched to his feet. He looked at Kian, and realized that his half brother's fate was out of his hands; Kian would live or die as the prophecy decreed, and all Kelvin could do was leave him alone. He would only get himself killed if he lingered here, and the guardsmen would drag Kian to safety and medical care soon enough.

He snatched up the left gauntlet, then tore the right one off Kian's unresisting hand. Then he whirled and followed John Knight, his heart beating hard, the memory of Kian's glassy eyes and last words all too sharp. Kian might be his enemy, technically, but he hoped Kian lived. But Kian didn't need the gauntlets at the moment; Kelvin did.

King Rufurt was running too, panting as he struggled to keep up. Now the steps were slapping beneath Kelvin's feet, and then there were no more steps and the three of them were on the balcony.

Below the balcony were walks and a garden and a beautifully cared-for lawn. Beyond the garden fence, quite visible from here, a battle was going on. Men in blue and gold uniforms were battling hard against men in green pantaloons and brownberry shirts. Men were hurting and men were dying, as were war-horses and plow horses. The din of the battle carried clearly, especially the cries of the wounded and dying.

His side was winning, Kelvin thought, straining his eyes to see through the dust. He had never thought the Knights would come here to fight, after losing the battle at Skagmore! But maybe they hadn't lost; maybe the tide of that battle had turned after he, Kelvin, lost consciousness. Was that big man Mor Crumb? It seemed to be. And with him, Les! Victory was, after all, within their grasp!

A frightful roar shook the very walls of the palace. Below, bright gold monsters smashed walls, trampled men, and lifted huge snouts holding men in brownberry shirts impaled on swordlike teeth. Horses

neighed and screamed as tremendous clawed feet
came down.

Dragons! At least twelve! Several times as many as
any living man had ever seen! How could this be?

Kelvin heard a gasp of astonishment and horror,
and realized that it was his own. The beasts were at
the back and flank of the Knights. The Knights of the
Roundear—*his* men! They weren't touching the
Queen's army, just his.

That explained how the dragons had come. Zatanas, the Queen's evil magician father, had summoned
them, just as he had for the first battle.

He looked at the gauntlets he had taken from Kian.
Were they really invincible? How could they defeat
that many dragons? Yet the monsters had to be
stopped. They had to be, or all was lost! He drew them
both on, and they made his hands tingle with their
special animation.

Kelvin looked at his father. John Knight was adjust-
ing knobs on the otherworld weapons. He lifted one of
them, aimed it like a crossbow, and pressed a trigger.

The red beam speared out. It jumped instantly to a
dragon, whose head was lifted high, golden scales
reflecting bright in the sun. The dragon was munching
a mangled red thing that had surely been someone
Kelvin had known and joked with. Blood was oozing
down from the morsel between the sword teeth,
dripping down from the dragon's golden chin, splat-
tering across its golden breast. Dragon's gold
—drenched in blood. There was a symbol of the
Queen's rule!

But as the beam struck, the dragon's head disappeared in a puff of smoke and steam and dissipating
vapor, leaving only a neck attached to a body. The
body and neck settled downward as the tail lashed;
the tail had not yet realized that the monster was
dead.

"One," John Knight said.

Both Kelvin and the King simply stared. No wonder roundear magic was legendary!

The man aimed his weapon again. The beam lanced through another dragon, burning into the great body, the scales reflecting a coruscating splay of light before the heat penetrated to the vital heart and the creature collapsed.

"Two." Then, in rapid succession, "Three. Four. Five. Six."

Kelvin wanted to scream. Those beautiful, terrible dragons! They would never have come here on their own; they normally left men alone unless men braved their wilderness fastness. The evil magician had used the lizard magic Heln had described to compel them to come, and now they were dying. One after the other, the red beam caught their raised heads or exposed breasts. One, larger than the others, retained part of a ruined head with a wide hole through it where the nostrils and eyes had been. One, caught lower down, simply collapsed with a great smoking, bubbling hole in its throat. They all were going down!

"Seven," John counted. "Eight. Nine. That will even the odds. Now if number ten will get into position so I don't have to risk hitting a horse . . ."

"I wouldn't have believed it possible," King Rufurt said. He was gasping for air, his chest still heaving from the run up the balcony steps.

Kelvin saw the magician before the rest of them. He appeared on the balcony with them, and his face was a study in fury and disbelief.

"My dragons! My lovely dragons! You're frustrating my dragons!"

John turned from the balcony edge, the offworld weapon still in his hand. He looked surprised to see the magician. Then, his face singularly grim, he raised the weapon.

At the same time, Zatanas raised his arms. He made a gesture and spoke a spell.

The red beam came from the weapon, stopped just before reaching its target, and made a bend. The beam went up into the sky and vanished. The magician stood there, unharmed. From a doorway behind him the hunchbacked dwarf emerged.

"What?" John said, amazed. He looked down at his weapon.

Zatanas pointed a finger. John Knight froze in the act of checking his laser pistol. He stood as still as a statue, seemingly locked in place.

King Rufurt moved. "Your evil sorcery—" he began.

The magician's finger moved again. King Rufurt froze in place, his mouth still open in speech.

This was potent magic! Kelvin knew that it was up to him to deal with the sorcerer. He raised his arms.

Once more Zatanas' finger moved. Kelvin felt a new tingle in all his body except his two hands, enclosed by the gauntlets. He could not move even an eyelid. He was off-balance, but his body did not fall. Only the gauntlets retained the power of action. But they held no weapon, and the magician and the dwarf were several horse lengths away, their backs to the balcony stairs. Despite the magic of the prophecy, Kelvin was helpless.

Suddenly a small white object struck the magician's pointed hat and head. Zatanas stumbled over to the railing, eyes unfocused, reaching a hand to the back of his skull. The pointed cap fell from his head, flipped over the railing, and dropped.

The dwarf ran to the magician and stopped him from falling too, bolstering him with outstretched arms. "Master! Master! What is it, Master?"

Behind the two, Kelvin saw a small figure drop out of sight on the stairs. Could it be? Had she come too? Suddenly Kelvin understood why Kian had gone out of control!

A great hissing sound came from below. A gigantic dragon reared its golden-scaled head up over the railing. Red eyes focused on the nearest human beings. Its mouth opened, gaping awesomely, and its long, forked tongue flicked out.

The dwarf screamed shrilly as the dragon's tongue yanked servant and master over the edge.

Kelvin found that he could move now, and he saw at a glance that his father and the King were similarly free. The sorcerer's spell had been broken by Jon's rock.

Without a thought for the danger of his action, Kelvin rushed to the railing, which was still dripping with dragon saliva, and looked down over the edge. The dwarf's shrill scream seemed to hang in the air long after it was uttered. Below were the mashed hedges and fences and men, and only the tail of the dragon as it ran around to the palace's east side.

It was John Knight who brought Kelvin's attention back to the balcony. The man's hand was on his shoulder, and the other hand pointed the offworld weapon at the golden tail. But no destructive beam emerged; it was pointless to make a strike that would merely wound, not kill.

"Father, I—" But Kelvin faltered. Could he tell John Knight about Jon? If the man learned about her sling, he would know what had happened to Kian. How would he react to that? What would he, Kelvin, do if that dread alien weapon were to point at his little sister?

"Damn," said his father. "A second earlier and I could have had him! But he did us a favor, that dragon did. Somehow he broke through the force field that held us. I don't understand magic, but I do recognize a force. A force field by any other name—"

"Kel! Kel! Kel!" Jon was running across the balcony. The sling was in her hands. Would John Knight see it and raise that terrible weapon now? If he did, could Kelvin or his gauntlets stop him?

The weapon did not come up. Jon ran right past John Knight and flung herself into Kelvin's arms. "Kel, Kel, I knew you'd come through alive! I knew it!"

"We haven't won yet," Kelvin reminded her. "There's still the battle. And the dragons."

"Speaking of dragons," John Knight said, still searching for one.

"How did you get here, Jon?" Kelvin asked, hoping to divert attention from the sling.

"The river," she said. "And a little help from some friends afterward. Brother mine, did you see that old magician reel when I conked him? I saved your lives, that's what I did!"

That did it! But John Knight merely turned to her and said, "I don't think you recognize me, just as I didn't recognize you at first. You have grown, and I think undergone a metamorphosis."

"A what?" Jon asked blankly.

"You were a girl when I last knew you."

She turned to Kelvin. "Who—?"

"I am John Knight," their father said. "You were named after me."

Her mouth dropped open. "But—"

"He didn't die," Kelvin said. "He was captured by the Queen. I found him in the dungeon."

"You were only two years old when I left," John Knight said.

"You have round ears!" she exclaimed abruptly.

He laughed. "Yours are like your mother's."

"So you must really be my—"

A hiss like that of escaping steam put all of their attention on the dragon peering over the balcony. The beast was looking at them, seemingly trying to decide which one to consume first.

"You use the laser like this, Kelvin," John Knight said. "Sight here, the same as a crossbow, squeeze this trigger, and—"

The bright red beam caught the dragon in its mouth and bore on through. As the beam vanished, so did most of the dragon's head. The rest of the beast collapsed into a golden pile on the palace's lawn.

"You really must learn to use this," John Knight said. "Ordinarily I'd say no, but now's the time, and if you don't finish off dragons before they finish your Knights, what's left for this land?"

Kelvin didn't know. He was astonished that his father was carefully placing the weapon in his hands.

"There's one! Watch until its head isn't in line with a Knight, then aim and press the trigger."

Kelvin shook, but his gauntleted hands were steady. He raised the weapon and squinted through the aperture, which, indeed, was not unlike a sight on a crossbow. The gauntlets animated his hands, making his aim confident.

He followed the dragon's head. He focused the cross so that it was between the creature's eyes. Then, firmly, of its own volition, his gauntlet pressed the trigger.

The dragon's head disappeared, exactly as the others had done.

"Good shot, Kel!" his sister exclaimed.

"You've got the warrior's eye and nerves," said his father. "Now I want you to get any others that are destroying your men. It's your responsibility, from now on."

"But—"

"You three go stop the dragons. I think we've gotten most of them, but we want to be sure. Tell the men the fighting's over. And, son, give me your word that when all of this is over, you'll destroy the laser. Get rid of it, as you get rid of dragons that destroy the people and the land."

"But the dragons don't really do that!" Kelvin protested. "They stay in dragon country, mostly. It's only when the evil sorcerer makes them come that they—"

John Knight smiled. "A conservationist! You, the dragon slayer!"

"But the dragons themselves aren't evil! They cultivate magic berries that—"

"I'll watch out with this other laser while you go out front. Your men will rally round you when they see it's you and the King. Kill any guardsmen who refuse to surrender. Only remember, it isn't good to kill helpless men."

"I'll remember," Kelvin said. It was evident that his natural father still didn't really believe in magic.

CHAPTER 27
Blood Sorcery

HELN REVIVED, AND FOUND her mother waiting anxiously. "I saw them!" she exclaimed. "All getting ready for battle, and Kelvin escaping, and Jon, and dragons—"

"I'm so glad you're safe!" her mother exclaimed. "I was so concerned—"

"But they don't know about the dragons!" Heln cried. "Those dragons will destroy them! I must warn them!"

Her mother shook her head. "There is no way, my child. We are too far from the palace."

"I know, I know!" Heln said impatiently. "But if I don't warn them, they'll die! Kelvin, and Jon, and all the brave Knights! And if they die, I will too!"

Her mother only shook her head sympathetically.

"The astral separation!" Heln exclaimed. "That's the only way I can reach them instantly! I've got to go back, find some way to warn them!"

"But you said you can't speak to anyone in your astral state!"

"I can't, but I've *got* to, this time! I've just got to! Otherwise everything is over, for all of us!"

"But isn't it dangerous? You said you had to rest between—"

"I ate three berries the first time!" Heln said, suddenly impatient with caution. "They separated me for longer, and it took me longer to recover, but I *did* recover."

"Still—"

"Mother, *I've got to help!*"

Her mother spread her hands, knowing better than to argue further. Heln took another berry, and soon sank back into her deathlike state.

241

It was different, this time, because she had not yet properly recovered from the prior berry. It was as if her body was eager to give up the spirit, and the spirit eager to be free. She seemed to leap out of herself, finding herself spinning in the air above the house. Then she willed herself to the capital, and she was there, looking down on the palace grounds.

The battle was in full swing. Men in brownberry shirts were fighting the blue and gold guardsmen, and the Knights seemed to be having the best of it, perhaps because of the element of surprise.

Then the dragons came, and tore into the Knights of the Roundear. Heln screamed inaudibly as she saw people she knew getting crunched in those terrible golden jaws. She had to stop it—but she was helpless. She was only tormenting herself by watching this!

She sought Kelvin. Somehow she had to find a way to communicate with him, to tell him—what? That there were dragons attacking? He surely knew it already! What could she do, even if she could talk to him? She had been foolish to think she could make any difference, regardless!

But she was here now, and she had about an hour to use up. She could look around, and maybe she would learn something useful. At least she would have a better notion how the battle was going.

She found Kelvin on a balcony. He was talking with one of the older men who had been in the dungeon with him. As she came close, one of the men pointed an object at a dragon. Red light appeared, and the dragon's head puffed into smoke.

That was a weapon! A powerful roundear magic weapon, for the man had round ears! Kelvin had found a marvelous ally! But—round ears? Who could that man be?

The man aimed at another dragon, and killed it. Then, in rapid succession, several more. Heln almost felt sorry for the monsters!

Then the Queen's sorcerer, Zatanas, appeared on the balcony, with his dwarf henchman. He pointed at

Kelvin and the men, and they froze where they were. The evil magician was overcoming them with his magic!

Heln went into a frenzy. *Stop Zatanas!* she screamed with all her being. *Go there, stop him, now!*

Huh? something responded.

Heln paused in mid-frenzy. Someone had heard her! Someone had answered! She oriented on that response, her spirit jumping instantly to that spot.

She paused, amazed. It was a dragon!

You heard me? she called to it, hardly believing.

The dragon's head whipped about, and its ears perked forward, as if it were trying to locate the speaker. It *did* hear her!

Actually, it made sense. She was using dragonberries for astral separation, and this was a dragon. If these monsters ate the berries, and used them for astral separation, they must have some sensitivity to the astral state. Maybe they could communicate with each other's spirits. So this one heard her, but because she wasn't another dragon, it was confused.

Well, she could certainly use this discovery. "Trouble by the balcony!" she cried, knowing that it was her thought, not her voice, it heard. "Go stop Zatanas!" She wasn't sure how much of this the dragon could understand, but the urgency of direction and action should be clear enough.

The dragon turned and lumbered for the balcony.

Heln jumped there ahead of it. This time she spied Jon Hackleberry approaching the balcony. Jon saw Zatanas, and brought out her sling, and heaved a stone. Her aim was true, and the evil sorcerer reeled from a strike on the head. So Jon was succeeding in helping her brother! Maybe Heln's effort had been unnecessary.

The dragon reared below the balcony, lifting its golden head. Its tongue whipped out and wrapped about the magician and the dwarf, pulling both over the edge. It ran off with its prey as the frozen men recovered. Maybe she had helped after all!

Now Jon ran up. There was a flurry of introductions—and, listening, Heln suddenly realized what should have been obvious before. The grown roundear was Kel and Jon's father! The round-ear from the other planet! No wonder he knew the roundear magic!

The man was showing Kelvin how to use the terrible dragon-slaying weapon. Then another dragon appeared at the balcony; perhaps it, too, had responded to her directive to the first one. She didn't know how broadly her thoughts were broadcast, or how sensitive the monsters were to them.

John Knight killed the dragon with the roundear weapon. Then he put the weapon in Kelvin's shaking hands and told him to use it on the next dragon. It was obvious that Kelvin was in no state to accomplish this; he seemed to be as much afraid of the weapon as of the dragons. Poor, dear, uncertain Kel! How she loved him!

"Hold it steady, Kel!" she cried, knowing he could not hear.

But *something* heard! She felt a quiver of response. Then Kelvin's hands became rock-steady. When he sighted another dragon, his aim was perfect, and he killed it.

What had responded to her this time? It hadn't been a dragon! Heln spread her awareness out, searching. She had to know exactly what her astral self could communicate with; it might make a big difference!

She didn't find what she wanted, but she did find a surprise. She was at the dragon she had first brought to the balcony—and it hadn't eaten the magician and the dwarf! It had brought the two to a hidden spot. Was it going to eat them now? She paused and listened, absorbing the scene.

Queeto dropped down from the slippery tongue and lit feet-first in a cluster of thornbushes. He seemed hardly aware of the smart of the scratches or of his torn tunic as he watched the sorcerer.

Casually, Zatanas was uncoiling the dragon's dark

purple tongue from around his own waist. He seemed quite oblivious to the golden-scaled face overhanging him, puffing forth moist, rancid dragon breath.

"It w-won't harm us, will it, Master?" Queeto asked. He looked as though he had never been more frightened.

"It won't hurt *me*," the sorcerer said, his voice carrying the strong conviction of the magic-protected. "Not my little brother."

"A spell protects us both, Master?"

"The dragon does my bidding." The sorcerer rubbed the back of his head where a red lump was showing. "Good thing it happened to be in the vicinity when I got struck; I hadn't summoned it."

Heln was mortified. Her effort had *helped* the evil magician? By bringing a dragon who carried him away to safety, when he would otherwise have been killed by the roundears? She should have left well enough alone!

The magician glanced about. "Let's go around to the courtyard and the three flights of stairs to our quarters," he said. "We've plans to make."

Plans? Heln knew she had to keep listening!

"But, Master, the dragon—"

"Ah, yes, the dragon," Zatanas agreed. He faced the monster. "You may go to eat more Knights. But not back to the balcony. Stay away from there."

As though it understood, the great beast drew in its tongue. Without a backward glance it strolled off across the grounds, knocking over statuary, crushing ornamental plants, hedges, and whatever it chanced to tread upon. Its great tail swished twice, and then it was doing the wriggle-run that in its small brother the lizard was so comical. It raced through the orchard, knocking aside bushes and splintering trees. Then, having reached the high wall, it stretched up, hooked its talons at the top, and pulled itself over. It perched there like a great, ungainly bird, then dropped out of sight.

Queeto sighed, evidently now feeling his scratches.

A dragon was a sight to behold, and few men ever beheld them so close and lived to speak of it. Heln was impressed, too; Zatanas really did have power! He was now doubly dangerous, because Kelvin and his father thought the evil sorcerer was dead, and were no longer on guard against him.

"Come!" the magician said.

Meekly, Queeto followed him. The dwarf licked his lips, as though the sour taste of fear had been replaced by the eager, peppery feel of anticipation. Nothing seemed to be able to destroy Zatanas, or even hurt him, not even the most powerful beast alive. Whatever evil he planned was surely a horror Heln had to spy out!

"Hurry!" Zatanas snapped. "You waddle so slow!"

They had come now into the courtyard at the back of the palace where all the trade goods were normally brought: the special foods and furnishings and supplies.

Queeto was muttering, talking to himself as he scurried to catch up. "From here that roundear boy tried to fly. Dangerous, having the roundear man teach the roundear son to do that. I knew that, I could have told them, but the Queen wanted it for some fool reason. I wanted to watch, but the Master had business, bringing dragons here to once and for all devour the Roundear and the Roundear's Knights. I could have told them that was even more dangerous, but did anybody want my opinion? No, nobody listens to Queeto!"

"Get moving!" Zatanas called back irritably.

"Only something happened that Master hadn't anticipated," the dwarf continued to himself, evidently getting some satisfaction from the narration. "The flying roundear boy fell, and the roundear man got the roundear weapons. I could have told them that something like that would happen! That lightning-hurler stick—look what it did to the dragons! Master had to stop that! But then he got conked on the head by a stone from nowhere—"

"Stop that muttering!" Zatanas exclaimed. "You drive me crazy with your nothing-comments!"

Queeto shut up, and followed the sorcerer up the three flights of stairs. By this time he was puffing too hard to mutter anyway. But Heln had learned some interesting things. She had seen the flying man, going right toward Jon, but had had to return to her body too soon. Now she knew that the man had fallen. Knowing how apt Jon was with her sling, Heln could piece together what had happened. Jon was making her presence count!

The stairs at the back of the palace led up to the sorcerer's quarters. Heln saw that three other flights ran down from those quarters to a secret anteroom adjoining the Queen's throne room. The sorcerer was really set up for spying!

"Hate these stairs!" Queeto wheezed briefly as his short legs carried him to the top. He sounded almost like the choking breath of the dragon that had carried them. He surely would have preferred to have the dragon carry them all the way here, if he hadn't been so afraid it was about to eat them!

An owlhawk greeted them with a squawk. Its huge yellow eyes looked for food, its talons pulling at first one and then the other leather thong that bound it to its perch.

Zatanas went straight to a dusty old book. He opened it, scanned its yellowed pages, then set it aside. He took a pinch of powder, tossed it in the air, and said, "Abidda bebop teevee a zee hop." At least, that was what it sounded like to Heln.

Smoke puffed as yellow grains of powder settled. A picture formed as the sorcerer held his arm out toward it and furrowed his uncapped forehead.

In the picture were Queeto and Zatanas, as well as the three others. It was the way things had been on the balcony, but now the view was from a spot that took in the balcony and part of the stairs.

On the top stair a small figure twirled a sling and sent a stone flying at the imaged magician's head.

The stone struck. The sorcerer staggered. Queeto helped him. The dragon came. The long tongue snaked out. It wrapped itself around the magician's waist, then Queeto's. They went over the side of the balcony. Heln was amazed at the accuracy of this vision; it showed exactly what had happened! Jon was quite recognizable as she ran up to join the others.

"Master! Master!" Queeto cried. "It's her! It's the girl I bid upon! The virgin girl the brigands took from me! The Roundear's sister, Master!"

"Yes," Zatanas said calmly. "I thought it might be. The fool came to help her brother."

"Will you bleed her, Master? Will you bleed all her blood out and skin her alive while she screams with horror and shrieks with agony?"

The magician's hand reached down to pat the bald spot on Queeto's head. *"We* will bleed them, little brother. I will put the silver needle into the virgin's arm, and you will catch the blood as it drips, drop by tasty drop, into the golden urn."

"Oh, Master!" Queeto said, licking his lips. "That makes me so happy!"

It hardly made Heln happy! This was worse than she had feared. They planned to capture Jon and take her blood!

"And at the same time we will bleed the other," Zatanas continued. "Not of his blood, but of his strength. As the sister weakens, so will the brother. So, too, may the roundear father."

"Like the lizards and the dragons, Master?"

The clawlike hand patted his head again. "Exactly like the lizards and the dragons, Queeto. This is the nature of sympathetic magic, of blood sorcery. It is the way I brought the roundears from Throod to Rud to help my daughter secure her throne, a generation ago. Stick-figure men, but the real ones had to follow, because the stick figures had round ears. Only it will not be dragon appetite the Roundear feels, but weakness, and then much, much pain, until finally, at long last, we allow him death. He cannot escape it, for it will stem from his blood sibling, whom we shall control absolutely. His gauntlets will not avail him then, and neither will the roundear weapons."

"Oh, Master! I wish we could make it last forever!"

"We will try, little friend. We certainly will try."

Abruptly, Zatanas returned to his book and began turning pages.

Heln, appalled, drifted from the chamber. She had to warn Kelvin of the threat to his sister, and to himself! But how could she? Not through the dragons, certainly!

She returned to Kelvin. He was now on the field, holding the roundear weapon, looking for dragons to slay. Jon was with him, but Heln was sure that the evil sorcerer was devising some way to abduct her. Kelvin's gauntlets would protect him, but Jon had no such security. They had to be warned!

But how? Heln's time was ending; soon she would be drawn back to her body, and she knew that it would not be safe to take a third berry. The second one had worked too well, sending her out too strongly; a third might vault her out so far she would never return. She had to do what she had to do now.

What about that response she had felt before, the one she had been trying to identify, when she found the dragon and Zatanas instead? It had been near Kelvin, but it hadn't been Kelvin himself.

"Where are you?" she cried desperately. "Answer me!"

She felt the response! It was near Kelvin again. She jumped over to it, and found herself hovering right in front of him, as if he were holding her with his gauntlets.

The gauntlets . . .

"Is that you, gauntlets?" she asked. "Do you hear me?"

She received the feeling of agreement. Was she imagining it? It was so hard to tell! At least the dragons could move in the direction she sent them, so she could tell by their actions. But these gloves—

"Left gauntlet, *lift!*" she exclaimed.

Kelvin's left arm came up, as though he were waving. He looked startled.

She could do it! She could command the gauntlets! It must be because she was another roundear, and they were attuned to roundears. That was why only roundears could use them; back at the camp, Kelvin had tried lending his left gauntlet to other men, but their hands had been rent by pain when they tried to don it. The gloves accepted *only* roundears.

But now she felt the first slow tug of her faraway body. She was about to leave; she had only a few seconds left. There was no time to try to make the gauntlets signal in air or write a note; what could she do?

The second tug came, drawing her away. "Zatanas' lair!" she screamed. "Gauntlets, Jon will be in Zatanas' lair! Take Kelvin there, when—"

But now the third pull was drawing her back, and she could say no more. How she hoped the gloves understood! If they could somehow guide Kelvin, so that he could save his sister before her demise brought them both low. . . .

CHAPTER 28
Sympathetic Magic

JON TIGHTENED HER GRIP on her sling as the horseman approached, but it was one of the Knights. The swirling dust had made it uncertain until the beast and its rider had drawn quite close.

"Gods!" Les Crumb exclaimed, recognizing them at the last second. "It's the Roundear! And Jon! And—"

"And your rightful King!" exclaimed Greenleaf as he strode on foot with bared and bloody sword. His dead horse lay next to the wall surrounding the palace grounds, as did half a dozen dead guardsmen.

"Then—" Lester began.

Kelvin raised the laser. "We've won!" he shouted. "With this weapon I can slay any dragon, any guardsman!"

"Hold up," Mor protested. "I haven't figured out what Jon is doing here, let alone all the rest. I sent the girls home—"

Through the dust rode a guardsman with raised sword, ready to chop. He was almost upon a startled Greenleaf before Kelvin acted. The red beam reached out, took away part of the Queen's wall and the man's sword and sword arm. The guardsman screamed as his horse barely missed running down Greenleaf.

They waited until the horse and one-armed rider had vanished in the swirling dust. Then Lester reached down and grabbed Kelvin's arm. "Come, Kelvin! There's dragons and foe to be slain!"

"But—" said Jon.

"You, girl, and you, Your Majesty," Mor said, "you should be safe here. See to it, Greenleaf, and—" He

251

paused as another figure loomed from the dust, but this one wore their colors. "We'll be back. See that these two are kept safe until we end the fighting."

Then he and Kelvin were away in the dust, leaving Jon and King Rufurt and the few Knights who had appeared.

Jon wanted to swear. Here she was, the hero who had helped destroy the magician and his apprentice, and helped save Kelvin and John Knight *and* the King. Here she was, being treated like a child or, worse, a girl who had to be protected.

"It shouldn't take long," King Rufurt said. "The guardsmen won't want to fight magic, and the dragons will either have to retreat back to dragon country or be slain. We've all but won!"

Jon knew the King was right. That was, after all, what Kelvin's father had said, and who, after all, would know better? Still, there was an awful lot of noise, and a lot of fighting remaining. She wished she could be at Kelvin's side, or at least somewhere where she could watch Kelvin. If only Kelvin had given *her* a fancy weapon! But such a thought, she knew, had never occurred to him.

Dust was so thick that it was hard to see even the nearer Knights, though so far she had recognized every one who came up. She wiped at her tearing eyes and drippy nose, hating the dust. Battle dust took the glory right out of it! That, and all the gore. Maybe it would be better just to be a girl, and leave the mess to the men. She had never actually fought in battle with a sword.

Jon felt a man's hand on her shoulder. Looking up, she saw a Knight on a horse. How had he come so close without her being aware of him? It was not one she recognized.

"Want up on the horse?" the man asked.

Why not? Maybe she would get to fight after all. Just so she could say she had done it, when this was over.

She threw her leg up as the man hauled on her. In half a breath she was astride the big war-horse. This reminded her of the time she had been on a black stallion with another man's big arm around her.

Another man?

She twisted to look in shock into the dark face, seeing the scar under grime, the gleam in the man's eyes. That could mean only one thing. The man was an enemy, and one she recognized!

"Che—" she started to say.

Cold steel touched her throat. "Shut up, or I'll decapitate you right here and throw your head to your friends. Keep your mouth shut, don't struggle, and you'll live to be of some use. *My* use."

It was humiliating and scary, but what could she do but keep silent? One little squeak on her part, and she felt certain the highwayman would do what he threatened. How had the bandit gotten here, and dressed like a Knight? Had he learned that she was not the boy he had sold to the Boy Mart? Of course she couldn't ask! All she could do was keep her mouth shut and try to stay alive.

Jon felt the horse leap forward, and then King Rufurt and the Knight guarding him were behind and there was dust swirling all around. An open section of wall loomed ahead. With a single tremendous leap the war-horse cleared the rubble. Behind them were shouts and the sounds of another horse.

The man holding her swung around. He slashed quickly at their pursuer, and then as the man drew close, he stabbed.

Greenleaf fell soundlessly from his horse, pierced through the heart. Jon stifled a cry; if only she had thought to jog the bandit's arm or something, she might have saved the Knight! She was a helpless female after all.

The palace's walls loomed. Then they were behind the palace, in the courtyard, the horse halting in response to the quick pull on its reins.

"Down!" Cheeky Jack ordered. "Slowly."

Jon moved slowly, the sword at her throat.

Her captor swung down, dropped the reins, and

slapped the war-horse's flank. Jon saw with astonishment that the beast raced into the orchard where
broken branches and downed trees suggested a dragon
had been. As it neared the first trees, the horse started
to change. It seemed to grow in size. It developed a
lizard's tail and a snout. It was turning into a dragon!

Jon shook her head, hardly believing what she had
seen. Had she really just ridden a dragon? She
couldn't have! Yet now a dragon was scrambling over
the orchard wall.

The highwayman laughed, and it was a cackle. As
she looked, startled, at Cheeky Jack's face, it seemed
to melt and flow. The scar vanished. The hair changed
from black to dark gray. The nose elongated. The chin
became sharp and protruding.

In a moment it was the evil sorcerer who stood
there.

Had she realized his true identity, she would have
screamed warning at the outset, no matter what! But
she had been sure he was dead! How could he have
survived the attack by the dragon?

The dragon. But the magician could tame dragons!
That was how he had survived!

"Wh—what are you going to do with me?" Jon
asked. Then she remembered to add "Zatanas," so as
not to aggravate him further. If he merely kept her
prisoner for a time, hoping to use her to bargain for
his life when the Knights won—

Again the cackly laugh. "I shall use you, of course,
in my magic. I shall use your blood and your skin and
your bones and your eyeballs and your stupid little
soul. I shall use you to gain, once and for all, full
control over this, my rightful land."

Jon shuddered. She felt certain that whatever else
the black magician might be, he was as powerful as he
was insane.

Regretfully, Kelvin sighted the laser at the charging
dragon. His gauntlet steadied his aim, and squeezed

the trigger. The red beam went out like the finger of a deadly lightning god.

The dragon collapsed in a golden pile, its head mostly disintegrated.

Kelvin felt real regret, and he hoped this was the last such killing he would have to perform. They had now ridden down three dragons. The real hero was the pair of gauntlets, which made his aim perfect. But he wished the dragons had fled back to dragon country, so that no more had had to be destroyed. There was a lot of dragon's gold on the battlefield, and some Knights were already hacking away at the precious scales, taking their spoils, but how much better it would have been to leave the dragons alone in their own haunts!

Kelvin squirmed in the saddle. It was a nice war-horse, and nice accouterments. The Crumbs had captured it for him. But all he really wanted was for the fighting and killing to stop. The guardsmen hadn't a chance against him, and once the word got out, they would realize it. How many guardsmen had charged him and been slain? How many had seen him destroy dragons, and had ridden to spread the news? Round-ear magic was indeed the key to victory!

"I think," Kelvin said, "that I weary of the fight." That was a dragon-sized understatement!

Lester frowned. His father, some distance away, had not heard, and therefore did not bellow his customary protest. "You want to go back to Jon and the King? Until this is over with?"

Kelvin nodded.

"All right. I'll cover for you. I'll get Father away from here, and when we're out of sight, you go back."

Kelvin appreciated Les's help. The elder Crumb had become so obsessed with the fighting that he seemed not to want to stop. Not that Mor killed guardsmen who weren't trying to kill him, but he didn't avoid meeting them either. For Kelvin to drop out of the fighting before the guardsmen had accepted defeat must be barely understandable to Les, and not at all comprehensible to Mor.

Already, Kelvin felt guilty. "But maybe I should—"

"No, I understand," Les said. "I get pretty sick of it myself. I almost got taken out at Skagmore, you know. Father dragged me back unconscious, and your sister nursed me back to consciousness. She's some little woman, when she wants to be."

Kelvin laughed shortly. "But she doesn't want to be! That's the problem."

Les shrugged. He shaded his eyes with a hand. "Over there!" he called suddenly. "Behind those trees! Someone in a guardsman's uniform!"

"Let's get him!" Morvin cried, wheeling his horse around. The Crumbs raced for the trees at full gallop. There was a cry of dismay from the trees; evidently the guardsman had hoped to remain undiscovered. Kelvin could understand that.

As he watched them, he felt a tingle in his gauntlets —both hands. Usually this meant danger, but now there was no danger. Once, his left gauntlet had lifted of its own accord when there was no enemy to fend off. Now the tingle was back, with no visible threat.

Kelvin locked the safety mechanism on his laser the way his father had done, and holstered it. It still didn't feel comfortable hanging from his waist.

The Crumbs disappeared among the trees. Was the tingle for them—a danger they faced?

As though in answer, the gauntlets grew warm. He felt them tug at the horse's reins. They were up to something, and he could not afford to assume they were mistaken. They often seemed to know best.

As the horse turned, the right gauntlet slapped its flank. The steed leaped forward, and proceeded to a full gallop away from the trees and the Crumbs.

He was going back to join Jon and King Rufurt —but the gauntlets were doing it, not himself. Were they tired of battle, too?

Then the gauntlets turned the horse again. An opening appeared in the wall, and they were racing for it.

Kelvin barely remembered to flatten himself and nudge the horse with his knees before the leap. Then they were over, on the palace grounds. Broken hedges and flowers and a tipped-over statue showed where another beast had run. A war-horse, or a dragon? Where were the gauntlets taking him, and why?

A man lay dead on the ripped-up lawn. As they raced by, Kelvin recognized the dead one as Greenleaf. How had he come to be here? Whom had he been chasing, and who had slain him? But the gauntlets did not slow the horse.

They were at the side of the palace now, approaching the rear and the courtyard. He recognized the side of the balcony and its stairs. The balcony was now empty, and there seemed to be no living thing near the stairs.

The horse's hooves clattered on cobblestones. The gauntlets pulled the reins. Now they walked, to another flight of stairs. The gauntlets, almost uncomfortably hot now, urged him to dismount. They had never before shown so much will of their own!

Kelvin swung out of the saddle, left his steed to wander or wait as it wished, and raced up the stairs. He slowed his steps as he neared the top. He felt uncomfortably weak and light-headed—weaker than he had felt at any time except when he was sick. He must have gotten more tired than he thought! Maybe that drug they had given him to make him sleep so long had weakened him. He had been quite active recently, and maybe shouldn't have pushed his limits.

An owlhawk tethered on a skull flopped its wings and snapped its beak as he entered a darkened room thick with unusual and unidentifiable smells. What *was* this place?

For a moment he stood weakly swaying in the doorway as his eyes adjusted and his gauntlets all but burned his hands. Then he saw the magician and the dwarf. The two he had thought devoured by a dragon! And—

Shock struck him, even as the sorcerer made a puff of pink-colored smoke appear. "Jon!" Kelvin whispered. "Jon!"

For there was his sister, strapped to a table. She was very pale. A needle was in her arm, and her blood was dripping into a golden vessel held by the hunchbacked dwarf.

Kelvin had sworn to protect her—and look what had happened! They were bleeding her to death!

Zatanas was mumbling something, gesturing as he had on the balcony. Instantly Kelvin felt frozen, paralyzed by the power of magic. His natural father had tried to convince him that such magic did not exist, but on this matter John Knight had been horribly mistaken.

Kelvin remembered the laser weapon in its holster. If he could reach it—if the gauntlets . . .

The sorcerer made a gesture. Instantly the mystery weapon slid from its holster and floated in midair. The laser turned, steadied before Kelvin's nose, poised there briefly like a hummerfly, then retreated as suddenly to the magician's waiting hand.

"An interesting toy," Zatanas said, moving the laser to a vacant shelf and dropping it. "But against me, worthless. It's not true magic, you see. Not like mine."

Kelvin tried to speak. There was no sound from his lips. In his ears, steadily, was the drip, drip, drip of his sister's lifeblood.

"I really hadn't expected you to be fool enough to come here," the sorcerer continued. "That is why I devised a demise for you that would strike wherever you were, inescapably. But this is even better."

Kelvin still stood, feeling weaker and more hopeless every moment. Why couldn't he even try to fight this man?

"Let me explain for you one of the basic principles

of sympathetic magic," said Zatanas. "Like affects like. As your sister and you share a parentage, so you share a bond greater than that of strangers. As her blood leaves her and she weakens, you weaken, too. Slowly, slowly, over a good long time. It would be inartistic to rush it! Every stage must be properly savored. When we skin her, you will feel some of the agony. When we pluck out her eyes, your vision will weaken until you are blind. When we——"

But Kelvin had ceased to listen. He was thinking only of Jon and the gauntlets, and of the necessity, somehow, someway, to overcome this horror. Yet he remained powerless.

Drip, drip, drip, drip . . .

CHAPTER 29

Queen

JOHN KNIGHT ROAMED THE palace rooms, searching. He had not told the Knights (he found the name entertaining) what he intended to do, knowing that would only have diverted them from the necessary business of winning the battle. This was an aspect of it he just had to do himself.

He was looking for the Queen. His son and hers lay outside, perhaps receiving the medical attention he desperately needed, perhaps already beyond the power of any such help. The Queen was not directly responsible for Kian's situation, but she was certainly indirectly responsible, for she had set him up to fight the Knights, and that had brought him crashing down. It was ironic that it was Jon's daughter's slung stone that had done it, but it had had to be done, because once Kian mastered the flying harness and the laser pistols, he would have destroyed the Knights and ended the threat to the Queen's evil dominance. John had had deep reservations about showing Kian the proper use of these items, but with Kelvin in the Queen's power, he had had no choice. Now the weapons had changed sides, and he had his daughter to thank for that, and only hoped that this had not cost him Kian's life. His hatred for the Queen was built upon such matters as this: that she had set John Knight's children to fighting each other.

He wondered whether he was quite sane, to hate her so. Yet he knew that the Queen and her consort had to be destroyed. They had brought this fair and wondrous land almost to total ruin, and if allowed to live would wreak further evil. It was Zoanna's nature to bring destruction on others; that was why she herself had to be destroyed.

Yet he had thought he loved her, once. Certainly he had fallen under her spell for a time. Her body—

John Knight shook himself. He could not afford to be distracted by that! The woman he had more truly loved was Charlain, even though he had had to leave her. So now he would eliminate the Queen, and if he lost his own life in the process, well, that would leave Charlain's life less complicated. She had remarried, thinking him dead, and he could not fault her for that. She and her second husband had done a fine job with the children, both of them.

He entered another room, a ballroom where once he had danced with the Queen. Crystal chandeliers hung above, and along the walls were heroic life-size statuary of royal family members from ancient days, and the floors were polished inlaid rare woods. What happiness he had had here for a time, when he had supposed himself a kind of king! He had thought he had the love of a beautiful Queen!

He paused, searching with narrowed gaze, holding the laser ready, willing himself to hate her as he had hated her every day of his imprisonment. As he had hated her when she acceded to Flick's demand that Kian try to be the Roundear of prophecy. As he had hated her when she forced him to train Kian. As he had hated her when Kian fell.

His eyes rested momentarily on a doorway he didn't remember, and a shimmer there made him think "ghost." Then she was there in all her beauty, undimmed by twenty years, hair undone, dressed in the filmiest of nightgowns. She beckoned him, and his hate evaporated; it was impossible to oppose such a creature! He knew that magic, another aspect of that sorcery he had tried not to believe in, kept her eternally youthful in body, if not in mind. Suddenly it didn't seem to matter. Despite himself, he took a step forward.

The floor vanished beneath his feet.

He landed in a painful heap, the laser still in his hand. Something struck his wrist, and his fingers opened involuntarily. The laser clattered to the floor. Something struck him on the head, dizzying him.

"Go ahead, Peter, finish him!"

It was her voice. Hers! He blinked, seeing her now, trying to see the reality he knew was there.

She stood before a reflecting mirror that sent her image up to the mirror placed in the ballroom, and to this cellar, too. She was no ghost! She remained hidden, physically, while her image supervised the action here. The floor had not simply dematerialized; above him, in the ceiling, was the opened trapdoor.

It had been a simple trap. Mirror and trapdoor. Planned for him since he agreed to teach Kian? Or just here, waiting for its time of need? Waiting for John Knight to come seeking her? Waiting for the laser in his hand and his heart full of hate? The Queen was evil, but no fool. She had known he would one day attempt to take her life.

As his sight cleared, he saw Peter Flick standing over him. The Queen's cruel consort had the sword turned flat side toward him, ready for another swing.

"Finish him, Peter! Use the edge!"

Was that the woman he had loved? No, it was just the illusion, the reality of her as deceptive as the mirror image. Magic enhanced her, and always had. He had fought so hard against a belief in magic because he had wanted the illusion to be real. He had tried, even after his first imprisonment, to believe that it was real. That refusal to accept magic had even misled Kelvin, and now—

"I want him to suffer," Peter said.

"Fool!" she retorted. "That man is dangerous! Finish him!"

John Knight tried putting his hands out, to brace himself against the floor. The floor seemed to spin. Then there was agony, as Peter Flick trod heavily on his right hand. He felt Flick's full weight. He heard a snapping sound, and knew that his trigger finger had broken.

"He can live a long time yet," Flick said. "Just as long as I'm willing to let him. Let's keep him alive a while and enjoy him, love."

"Peter," Zoanna said icily, "remember who you are! *I* am the one to say, and I say kill him."

John Knight realized that because the Queen wasn't here physically, being present merely in mirror image, she had to act through her consort, and Flick was taking advantage of the situation. Evidently the man was too stupid to realize what that would cost him, the moment the Queen didn't need him anymore. He saw Flick's evil grin, and then he saw him pick up the laser.

"No! No!" John said. He was trying to play for time; he wasn't really that weak.

"Yes, yes," Flick taunted. "Yes, I will fix you with this. That's more appropriate, don't you think? To be slain by your own offworld weapon. Offworld magic, offworld science, as you call it—it's all the same to me."

"Peter, that's dangerous!" the Queen said.

Peter Flick examined the weapon, turning it over and over in his delicate fingers. His hands were more accustomed to the touch of fine linen and fragile art objects.

"You don't know how to use it!" the Queen said. "Remember what it did!"

"I'm remembering. I think I'll start with his legs."

John watched his enemy turn the laser until it pointed at his feet. He saw the grin he had come to know so well, and knew that Flick would take his time squeezing the trigger. More time than he needed.

He watched the finger start to tighten. He took a deep breath and kicked out. His heavily booted foot struck Peter's left kneecap.

Peter gasped and lost his balance. His arm came up. His finger tightened involuntarily.

The ruby beam cut halfway through the supporting

column at John's back. A chunk the diameter of a dragon's neck vanished. It left a hole between the column's base and the rest of it.

The column dropped, its end smoking. It twisted sideways and fell, breaking apart in segments.

But Flick was not paying attention. His finger still pressed the trigger, and the beam still shone. It raced on, cutting a trench through the overhead floor. Flick's right arm went all the way back as he fell.

The ceiling gave way with a crack louder than a pistol shot. Bits of statuary rained down. The floor sagged where a jagged, zigzag cut had been made. It shook, starting to collapse from the center.

It was coming down, John realized. The ballroom floor was crashing down on Peter Flick's head!

"The Queen was right," John said as he scrambled for the relative safety of an arch. "That thing is dangerous."

Then, with a crunch like that of a gigantic dragon's jaws, the ballroom floor gave way completely and crashed into the basement.

John Knight saw Peter Flick caught under the descending roof. The man had not had the wit to seek immediate shelter. Dust rose in choking clouds so thick that John could not see, and his ears felt as muffled as his eyes, and it was hard to breathe. He curled up, covering his ears as well as he could, closing his eyes, and putting his mouth against his shirt to inhale.

Finally, as the noise ceased to reverberate and only a great ache remained, he crawled through the settling dust to the region where Flick had disappeared. There was a large timber there now, with something sticky beneath it. The laser had stopped showing; evidently the weapon had been crushed, too. Well, he had planned to dispose of it anyway, in due course.

That left—

"Zoanna!" he called gently.

There was no answer. He strained his eyes to see in the dim light coming through a break from above.

The entire palace must have collapsed, or at least the main section. The wings, including the one where Zatanas had his quarters, might still be standing. The evil sorcerer had to be eliminated, too, for he was the power behind the Queen.

"Peter. Pe-ter." Her voice, very faint.

Damn her! So he would have to kill her after all! Why couldn't she have been crushed with Flick? John didn't have his laser now, or even a sword. He would have to kill her with his bare hands, and he wouldn't have liked that even if his right hand hadn't been crushed.

He felt his way over broken picture frames, torn canvases, chunks of statuary, and wads of drapes. He located her by the sound; she thought it was her consort coming.

He saw her left arm, pinned by part of a fallen column. Her mouth was wide now, as were her eyes, but there was no blood that he could see. She appeared to be hurt mainly by shock. This was the real Queen, the physical one; the mirrors had been broken.

"Peter," she said. "Peter, help me." It was her old voice, almost. The voice that had weakened him and hypnotized him. It was a voice as could work enchantment even without the help of magic.

He knew he should throttle her. But he couldn't do it one-handed.

"There's a passage," she said. "Trapdoor. River. Escape."

Did she know to whom she spoke? Did she even know where she was? Her eyes seemed to suggest no, but her words could be taken either way.

He hardly knew where he found the strength, but he worked until he pulled her arm free. She had been lucky; the full mass of the column had not come down on her. It had fallen across statuary that supported most of its weight. He only needed to excavate around her arm, making more room, to work it free.

The arm hung loosely from her shoulder. Certainly

it was damaged, but at least it was there. He got one of his own arms around her and helped her to stand, bending slightly because of the sagging ceiling here. Her body was light, and its contours sweet against him; how he wished that—

"Trapdoor. There. There," she said. Her good arm pointed to the far right corner of the room, and at a statue of a dead hero whose head was now detached and whose sword arm was broken. That seemed appropriate!

He half dragged, half carried her as he made his way step by step to the spot she indicated. When he got there he had to put her down and drag aside the statue. Then he had to pull back the rug with its fighting-dragons motif, to strain to lift the trapdoor by its iron ring.

When the trapdoor opened all the way, he gave out an involuntary groan and almost plummeted head foremost down the crumbling wooden and moss-grown stairs. The cool, moist air of an underground river came up to meet him. Of course—the capital was beside a river, and this would be a tributary.

He shook his head, fighting off the dizziness that assailed him. Somehow he got her to her feet again. Somehow he got started down the stairs. It seemed a long, long way down. Longer than he had ever climbed down before. He felt weaker and weaker by the second, as though his blood were leaving him. But his body was intact except for his broken hand; he wasn't bleeding.

"Raft. Raft," she said. "Hurry. Hurry."

He hardly knew what to answer, and didn't try; he needed all his remaining strength to do the job.

Step by step, downward, they went. Her thigh against his, her body close against him. She was a middle-aged woman now, and surely she had no magic enhancing her anymore, yet she was alluring in every aspect. He couldn't hurt her!

His feet slipped, and he stopped, steadying himself

with grim determination. Then he went on, step by slow step down, and she went with him.

At the bottom of the first flight there was a landing, then a second flight of stairs. John dragged them down. At the bottom of the second there was another landing and a third set of stairs. How deep *was* the stream? But finally they were there at a crumbling and moss-covered dock. There was an old raft tied here that appeared to have remained for an eternity.

He stopped, tottering, half collapsing on the dock. He felt the water lapping, lifting and lowering about him, and he knew he hadn't finished, but he was too exhausted to do any more.

Now she seemed to be supporting him, bearing him up, helping him onto the raft. His feet obeyed her, as once his whole body and mind had done. Now this foot, now that foot, and now he seemed to be on the raft with her and she seemed to be lifting a pole attached there by a rope, and she seemed to be poling them out into the current.

He struggled to sit up, to make sense of what was happening. He thought he heard a splash.

Pulling himself up to sitting position, he saw a string of silvery bubbles in the dark water behind the raft. Nothing else. He was alone.

He was too weary and disoriented to think or ponder anything. He couldn't even feel the pain in his hand.

The raft drifted. It passed between rock walls covered with eerily glowing moss that gave a strange green color to everything. The stream didn't seem to be flowing into the river that served the capital.

John Knight moved on to an unknown and perhaps unknowable destination.

CHAPTER 30
Recovery

KELVIN WATCHED THE BLOOD dripping into the golden urn, feeling, thanks to Zatanas' magic, that it was his own blood as well as his sister's. Jon, wide awake, unable to move because of the straps, whispered softly, "Kel, Kel, save me."

"Yes, why don't you save her, Kelvin Roundears?" Zatanas inquired. It was almost as though he expected an answer.

"He can't, Master," Queeto said, and swished the blood in its vessel, shaking all over as he croaked his laughter. "Not ever. Not him. He can't move, Master. And he's getting weaker. Weaker and weaker and weaker!"

Kelvin knew that the vicious dwarf was right. Queeto was having his revenge for the way they had taken Jon from him, after the sale at the Mart. There would be no mercy there. But if he willed the gauntlets to move, and if they did so, and brought along the rest of his body . . .

But there was little use. Zatanas had his laser on a shelf and he hadn't acquired a sword or even a dagger since leaving the palace balcony. There was little even the gauntlets could do as long as Queeto and Zatanas stayed out of reach. Only if he could reach them, he thought. Only if—

A great crashing, splintering noise came from below the floor. Clouds of dust rose in the room, books fell, glassware rattled. Something crashed over and made a foul stink.

The room shook violently. Almost as if a quake had come.

268

Queeto stumbled back, still on his feet but losing his balance. He pulled the golden vessel away from the tube in Jon's arm, splashing Jon's blood on himself. His hump seemed to pull him over, on his back, against Kelvin.

Instantly the gauntlets acted. Pulling Kelvin's unfeeling arms along, the gauntlets fastened on the dwarf's thick throat.

"Master! Master!" Queeto cried. His short, powerful arms reached back but couldn't stretch to the gauntlets and Kelvin's arms.

Kelvin willed strength to the gauntlets. Never before had he wanted to destroy any living thing as badly as he wanted to destroy this dwarf!

Queeto made a choking sound. His eyes bulged. It was magic strength squeezing the life out of him. But the gauntlets did not wait for him to suffocate; they crushed so hard that his neck collapsed, and he was dying.

Zatanas struggled up from the corner where he had been flung. His breath came in shallow, whispering drafts. His eyes bulged in sympathy with the dwarf's.

"Lit-tle bro-ther," he whispered. "Like links like. The spell I cast—it's affecting us!"

He choked, wheezed, and gasped horribly. On his feet, he rose unsteadily to his height. He began to raise a hand to gesture.

"Kel," Jon whispered. It wasn't much, but it distracted him for a moment. He had to save her!

Kelvin felt a bit of strength. He could move now! He concentrated, trying to aid the gauntlets in their grisly task. He put all his remaining strength into it—and the terrible fingers crushed in so hard that they pulped the tissues of the dwarf's neck, and Queeto was abruptly dead.

Zatanas tottered. Then, with no sound, no real warning, dwarf and master crumbled into unequal piles of dust. Only their clothing remained with the dust rising up from it and then settling down again.

Kelvin stepped on the dwarf's clothing and the dust as he fought to get to Jon. It was only his own weakness that slowed him now, instead of the sorcerer's magic, but that was enough. He struggled to her, almost falling, and clawed at the needle in her arm. He hauled on it, trying to pull it out; the gauntlets were clumsy for this.

He wrenched it out, and blood flowed across her arm. He reached down for the dwarf's sash and brought it up to make a tourniquet for her arm, but couldn't get it right, and still the blood flowed.

"Just untie me," she said. "I'll take care of my arm."

He put the gauntlets on the straps, and the gloves ripped the straps apart. Jon sat up unsteadily, and put her free hand on the wound, stanching the flow at last. Then she glanced at the floor, where the dust was. "Kel, what—?"

"Dust," he said. "Magic kept them alive, and now magic has destroyed them. The prophecy was right: 'And the gauntlet great, shall the tyrant take.' You remember those words, Jon?"

She raised her gaze. "Well, you saved me, Kel. But the Queen may still be lurking."

Kelvin picked up his father's weapon from the shelf. He made certain the safety was on, then placed it in the holster.

The room shook. More books hit the floor. More glassware trembled and fell. The odor got worse. The floor seemed to give a little. Below, something creaked and grumbled.

"The palace!" Kelvin said. "I think it's collapsing!"

The owlhawk fluttered. The poor creature was a victim, he thought, just as Jon had been.

He untied the leather thongs holding the bird to its grisly perch on a human skull. He watched it fly to the window overhead, then go through to its freedom.

He put his arm under Jon's shoulders and helped her sit up. His strength was returning, but hers was not. "I'm so tired, Kel," she said. "So very tired."

"Yes, I know." He had felt the power of the linkage, and knew exactly how tired she felt. He understood how the evil magician had died when the dwarf did; the magic transference was potent.

Jon pushed her legs over the side of the table. "We have to get out of here, Kel," she said faintly. "Before they—" She nodded at the dust. "Before they return to life."

"They won't return to life," Kelvin said. But he had seen and felt the power of Zatanas' magic; now he was no longer sure of its limit.

Jon rubbed at a cheek. "They won't, will they? Never again. You—you've killed them." Yet she, too, sounded uncertain.

"Say rather that the gauntlets killed them. Lean on my shoulder and I'll walk you out."

"I'm very weak, Kel."

"I know." *How well he knew!* "But you'll make it. We both will." He hoped. His confidence in things was only a shadow of what it had been, back before they went hunting for dragon's gold.

It seemed to take forever to cross the room and descend the stairs. In the courtyard, his superb war-horse waited for them, the only living creature remaining there.

Jon, recovering slightly, pulled herself up to the front of the saddle, while Kelvin sat behind her with the reins. It was good to be mounted again; this entire region made him nervous. Of course the evil sorcerer was permanently dead! Yet, somehow . . .

"Master! Master!"

"Courage, little brother apprentice. We will regain our bodies. Do as I do."

Dust motes drifted in the silent room. Slowly they settled downward. Heaps of dust began drifting together, eddying into larger and larger clumps.

More dust swirled, coming together. Slowly the particles attached to others of their kind. Bit by bit, a skeleton formed. A shape that was as yet nothing *but* form.

A lizard, escaped from its cage, raised its head, flared its hood, and scuttled for the corner.

With agonizing slowness, the skeleton assumed greater solidity. Other dust particles attached to it. A figure began to shape. It was a faceless mannequin, and then a faceless corpse. Tiny whirlwinds moved about the floor, sucking up dust that had once formed the sorcerer Zatanas.

"Master! Master!"

"Try, Queeto. It is your only chance."

Now other dust particles at the other side of the room began to move. Slowly, slowly they lifted, then swirled, then formed. "Master! Master! I'm doing it!"

"I knew you would. Apprentice like Master, always." The dust whirlpool swirled, moving hither and yon, questing for dust in obscure corners.

Slowly, ever so slowly, the two bodies formed.

"Will there be enough, Master? Will there be enough?"

"There will be. If not enough from us, then enough from other sources. Dust is dust."

"How much time, Master? How much time?"

"Enough. Work, Queeto, work!"

Now the body of Zatanas lay stark on the floor by a broken gold vessel and a slash of crimson. An opened book lay almost beneath the magician's form. Hair grew, fingernails, eyelashes. But the body did not breathe.

Queeto's hump was finished. His short legs and powerful forearms appeared as they had in life. The whirlwinds fed the form at an increasing pace.

"When can we enter, Master? When?"

"When the bodies are set. For now they are only forms. Mine is almost ready; yours is not."

The body of Queeto emerged from the dust. Organs, blood and bone, ugly, misshapen, monstrous, all dust. But the dust was being set by the solidifying action of agglutination. Magic was converting it to form. Soon it would be living flesh.

"I'm done, Master! I'm done! I'm whole!"

"Almost. There must be time for setting."

The owlhawk's shadow touched the window. Then it was inside the room, diving for a lizard on the floor.

The lizard ran into a pile of clothing. The owlhawk swooped, caught the lizard up in its talons, and carried it to its perch. It lit on the skull, opened its beak, and with one swift motion bit the lizard's head off.

"Master! Master!"

"It will go away. It must!"

The owlhawk devoured its repast. Another lizard crawled along the wall. The big bird flopped its wings, scattering dust, dislodging particles, making of two apparent corpses two apparently faceless mannequins. But it caught its prey.

"Master!"

"It will go away, Queeto. We can live again as long as there is our dust."

Again the owlhawk returned to its perch. Again it devoured its dripping repast, this time more slowly. Bits of lizard blood and lizard juices dripped from its opened beak.

"Master! Master!"

"When it has fed, it will sleep. Owlhawks sleep in the day."

The bird finished its second lizard, rotated its head, and stretched its wings.

"Master, it—"

A third lizard ran along a shelf of glass bottles and retorts. This was too much temptation. The owlhawk flew, talons extended. The wings stirred up dust in a swirling cloud. The talons touched the lizard, and needle claws sank into its greenish sides.

The blood dripped as the bird dropped, lizard clutched in its claws. As it dropped, its wingtips fanned and brushed bottles and glassware.

A beaker fell. A bottle tipped, rolled off the shelf, and burst explosively on the floor. Another bottle followed.

Fanned by the commotion, the dust figures collapsed inward on themselves.

Unperturbed, the owlhawk carried its prey to its longtime perch. Green flames shot from the broken bottle. They rose high, crackling, giving off smoke.

"Master! Master!"

"Fear not. If I live, I will bring you back. If not as Queeto, then as an object. A magical staff, or—"

"But, Master, I don't want to be a staff!"

"You will take what you will get! Cursed bird, I will enter you and—"

The bird lifted from its perch, dropping the mangled lizard in its wake. It rose to the highest shelf, its wings dislodging boxes and containers and bottles that fell and burst with hideous noise.

Now it was flying for the window, and outside.

"Master! Master!"

"Cursed bird, why didn't it wait?"

Now the room was filling with dancing green flame. The flame grew, devouring what it reached. Clothing charred and blackened. The owlhawk's perch burned, and so did the dust.

"Master, Master, I fade."

"Oh, the ignominy of it! Destroyed by a bird!"

*"Mas-ter. Mas-*t-er . . ."

The green flames licked up the walls, shot out of the windows, and then onto the roof.

Soon the crackling flames were being witnessed by nothing living, semi-living, or with any hope of living.

EPILOGUE

THEY GATHERED IN THE great tent that had been pitched on the Hackleberry farm, the temporary headquarters of the new government while the palace was being rebuilt. The Hackleberries and the Flambeaus had met, and liked each other, and were cooperating in the plans for Kelvin's marriage to Heln. King Rufurt had decreed that all back taxes on both farms were excused, in return for the services that members of these families had rendered in restoring the rightful government. The scales from the slain dragons had become part of the royal treasury, and were backing the new currency and paying for the rebuilding and all other obligations. A program of tax reform was being instituted, so that no longer would farmers be impoverished by taxes, and of course the Boy and Girl Marts were abolished.

Yet certain mysteries remained, and it was to investigate these that they were here. They had discovered, because of certain remarks made by Heln's mother, that a person who touched Heln while she was astrally separated could pick up some of what her spirit was doing. Indeed, it was possible to communicate with her when she knew that the person was there to hear; she could not see or hear the person when her spirit was elsewhere, but she could send her thoughts to that person through her unconscious body. They had tried it experimentally, Kelvin lying beside her and holding her hand while she separated, and he had received an ongoing narration of her experiences.

After the palace had burned down, workers going through the wreckage, preparing the site for the new palace, had discovered flights of stairs descending to a nether dock, where a subterranean river passed. There were signs that suggested that John Knight and Queen Zoanna had fled the collapsing palace by that route, and taken a boat down the river. But the stream did not flow into the surface river that flowed by the capital; it wended its way elsewhere. Men had searched as far as they could along it, but it wound so deviously through its channels that they had been unable to trace it far, and their labors were needed for the work on the new palace. There had been no sign of either John Knight or the Queen; possibly they had drowned, or floated far away. But it was necessary to know their fate, for if John Knight lived, Charlain's marriage to Hal Hackleberry was in question, and if the Queen lived, the kingdom itself was in danger. So now, a week after the victory of the Knights, Heln was going to explore the river labyrinth astrally, and Kelvin was going to report her findings as they occurred. Everyone who counted was here for this quest.

Heln swallowed a dragonberry. "Stay with me, dear," she said to Kelvin as she sank back on the bed.

"Always, dear," he agreed. He held her hand firmly and sat on a chair beside her. Much had changed, but this had not: the use of the endearment still caused him to blush. The others pretended not to notice.

"I wish I had someone to call me 'dear,'" Jon murmured. She was seated on Kelvin's other side. She remained pale from her loss of blood, and was weak, but was otherwise in good condition.

"What about that boy who helped you get into the palace grounds?" Les Crumb asked, standing on her other side.

"Tommy Yokes?" She smiled briefly. "I liked him, but he went back to his girlfriend the moment the King freed the bound boys." She shrugged. "I guess I wasn't cut out to be anyone's girlfriend."

Kelvin's eyes were closed, as Heln's breathing slowed and her hand grew cold. But though he felt the impact of the transference, he remained conscious in the tent. Jon was speaking quietly, so that only those closest to her could hear, but he was one of them.

"When I was knocked out in battle," Les said, "I felt myself sinking down and down, and I did not know whether I would ever rise up again. When I woke I couldn't move at all, and I felt terrible. But then I felt a hand cooling my brow, and I knew someone was taking care of me, and I knew that if I recovered I would owe that person my life."

"That's silly," Jon said. "Your father brought you in. I only helped clean you up."

"Yes. I was delirious. My thoughts made no sense. When I opened my eyes and saw you, it was as though I had never seen you before. You were absolutely beautiful."

"Oh, shut up," she said, embarrassed.

"That vision remained with me after I recovered," he continued. "You are as lovely this moment."

"What are you saying?" she asked, disturbed.

"I thought your interest was elsewhere. After all, you are young. But you showed great courage when you went to rescue your brother. When it seemed you were dying, I—"

"Please, I don't like to think about that blood."

"When you recover, if—what I'm trying to say is—you don't seem that young anymore, to me—"

Jon finally got his drift. "You mean—you see me as—as—"

"As a woman," Les finished. "And if you were to find it in you to consider me as a man—"

Then Kelvin received the first signal from Heln. "I'm at the underground river now," he said, verbalizing her thought as he received it. There had been stray murmurings in the tent, from several conversations; now it was abruptly quiet. "I jumped to this site as soon as I got fully separated, but now I shall have to move more slowly, or I might miss something important. I hope you are receiving this, Kel."

There was a brief wave of mirth in the tent; obviously he was receiving it. He kept his eyes closed, to concentrate entirely on her thought.

"The water winds about," he continued, speaking for her. He began to glimpse it himself: the dark water, the cold cave walls. "It splits into several channels, but I see they merge again farther down, and there's only one big enough for a boat. I'm following that one. I'm sort of flying just above the water, moving faster now; I'll spot any boat if it's here."

She was silent for a time, evidently having nothing to report as she followed the buried river.

"You mean it?" Jon whispered, and Kelvin knew she was not talking to him.

"With all my heart," Les whispered back.

There was a disturbance at the tent entrance. "Am I permitted?" Kian asked. "I know I was on the wrong side, but those are my parents you seek."

"Permitted," King Rufurt said gruffly. "You behaved as you had to, and you are Kelvin's kin. We are glad you survived."

It grew quiet again. Kelvin could tell by the sound of his sister's breathing that she was deep in thought. Les Crumb had certainly caught her by surprise! But Kelvin remembered how the man had remarked favorably on her; it seemed he had been serious.

"I just don't see any boat," Kelvin said for Heln. "The current seems stronger now; I suppose it could have carried the boat quite far. I've traced the river a long way—oh!" She was uncommunicating for a moment; then: "It drains into The Flaw! The Flaw! The water just, just—falls in. Into the starry dark! I don't know how far I can follow it, there; I think it's not safe for me."

"Get away from there!" Kian cried. "Zatanas said something about The Flaw once—it's an astral bridge as well as a physical one!"

Get away! Kelvin thought as hard as he could, hoping he could reach her. So far the communication had all been one way, but if it was humanly possible to reverse it—

"Suddenly I'm very nervous," Kelvin said for Heln. "I don't trust this place at all. I'm going back up the river; maybe I missed something."

Kelvin heard a general sigh of relief. They had thought that only Heln's body was vulnerable when she separated, because she had no control of it then, but now it seemed that there were places her spirit could not safely go.

"I am feeling weak," Jon said. "Would you help me walk back home, Les?"

"Certainly." There was a smaller disturbance as they walked from the tent, Les supporting Jon with his arm about her waist.

That was interesting, Kelvin thought. Ordinarily his sister would have fainted rather than admit any feminine weakness. But of course she had lost a lot of blood, and a week wasn't nearly time enough to replace it.

"I *did* miss something," he said for Heln abruptly. "Not the boat; I'm afraid that's gone, and if they were in it, they're gone, too. But there's another channel of the river, or maybe it's a tributary. I must have overlooked it because I was going the other way, and it comes in at an angle. It's actually larger than the other; the caves are rounder here, almost polished, as if this is an artificial channel. And it leads—oh!"

Every breath in the tent seemed to be held. Kelvin strained to see what Heln was seeing, and made out a round door of some sort.

"There's a door here, perfectly round, like round ears," she said, chuckling. "I'm going through; it can't stop me, though it seems to be locked tight. Inside —it's a chamber, in the shape of a sphere, and there's—why, there's a parchment sitting on a table. Let me look—yes, I can read it! It says: *To whom it may concern*—I suppose that's me!—*if you have found this cell, you are a roundear, because only a roundear could penetrate to it without setting off the self-destruct mechanism.*" She paused. "I *am* a round-ear; this message is meant for me! But this chamber must be hundreds of years old! How could it—oh, I'd better keep reading it! *I am Mouvar—*"

"Mouvar!" King Rufurt exclaimed.

"*And I am a roundear.*"

"A roundear!" everyone exclaimed.

"*But because the natives look with disfavor on aliens, I masked my ears so that I could work among them without hindrance. I used the technology of my home frame to set things straight, then retired, for it was lonely. I set up the prophecy of my return, or the appearance of any roundear, to facilitate better acceptance in future centuries. The tools of my frame are here, and you may use them as you find necessary. If you wish to contact me directly, seek me in my home frame, where I will be in suspended animation. Directions for using The Flaw to travel to the frame of your choice are in the book of instructions beside this letter. Please return any artifacts you borrow. Justice be with you.*"

"Mouvar—a roundear!" Mor Crumb exclaimed. "Suddenly some funny things make sense!"

"There's another pair of gauntlets," Kelvin said for Heln. "And something that looks like a roundear weapon. And a jar of seeds—they are labeled 'Astral Berries'—and something labeled a levitation belt, and—oops, my time is running out; I must return."

Then, after a moment, "That's funny! They're kissing! I didn't know they felt that way about each other!"

And, finally, Heln's hand warmed, and Kelvin knew she was waking.

"Kissing?" King Rufurt asked. "No one's kissing here! What does she mean?"

Then Heln's eyelids flickered. "Did—did you hear?" she asked Kelvin.

"Everything!" Kelvin agreed excitedly. "You found Mouvar's retreat! He was a roundear!"

"Yes—but I think not from our fathers' world. He

spoke of frames, and that big book of instructions—I think The Flaw leads to many worlds, and on some the people have pointed ears, and on some round ears—"

"We'll learn it all, now we know the chamber exists!" King Rufurt said.

"Not necessarily, Your Majesty," Mor Crumb rumbled. "I don't know much about alien magic, but I know what 'self-destruct' means! Only a roundear can get in there!"

"But we have roundears!" the King said.

Kelvin exchanged a glance with Heln. "We shall do as we feel best," Kelvin said. "Those tools are too powerful to let loose on this world. We've already gotten rid of the bad government; we don't need even the gauntlets Mouvar lost anymore. In fact, I'll be happy if I never kill another dragon."

"The dragons guarded the astral berries," Heln said. She was weak from her experience, but animated. "They should continue to guard them, so that if things get bad again, centuries hence, the berries will be there for the next Roundear of Prophecy."

"Then I'll appoint you Guardian of the Dragons!" the King said. "You can use the berries to check the whole of dragon country, and warn me of any poachers; we shall take the gold only of dragons who die of natural causes. We won't use Mouvar's magic at all."

"If I may—" Kian said. He was bandaged and weak, but intense.

The King looked at him. "I don't think we could afford to trust you with—"

"My father—and my mother," Kian said. "They were in that boat on that river. They must have floated into The Flaw. They must be in some other world —some other frame, as Mouvar calls it. If I could go there to search for them—"

"That seems fair," Kelvin said. "You know the danger, Kian. You may never return, if you lose yourself in The Flaw."

"I realize the danger," Kian said. "But there really

is no place for me here, and if I have a chance to find them—"

"Granted," King Rufurt said quickly. "Heln will read the instructions for you, so you can travel through The Flaw."

"Thank you, Your Majesty," Kian said.

"Now I am very tired," Heln said.

"Everybody out of the tent!" the King said, and immediately there was motion as the people moved out. "We have much to think about, and much yet to learn." And the King, too, departed, leaving Kelvin alone with Heln.

"But one thing more, before I sleep," she said.

"Anything!" Kelvin agreed.

"Just give me what Les is giving Jon."

"What?" But then he caught on, and bent down to embrace her and kiss her.